Called to the window by a provocative moon-beam, Steven moved to stare out across the yard, now covered by a soft snowfall. Large, feathery flakes floated down past the window glass, sometimes pausing suspended for a moment on an errant breath of wind.

Movement below caught his eye. A bundled figure moved across the expanse between the house and the barn. Then, as Steven watched, the figure stopped abruptly and fell backward in the snow, spread-eagled beneath the cold gaze of the moon. Arms moved up and down; legs moved side to side. Snow angels. Someone was making snow angels.

He peered closer, enchanted. Hat flung aside, the figure sat up and glanced around furtively, dark hair spilling across her shoulders.

Willow.

She scrambled to her feet, moved over a short distance, and flopped back in the snow again, repeating the process until a choir of heavenly beings came to life side by side. She then stood, shook off the snow, and held her arms out to her sides. Head flung back, she offered her face to the falling flakes as she whirled around, her buffalo coat flying out behind her.

Palms against the cold glass, Steven leaned his forehead against the window frame, watching the snow nymph below him. Instinctively he sensed he was watching a very private moment, a bit of time she stole for herself. And in this private moment, she laid open her soul to the heavens above and allowed herself to indulge in whimsy uncharacteristic of the face she presented to the world.

All thoughts of kissing Emily Dawson fled his mind.

Dear Romance Reader,

Last year, we launched the Ballad line with four new series, and each month we'll present both new and continuing stories set everywhere from medieval England to the American West—the kind of passionate, romantic stories you love best, written by the most gifted authors. At the back of each book, we'll tell you when you can find subsequent books in the series that have captured your heart.

This month, rising star Martha Schroeder returns with the final book in her *Angels of Mercy* series. In **A Rose for Julian,** a young nurse with a painful past agrees to care for a nobleman's wounded son—but never imagines that she will come to love him, too. Next, Linda Devlin offers the next installment of *The Rock Creek Six* with **Jed.** What happens when an independent man and stubborn woman must work together to solve a crime? Teamwork, of course—the married kind!

In the last entry of RITA-nominated author Elizabeth Keys's atmospheric *Irish Blessing* series, the youngest Reilly sibling believes she's immune to the family Blessing because she's a woman. But one kiss from a certain man changes that immediately—and she vows to show him the power of *this* **Reilly's Heart.** Finally, Kathryn Fox concludes her adventurous *Mounties* series with **The Third Daughter,** as a new mounted officer makes a business arrangement with a local ranch, and finds that he wants something far more personal from the rancher's oldest daughter—her love. Enjoy!

Kate Duffy
Editorial Director

The Mounties

THE THIRD DAUGHTER

Kathryn Fox

ZEBRA BOOKS
KENSINGTON PUBLISHING CORP.

http://www.kensingtonbooks.com

1036 8942

ZEBRA BOOKS are published by

Kensington Publishing Corp.
850 Third Avenue
New York, NY 10022

All Kensington titles, imprints and distributed lines are available at special quantity discounts for bulk purchases for sales promotion, premiums, fund-raising, educational or institutional use.

Special book excerpts or customized printings can also be created to fit specific needs. For details, write or phone the office of the Kensington Special Sales Manager: Kensington Publishing Corp., 850 Third Avenue, New York, NY 10022. Attn. Special Sales Department. Phone: 1-800-221-2647.

Zebra and the Z logo Reg. U.S. Pat. & TM Off.

First Printing: December 2001
10 9 8 7 6 5 4 3 2 1

Printed in the United States of America

Chapter One

"C'mon, Mary, I've gotta raise your skirt."

"I can't concentrate on giving birth with that damned clown's face staring at me!"

Constable Steven Gravel whipped off the clown's wig and glanced over his shoulder at the sea of children's faces standing behind him, their eyes wide with amazement at the lady stretched out on her lace-draped dining room table.

"Mrs. Morton, I think this would be a good time to serve the birthday cake," he suggested to the elderly woman at his side. "In fact, take them *and* the cake over to Abraham's. Mary and I need a little privacy here." He wiped his face on his sleeve, ridding his skin of half the pasty white clown's makeup.

"Constable Gravel, it just wouldn't be proper. . . Someone should be here with you and Mary. . ." Mrs. Morton wiped her forehead with a trembling hand.

Mary gripped the edge of the elegant cherry dining table, arched her back against its smooth, polished top, and groaned.

"I believe, Mrs. Morton, that is comparable to shutting the barn door after the horse is out."

Her expression was so stricken, Steven smiled. "I assure you, Mrs. Morton, Mrs. Saunders's reputation is safe with me," he said with a wink to Mary, who answered his comment with another long, low groan.

"*Now*, Mrs. Morton, without delay, please."

As Mrs. Morton herded the children out of the room, Steven whipped away the tablecloth that had covered Mary and tossed her skirts up to her waist. "It's just you and me now, Mary. Scream all you like."

"I'm not going to scream. I'm not," she said through gritted teeth. "But when Charlie gets home, I'm going to kill him, the bastard." Before the words died on her tongue, her body tensed and she moaned.

"You picked a fine time to deliver this baby. You interrupted one of my finest performances." Steven stripped back his shirt sleeves and dipped his arms into the steaming water Mrs. Morton had brought.

"The children?"

"Safe over in Abraham's with Mrs. Morton."

"Abraham's! A saloon?"

"Abraham's very good with children. He'll keep them amused. We can't send them outside into a blizzard, now can we?"

Mary stared out the lace-draped window at the fat November snowflakes that drifted down and stuck to everything in sight. "I wonder where Charlie is?"

Steven ripped apart a soft white rag and made a stack of strips on a chair at his side. "A snowstorm never stopped Charlie."

"I can never serve guests on this table again. Owww. The baby's coming." She laid a hand on her bulging stomach.

Steven positioned her feet to deliver the baby. "Charlie hauled this table a thousand miles for you. It'll clean up just fine and nobody need ever know."

"I'll know."

"There's not a squeamish bone in your body, Mary. You'll sit at the head of this table and serve angel food cake without a qualm."

"After four children, I *would* have to have the last one on my cherry dining table."

"There was no time to get you upstairs, so the dining table it is. Now, stop fretting and keep your mind on what you're doing. We have to deliver Charlie a healthy baby."

"Charlie can go to hell."

Mary Saunders was a lady—kind, genteel, feminine—up until today, that is. Right in the middle of her six-year-old son's birthday party, her fifth child had decided to make a hasty entrance.

Steven leaned forward and the finely crafted edge of the elegant cherry dining table drove his belt buckle into his stomach. Mary's eyes were closed as her body relaxed between pains. If he'd only known four years ago when he enlisted in the Northwest Mounted Police that he would become a sort of all-purpose midwife, he might have thought twice about etching his name on that oath that swore him into service to Canada. Especially since the Fort McLeod surgeon, Colin Fraser, had decided to take his wife on a holiday to Benton, Montana.

Mary raised her head slightly and her eyes met his for a moment. Fear darkened their blue depths. He patted her knee. "It'll be all right. Your secrets are safe with me."

Her eyes clung to his, pleading for reassurance. "Have you ever done this before—delivered a baby, I mean?" she asked in a small voice.

Shaken, he looked away from her probing gaze for fear his eyes would not relay the confidence she needed from him. "Yes, a time or two."

Her smooth, soft hands gripped the edge of the table one more time, her knuckles whitening.

"One more time, Mary. One more time and we'll have a baby here."

Mary grunted in a most unladylike manner, bore down, and delivered her son into Steven's waiting hands. He sliced through the cord with his knife, held the baby upside down by his ankles, and gently swatted his tiny backside. "A fine lad, this one. Aren't you, little fellow?"

The baby whimpered, then belted out a lusty cry.

Mary dropped her head to the table, laughing with relief.

"A fine, dark-haired lad," Steven said softly as he wrapped the baby in clean sheets and moved around to Mary's side. "Too bad he looks just like Charlie."

Mary shot him a scolding glance that dissolved into a smile. Mrs. Morton bustled into the room, a rustling cloud of gray calico. "I'll take over now, constable," she said with authoritative calm that belied the fact that a few minutes ago she'd teetered on the edge of hysteria.

Steven nodded, then held out a finger to the

baby, who grasped it in his damp, tiny hand. The soft touch strummed a long-forgotten string in Steven's heart, an old pain so acute, he withdrew his finger. When he looked up, he found Mary watching him. "I'll be back in a few minutes to get you upstairs."

Mary stopped him with a hand on his arm. "How can I thank you?"

He shrugged and smiled. "I'll think of something. Tell Charlie I have a whole list for him for not being here."

Mary swiped a weary finger at his still-white painted cheek. "You look ridiculous."

"And you don't, stretched out on your dining room table?"

Mary laughed and shook her head. "So much for maintaining a presence in the community."

Steven lifted his scarlet jacket off the back of a chair and slung it over his shoulder. "A month from now, none of this will matter . . . except for the fact you have a fine son."

"Abraham said to tell you he's got a drink waiting for you." Mrs. Morton wrinkled her nose in disgust.

"Thank you, Mrs. Morton." He winked at Mary.

Abraham's tent was buzzing with men eager for any chance to drink, and the birth of a son for Charlie Saunders was as good a reason as any. Heads turned when Steven stepped inside and Abraham hurried to hand him a rag. Steven slipped his arms into his scarlet uniform jacket and wiped the remaining flour, soot, and water off his face.

"You done right good for old Charlie, I heard," a fat little man said around the cigar clamped firmly in his teeth as he clapped Steven on the back.

Abraham shoved a glass of whiskey under his

nose. "Legal spirits, constable, legal and paid for. You deserve a drink."

Steven took the glass, looked down into the amber depths for a moment, then downed the shot in one gulp that burned all the way down his throat.

"I heard Mary Saunders birthed that baby right on that there table she's so all-fired proud of. Reckon she ain't so highfalutin now, is she?" the little man said with an elbow dig to Steven's ribs.

Steven winced from the blow, handed Abraham the glass, and buttoned up his jacket. Then he turned to stare down the cigar-smoking busybody. "You're mistaken, sir. Mrs. Saunders delivered her son in her own bed."

They locked gazes for a moment; then the man looked away. "I didn't mean nothin' by that," he muttered. "Just thought it was funny seein's how she's always goin' on 'bout things."

Steven touched the man's shoulder, "I'm sure you meant no harm."

"But Earl there said—"

"I delivered the babe, sir, and I can assure you there was nothing unusual at all about his birth."

The buzz of voices dropped a notch and Steven sank wearily onto a waiting stool.

"You want another one?" Abraham asked, waggling a half-full bottle of liquor.

Steven shook his head and stared down dismally at his bloody buff-colored pants.

"You're a good man, constable," Abraham murmured.

Steven lifted one corner of his mouth in a half-hearted smile.

"I sent the young'uns home to their mamas before the crowd gathered," Abraham said with a nod to the raucous clientele.

"Thank you." Steven scraped off an overlooked patch of the flour and water he'd mixed to paint his face white. He'd used soot to accent his eyebrows, and some of Mrs. Morton's berry preserves to paint an exaggerated smile onto his face. He hadn't performed as Bubbles in years and had relented only because Mary Saunders begged him for her son's sixth birthday. Somehow, despite his best efforts, his days as a professional clown had become common knowledge in the community that had sprung up outside Fort McLeod.

Ever since joining the Northwest Mounted Police, he'd struggled to leave Bubbles and all he represented behind him. But true to the vein in him that had drawn him to work as a clown before, he couldn't resist a child's smile. "I better get back and help Mrs. Morton." Steven fished in his pocket for a coin, but Abraham reached across the plank bar, gripped his wrist, and shook his graying head.

"Your money ain't no good here today, constable."

Steven strode across the street and found Mrs. Morton helping Mary to her feet. Blood-streaked and wobbly-legged, she turned a grateful face toward Steven when he stepped in the door.

"You're a strong woman, Mary Saunders. Don't overdo your reputation." He scooped her into his arms and trudged up the steps, shoving open her bedroom door with his foot. He laid her on her elegant carved bed and stepped back. She looked so very pale and vulnerable amid the fluffy pillows, and a sharp, poignant memory rose unbidden to sting him.

Charlie Saunders had done very well for himself as a representative of I. G. Baker and Company, hauling freight and supplies to the fledgling settlement James McLeod had built five years ago. Mary and his children were Charlie's whole world, and tomorrow morning he'd come charging into town, driving his team like a madman. He'd haul the horses to a stop, kick open the door, bellow Mary's name, and bound up the stairs. Charlie's routine was well known, as was his deep love for the tiny wife who was, underneath her delicate facade, as tough as an old bull buffalo.

"Take care of the baby," Steven said, turning to go.

"Steven?"

He stopped with a hand braced on the door facing; something in her voice warmed him. Mary watched him from the bed, the baby held tightly in her arms. "Just now, with the baby. There was a look on your face . . ."

Charlie and Mary were his friends. He'd eaten meals in their home and played with their children. They'd never once asked him a personal question, perhaps sensing the pain that lay just below his skin. But now, it was just he and Mary, connected by an odd bond of intimacy, a joint accomplishment of having successfully brought a life into the world.

Lying there, so small and delicate in the large bed, the sleeping baby tucked safely in her arms, she reminded him of days and years past when such a tender, domestic scene was a gift easily taken for granted, a miracle lost in the shuffle of everyday life.

He knew her secrets; she deserved to know one of his—just to make things even. "I lost my wife in childbirth, the baby soon after," he confessed softly.

"Oh, God," she whispered. "I'm sorry. How long ago?"

"Six years."

"Is that why you joined up?"

Steven nodded. "I'd forgotten . . . a baby's little hands. So moist." His throat closed and he turned away from the compassion he saw in her eyes. "Gotta go, Mary."

A frigid wind tore across the prairie and slammed into the shorthorn cow's heaving sides. Willow Dawson huddled behind the cow, hat pulled low to deflect the now-vicious snowflakes.

"Come on, Lady, pop her out so we can both go back home."

Lady only rolled her eyes in fear and breathed faster, heavier, her slick, brown sides heaving with the effort. Willow Dawson squinted across the rolling landscape, now a blurry sheet of driving ice, and fought down the familiar panic. She patted the cow's hip. "What a stupid cow you are to have a calf in November. Guess it was love, huh?"

Lady bunched her body and grunted. A tiny rump appeared, then slid back inside.

"Damn, a breech." Willow closed her eyes and breathed deeply, coughing as the biting air filled her lungs. Lady needed her. Willow opened her eyes, squinting against the stinging ice. This was a cow and she'd delivered breech calves before. There would be little blood. No screaming. No pleading for death. Vivid images ran through her mind like tiny demons.

Shaking off her fear, she scrambled to her feet and stumbled against the howling wind to her waiting horse. Head bowed against winter's onslaught, the mustang rolled his eyes at Willow when she touched his neck. "Just a little longer, Pat, and you and Lady will both be home safe in the warm barn."

She untied a roll of rope from her saddle and pulled a tin of grease from the saddlebag. Oilcloth coat drawn tight around her, Willow trudged back to Lady's backside and dropped to her knees. She shed the coat, acknowledging briefly that she'd had the good sense to wear two sweaters, shoved up her sleeves, and slathered the grease onto her right arm above her elbow, then coated the rope.

With one hand on Lady's rump, she slid her hand inside the cow's warm womb and searched the lumps and bumps until a tiny, wet tongue licked at her fingers.

"There you are, you little troublemaker. You stay right there." Gently she looped the greased rope over the tiny snout, then felt for and found two tiny front feet. Drawing the noose tight, Willow braced her boots against Lady's hips and pulled gently. The rope gave a little and Lady hunched her back and pushed again. Another tug and the rope gave more. Lady groaned, bore down, and a wet, brown calf slid out, torn bag and all, right into Willow's lap. A gush of blood and water coated her already damp pants. Willow sobbed, relief pouring through her shivering body.

Lady shoved herself to her feet and turned to sniff first at Willow's hat and then at the calf. Willow's hat rated a small lick, but the calf got an all-over bath with Lady's wide, warm tongue.

"Sorry, Mama, but I gotta get you two home before this storm gets any worse." Willow wrapped her arms around the calf and hefted him onto her saddle, then swung up behind him.

"Let's go, Pat," she said, gathering her reins and turning into the storm.

The voice of the wind soared and the storm closed in around them, swallowing them. Pat plodded ahead, no hesitation in his steps. Willow pulled the brim of her hat lower and ducked her head, trusting Pat's innate sense of direction. She pulled the oilcloth coat tighter around her and draped the trailing edges around the damp calf.

Mixed with the whine of the storm, a wagon's rattle and clang soon rose above the wind's howl. A faint light poked a hole in the murk, and Cletis Dawson emerged from the snow like a large, frosted, hairy angel.

"Girl, what are you doing out here?" He jammed the wagon brake down with a huge boot and threaded the reins through beefy fingers.

"One of the cows didn't come in. I knew she was due to calve any day. Found her just over the edge of the coulee."

"Gimme the calf. I got some blankets in the back."

Willow maneuvered Pat closer to the wagon and handed the calf to her father. He turned and laid the bawling calf in the wagon bed. A shrouded figure hunched in the back threw back a blanket from its face, and thirteen-year-old Libby grinned at Willow from her swathed nest. "Pa said I could come and hold the calf."

"You hold him tight, Libby, or he'll try and jump out the back to get to his Ma," Willow cautioned.

The cow plodded to the wagon's side and stuck a wet nose into Libby's hair.

"Go on, Lady. You'll get your baby when we get home," Libby said, swatting at the cow with the end of her quilt.

Pat danced to the side, eager to be on his way to his warm stall and waiting supper.

"Any more of 'em out?" Cletis asked.

Willow shook her head. "Nope. Lady was it."

"Git yourself on home and get out of those wet clothes."

"I'm not cold. I put on extra layers."

"Same and all, your Ma'd come back and scalp me if I let one of her girls catch pneumonia."

Willow nodded, her face growing too cold to stretch in conversation. She let Pat have his head, trusting the rugged little mustang's instincts, and he eased into a lope that brought the wind's sting faster and harder. Willow leaned over his neck, using him to block the wind, and heard the wagon team break into a harness-jingling trot behind her.

When the glow of the barn lamps came into view, she was so cold she wondered if she should dismount or surrender and fall out of the saddle. Pat nudged the barn door, which was already ajar, and trotted inside, stopping by his stall and looking longingly at the ration of grain waiting just over the rails.

Willow swung a stiff leg over the saddle apron and ground her teeth as her numb feet touched the earthen floor. Clinging to the saddle as sharp needles stabbed her legs, she endured a shove from Pat and a warm sniff.

"In a minute, boy." She released the latigo straps on the saddle and stepped away, testing the integrity of her steps. With her teeth, she pulled off her gloves and wriggled her numb fingers. Then she shoved her hands underneath the saddle's apron and absorbed Pat's sweaty warmth.

A blast of cold air swept in as the double barn doors swung open and Pa drove the team inside.

Melting snow dripping off their manes, the matched horses hung their heads and waited patiently to be unhitched.

Cletis stepped down, lifted the calf out of Libby's lap, and pushed it into an empty stall. Lady shoved past them all and herded her baby into a far corner for another licking.

"Willow, you want me to unsaddle Pat?" Libby asked, poking her blanket-draped head over the wagon bed.

Willow bit back a laugh at the picture she made. "No, I'll take care of him. You go inside and get warm." She tossed a stirrup over the saddle, loosened the cinch, and dragged the saddle off Pat's back.

Wearing her quilt like a sarong, Libby climbed out of the wagon and scurried for the house. Willow removed the bridle, brushed down Pat, and opened the stall door. He pushed by her with a throaty whicker and shoved his nose into the waiting grain.

"Thanks for leaving grain for Pat." Willow heaved the saddle onto a saddle tree in the tack room and hung the bridle on the saddle horn.

Cletis unharnessed his team and sent them plodding toward the dark depths of the long barn, their plump backsides shifting from side to side in synchronization.

"Lady have much trouble birthing?" he asked, hanging the harness on a peg on the wall.

"The calf was a breech, but I turned him." She felt her father's eyes on her back. "I didn't have a choice."

He swore softly under his breath, then paused for a span of silence. "You should have come and got me."

Willow walked to his side, removed her coat, and shook off the beads of water. "There wasn't time. She'd have died in this storm before I could get here and back."

Her father studied her for a moment; then he shook his head slowly. "You had a rope with you?"

Willow nodded. "Put it in my saddlebag last week. I thought she was carrying a little odd. Put in some grease, too."

A small smile played with the floppy ends of his moustache. "So you thought so, did you? Well, you were right . . . this time."

"Ain't I usually right?" Willow rocked back on her heels, lightheaded from the relief pouring through her. Pa wasn't angry with her for taking things in her own hands.

"Aren't."

"What?"

"Aren't you usually right."

Willow nodded concession.

Cletis put an arm around her shoulders and pulled her against him. "Let's go see what Emily's got on the table. There were some awful enticing smells coming from the kitchen when I left."

Together they stepped back into the storm and followed a rope strung from house to barn. The two-story house glowed through the snow like a beacon, calling home all who had wandered. Willow loved its fancy woodwork and whitewashed sides, its wide front porch and many windows. And yet she felt out of place the moment she stepped through the door.

Pastel rugs covered the floor and delicate vases sat on every table.

All Emily's doing.

Willow felt more at home in the barn.

Cletis Dawson had done very well for an old buffalo hunter. Faced with the necessity of providing a home for his Blackfoot wife and three tiny daughters, he'd stolen some cattle, staked out a piece of land, and built himself an empire. He'd prospered for love of the challenge until his wife died seven years ago. Now he prospered to bury his pain.

Willow swung open the back door, and the aroma of apple with brown sugar reached out its fragrance and drew her in. Cletis banged the door shut behind him and stamped the snow off his boots.

"Tell Willow to knock the snow off her feet, too," a sweet voice sang from the kitchen.

Willow obliged with a glare to her father.

"You know how she is," he said with a weak shrug.

Willow hung her Stetson and coat on a nail hammered into the wall and stepped into the kitchen onto one of her sister's brown-and-red hooked rugs.

Emily stood by the kitchen table, a pristine white apron tied around her waist in a delicate, even bow. She raised her head and the lamplight sprinkled streaks of copper into her deep-auburn hair, a gift from their father.

"Oh, my. Look at you." Emily's perfect mouth widened into an O and she began to dust the flour off her hands. "Take off those filthy clothes right here. Don't you track that dirt and . . . and . . . whatever that is through my clean house."

Being chastised by Emily was like being scolded by a butterfly. She might flutter and flop, buzz and circle, but she never turned a sharp tongue on anyone. It was her house. She'd been their mother and housekeeper for seven years, sliding neatly into the job, effortlessly taking up where their mother had left off.

"I can't just strip naked right here, Em."

"Sure, you can. I'll get your wrapper first. Pa, you go on into the parlor. I laid out your coffee and pipe.

"Libby's already in the tub. She was nearly as filthy as you. Here, let me do that." Emily pushed away Willow's cold fingers from where they fumbled with the buttons on her shirt. "Did you get Lady home? Libby said the calf was cute."

Willow nodded tiredly. "Lady's all right and so is the calf. It was a breech birth. As many times as I've seen it, I never get over the wonder of it. Birth. Life giving life to life." *Or the horror it brings back to mind,* she mentally added.

"I'll never get these bloodstains out." Emily held up the ragged shirt and clucked over the wide, rust-colored streaks.

Willow sighed. Despite her sweet nature and compassionate soul, Emily wasn't the least bit interested in cows. Or ranching. Or the outdoors. Oh, she appreciated it all on a grand scale as a whole, but she never stopped to consider the gift of a sunrise or the elegant delicacy of an absolutely clear night sky, or the amazing variations in color of the northern lights.

"You've always had the prettiest skin, Willow; I do wish you'd take care of it. So smooth and even, just like Ma's. I wish I had your coloring and not Pa's. My nose gets red every time I get out in the sun. Don't you think a peeling nose is a horrid thing to look at?"

"What's for dinner?" Willow asked, standing in her suit of baggy winter underwear, sniffing the air.

"Did you hear a thing I just said?" Emily asked.

"No," Willow admitted. "Did you hear what I said about the cows?"

Emily slowly shook her head. "No, I'm sorry. What did you say?"

Willow smiled and shook her head. "It doesn't matter." She stepped forward to the staircase.

"Wait! Don't you want me to go up and get your gown?"

Willow never slowed her gait. "Why? Like you said, nobody's here but us."

Emily followed her to the bottom of the stairs and looked up as Willow concentrated on putting one foot in front of the other to climb. "What if somebody comes to the door?"

Willow stopped on the first landing with her hand on the banister. "When was the last time somebody other than one of Pa's hands came to our house?"

Emily looked crestfallen and Willow felt a prick of guilt. "Not in a long time. But a lady should always be prepared to receive company."

Willow started up the stairs again, pulling herself along with the banister. "I'm sorry, Em. I'm just too damned tired to care."

Chapter Two

The bull buffalo pawed the snow, uncovering clumps of brown grass with the nonchalance of one in command of its kingdom. Two cows trailed along behind, each followed by a yearling calf. Steven centered the beaded sight of his gun on the buffalo's withers. A shot through the lungs would bring instantaneous death.

He paused and lowered his rifle. Even though the fort needed meat, killing the beast seemed almost a shame. So few of them roamed the prairie any longer. With the influx of the American Sioux last year, the numbers of returning buffalo had dwindled to a trickle, then to almost nothing. The absence of the Indians' primary food source set off ripples that went through not only the villages and families of the refugee Sioux, but through the homes and lives of the Canadian Indians: Blackfeet, Assiniboins, the Saulteaux. Cultures that both worshipped and preyed upon the beasts suddenly found themselves wondering what Wankatakan had in mind.

Steven raised the gun, settled the sight on the unsuspecting bull, and squeezed the trigger. The discharge reverberated off the rolling hills in a throaty voice of despair. The buffalo flung up its head, leaped forward, and then plowed face-first into the snow.

" 'Tis a shame to kill the last of the beasts, isn't it?" Braden Flynn said with a shake of his head.

"It is, indeed." The cows and calves trotted out of sight over a rolling hill, tails flung over their backs.

"There's ranches along the border now. Walsh is figuring on contracting with some of them for cattle to supplement our herd."

Braden shoved back his Stetson hat and crossed his hands over his saddle horn. "Sure, and herding beef back beats huntin' and butcherin' the beasts here."

Steven jammed his rifle back into its scabbard and kneed his horse forward, leading a pack mare pulling a travois.

Braden swung down as he reached the great dead bull and put another bullet through the skull to assure he wouldn't suddenly come to life and gore them both with his heavy horns.

"Do you want to take the liver back to Dancing Bird?" Steven asked as he pulled his skinning knife from a pouch on his belt.

Braden nodded. "She asked if I could bring it home." Then he smiled slowly. "She thinks it's good for the baby."

Steven slit the throat and watched blood pour out in a smooth, dark river. He glanced at Braden's smile, and a prick of envy rose to irritate him.

Despite disapproval by the headquarters of the Northwest Mounted Police, Braden had married Sitting Bull's niece last summer, having fallen in love with her when her people came to Canada fleeing persecution by American troops after the death of General Custer. Once danger from Sitting Bull's battle-weary people seemed a thing of the past, Braden and Steven were transferred back to Fort McLeod, their first posting. Seven months along with child, Dancing Bird seemed happy in her adopted world. And Braden was at peace. Steven and Braden had each served a three-year term with the Mounted Police, then signed up for a second. For Braden, it was a matter of pride; for Steven, a matter of necessity. Where else, here in the hundreds of thousands of acres of unsettled land, would an out-of-work ex-clown find a job?

When the travois was loaded with buffalo meat and the skeleton lay waiting to be bleached by the sun, they began their long trip back to Fort McLeod. As the numbers of buffalo had dwindled, they had also moved farther away from the fort, never venturing closer than a half day's ride, eliminating completely the possibility of hunting during warm months and returning to the fort with usable meat. The herd of cows kept by the police had dwindled from severe winters and predators. With more recruits reporting as the weeks went by, a close and reliable source of beef would be a godsend.

They were at the westernmost point of their patrol area, just beyond a high ridge of the Cypress Hills. The barrier that reared forested slopes into the sky had become their stopping point. As they rode past it today, Steven noticed a well-hidden but much-scuffled trail winding up the side of the incline.

"I never noticed that before," Steven said, nodding toward the path.

"I've never noticed it either," Braden answered, dropping back for a closer look. "Blackfoot trail, you think?"

Steven shrugged. "Could be."

"Makes a man wonder what's on the other side."

Steven glanced back at the loaded travois. "If we didn't have to get back with this meat, I'd find out."

"I'm due to ride this patrol tomorrow. Want to take my place?" Braden asked.

Steven glanced up at the rugged height, the tall, dark evergreens staring down on him, their snow-flocked branches beckoning him to come closer and see what their dark-green skirts hid on the other wide. A sudden case of wanderlust gripped him. "Yeah, I do."

Willow turned over in her tumbled bed and groaned. Long-underused muscles now complained over their outing yesterday, and her cheeks burned from wind chafing. She flopped over onto her back and stared up at the ceiling. Bright sunshine poured in the window, its yellow beams feigning innocence of yesterday's snowstorm.

The scent of frying bacon wafted up the stairs to tickle her nose and lure her from her warm nest of quilts. But she resisted the seduction for a moment and listened to the sounds below.

Libby was banging out her lessons on the piano, giving new interpretation to Beethoven's carefully thought-out symphonies, and probably eager to be away from Emily's vigilant eyes.

Emily was fussing in the kitchen. That observation didn't take much imagination, Willow thought with a small smile. Emily was always fussing in the kitchen. Dishwater and flour seemed to hold an odd fascination for the older of Willow's two sisters. Pa would be in the parlor, reading a newspaper that was several weeks old. She opened her eyes and abandoned the cocoon of satisfaction she'd spun for herself. Even though he'd not said anything last night, Willow knew she was in for a tongue-lashing today.

Setting her mind against the inevitable, Willow swung her feet over the edge of the bed and sat up, shoving her hair out of her face. She rose and crossed to the dressing table. Bending down to peek into the mirror, she ran a hand over her red and tortured skin. The chapping would hurt like the devil when she rode out into the wind again this morning. Unless Emily smeared some of her cream on the irritated area. Willow wrinkled her nose at the reflection in the mirror. The thought of going the whole day smelling like one of Emily's cream concoctions was not a pleasant prospect.

Willow combed her fingers through her black hair and smoothed her palm down the side of her injured face. Emily and Libby were so fair, their skin smooth and flawless and totally unsuited for life on the prairie. She, however, had inherited her mother's coloring and complexion. Dark skin and a triangular face, evidence of her Blackfoot background. Her hair hung down to her waist only because Willow abhorred the idea of having to fuss with it. Much to Emily's dismay, she wore it either

braided or twisted up on top of her head in no
style at all.

Willow bent to reach for the pants she'd pulled
off last night, then sniffed the stiff fabric. Remembering the calf in her lap, she dropped the offending article and took another pair of brown
men's pants from her armoire and pulled them
on over her suit of long, knit winter underwear.
Topping the ensemble with an old flannel shirt
that she hastily tucked into her pants, she bounded
down the steps, bracing herself for a scolding from
Pa and Emily.

The breakfast table was set with pretty dishes and
neatly folded napkins, and Willow wondered, as
she did every morning, why Emily went to all that
trouble. The four of them would consume the meal
in minutes and Emily would be left with a stack of
dishes, and the napkins, to wash. But as she slid
into her chair and watched Emily, in her impeccably neat clothes, bringing steaming plates to the
table, she knew that this was what kept Emily alive
in a place as isolated and windblown as the Dawson
Cattle Company.

"Oh, Willow, dear, your face." Emily's cool fingers touched her tortured cheek.

"It's all right," Willow said, moving her head a
small distance away.

"I mixed up some rose, chamomile, and willow
bark this past fall."

"No, really, Emily, it'll be fine."

"Listen to your sister," Pa said as he slid into
his place at the head of the table. "Libby! Stop
that infernal banging and come to breakfast."

The torturing of the piano ceased and Libby
appeared in a flurry of hair, dress, and smiles.

"Young lady, what have I told you about running

every place you go?" Emily scolded as she ladled out fluffy yellow eggs.

Libby sighed exaggeratedly. "You said don't do it."

"And why did I say that?"

Emily forked onto their plates delicately pieces of bread, still warm and yeasty, and Willow wondered, with a wave of sheepishness, what time Emily had gotten up to prepare this feast.

" 'Cause ladies don't run; they glide."

"That's right. If you want to grow up to wear all those pretty dresses you were looking at in the magazine, you have to learn not to run. Can you see those ladies galloping across the yard like hooligans?"

"They couldn't run in those goldarned dresses even if they wanted to."

Emily's mouth fell open and her eyes widened. She set down the platter of bacon just in time and folded her arms across her chest. Willow nearly choked on a fork-full of eggs and hid a smile behind her napkin. The conniption fit was about to begin.

"Where on earth did you hear such a word?" Emily asked in a gush of breath.

"What word?" Libby said around a mouthful of eggs.

"Don't talk with your mouth full," Emily shot back.

"Bumf you askf me a quefton."

"Don't sass me."

"But—"

Pa laid a hand on Libby's arm. She slanted her eyes toward him, swallowed her eggs, and turned an innocent gaze toward Emily. "What word?"

"You know perfectly well what word."

Libby looked down at her plate. "From Wilbur."

Emily whirled on her father and he shifted uncomfortably in his chair. "This is what happens when she's allowed to play out in the barn with the cowhands."

"This is a ranch, Em."

"That's no excuse for her to run wild."

"She's not running wild, she's just . . . enjoying being a child."

"In case you hadn't noticed, she's no longer a child. She's a young woman in need of guidance and molding."

Willow eased back her chair, hoping for a chance to make an escape, for she knew she was next on Emily's list.

"Don't you even try to walk out on this conversation," came the anticipated admonition.

Willow silently raised her eyes to Emily's blue ones, concentrating on not losing her temper.

"And you're not even trying to set an example for her. You're the oldest, Willow, and you live like . . . like . . . like you were one of the cowhands."

Willow glanced at her father, who frowned and shook his head slightly. Emily wasn't like her and him; she didn't love the overwhelming solitude and harsh wind. She wasn't like Libby, curiosity with legs and examiner of life. Emily was like a hothouse flower thrown out among the tough, blue lobelia that reared blue flower spikes toward the summer sky.

"I'm not like you, Em. I never took to sewing and cooking. Ma tried, but I wasn't any good at it. I'm good with horses and cows. I figure I'm more valuable to the ranch out there."

"But she imitates everything you do." Emily dropped into her chair. "She worships you, wants to be just like you. Don't you see you're undoing everything I'm trying to accomplish with her? I don't want her to have to live out her life here, isolated, without even a peek at another human being except ... cowhands. I want her to be prepared to live among civilized people, to be able to go to parties and dances and dinners."

There was a yearning in Emily's voice that twisted at Willow's heart, and she knew her words described more than Libby. "I never knew you hated it here so."

Emily swiped at a tear that ran down her cheek. "I don't hate it here. This is our home. I just wish there wasn't ... so much of it."

A sadness crept into Pa's eyes. "Em, why don't you take Libby and go to your aunt Carrie's in Ottawa for a spell. She's been after you to come for the better part of a year now."

Emily shook her head. "I don't want to go to Ottawa. The two of you would starve to death or else drown in dirty clothes. I'm very happy here; I just wish ..."

When she didn't continue, Willow leaned forward. "Wish what?"

"Don't you ever think about getting married, Willow?"

Willow fell back in her chair. "Married? Heavens, no! What would I want with a man to look after and pick up behind?" *What would I want with a man who would get me with child, who would pace an outer room while I arched in pain and cursed his name.*

"Well, I do. I want a home of my own, children of my own, a husband of my own."

Discontent had apparently been simmering for some time behind Emily's calm exterior. Willow put down her napkin and folded her arms across her chest. Discussing intimate matters with Emily made her skin crawl. Discussing intimate matters with anybody made her skin crawl. She'd never had the urge to curl up on the bed with her sisters and swap secrets. Not that she didn't love them both dearly, but she'd always kept matters of her heart close to her heart. And her fears even closer.

"What's really the matter, Em?"

Emily suddenly pushed to her feet and walked to the wide window that looked out over the rolling hills. "Sometimes, I feel like I'm going to smother here."

Willow glanced to the endless rolling land just beyond the sparkling glass, then to her father. "What do you want us to do?" Sometimes her sister was a deep and unsolvable mystery.

Emily turned, her calm mask back in place. "I'm sorry; I'm just out of sorts this morning. Libby, eat your breakfast, then finish practicing."

"But, the calf—"

Pa shook his head.

"Yes, ma'am."

"I'll be back to get the dishes." Emily drifted away toward her room on a cloud of lavender scent, leaving her breakfast growing cold in a puddle of butter.

Buck scrambled up the last few feet of the rocky ridge and stopped atop the summit. Below stretched a flat, immense valley. Cattle grazed on the brown grass. A house and collection of outbuildings sat in the lee of the ridge, protected from the vicious north wind. Fencing criss-crossed the pastures like fine hand stitching.

"Well, I'll be damned," Steven said, pushing

back his Stetson. Figures moved below, and one in particular caught his eye. A long dress wrapped around her ankles as she struggled to hang a sheet on the clothesline.

He heeled Buck in the sides and rode down the ridge, loose rocks rattling down behind him. The ranch was well kept and impressive to be so isolated. The house with elaborate woodwork and a wide porch was stylish and out of place on the windswept prairie. A new barn sat some distance behind it with neatly painted double doors.

The figure that had caught his eye was indeed a woman, and a pretty one at that. Fragile and slim, she wrestled a dripping sheet onto a rope strung between the house and the barn, the front of her dress soaked through. As enticing as the sight of her was, it was the struggle going on in a small corral just to the right of the barn that made him draw Buck to a sudden stop.

A yearling calf bucked and plunged, trailing a rope behind him. Clinging to the end of the rope was another woman, this one in tight men's pants. Sliding along on her shoulder, she abruptly yanked on the rope, scrambled to her feet, and dug her heels into the dirt. Two men hung on the top rail of the corral, waving their hats and laughing.

The young bull stopped, looked over his shoulder, then hopped along as if he had springs in his legs, dragging the woman behind on her finely shaped backside.

She endured this punishment until the calf circled close to a post in the center of the corral. Then, she stumbled ahead of him, snubbed the rope around the post, and brought the frisky youngster to a short stop.

"Took you longer than last time," said one of the men.

The woman's comment was lost to the distance, but not the gentle curve of her hips as she strode over to an abandoned hat and snatched it off the ground to plop it onto her head.

Steven rode into the center of the yard and shifted in his saddle as shocked faces all around stopped their tasks and stared at him. The woman at the clothesline moved first. Drawing her over-sized coat across her damp chest, she moved toward him with a graceful step.

"May we help you . . . constable?" She glanced at his scarlet uniform, then back up to his face.

Her cheeks were smooth and pink, her skin soft and unblemished, reminding Steven of a ripe, pampered peach.

"I'm Constable Steven Gravel of the Northwest Mounted Police. I'm stationed at Fort McLeod, about a day's ride from here. I'd like to speak with your . . . husband, if he's around."

She smiled demurely and a blush ran over her face. "I'm not married, constable. You'll need to speak with my father. I'm Emily Dawson. Please, come inside. I have some currant bread fresh out of the oven."

Steven swung down and looped Buck's reins over the gnawed hitching rail. He cast a glance toward the group at the corral, who stood with chins propped on crossed arms resting on the top rail.

"Willow, please come see to the constable's horse," Emily called, and the young woman in the tight pants turned away from her companions and walked toward him with a gentle sway.

"Constable Gravel, this is my sister, Willow."

Emily seemed completely at ease that her sister

was wearing the most tantalizing pair of pants he'd ever seen.

Willow nodded, watching him from underneath the battered brim of the old Stetson. Her complexion, what he could see of it, was as dark as her sister was light. Hair, black and full, was drawn back and bound with a bit of frayed rag. Her skin was smooth but tanned, her square face hinting at Indian heritage, and he compared her to Braden Flynn's wife, Dancing Bird.

Without a word, she untied Buck's reins and led him toward the barn, one hand resting on his shoulder. And as he watched her walk away, some instinct stirred to life inside him.

"What brings you here, constable?" Emily was asking as she preceded him through the door.

In a land filled with shacks and log cabins, the house was a small miracle. It looked as if it had been picked up in Toronto and dropped here intact. Soft hooked rugs covered a shiny wooden floor. Wispy curtains hung at paned windows. Carved, modern furniture filled the rooms, and lacing it all together was the enticing odor of freshly baked bread.

"Please forgive my appearance," she apologized as she directed him into the parlor. "We have guests so seldom."

A large bear of a man sat hunched at an immense desk, poring over a stack of papers. He looked up at the sound of her voice.

"Pa, this is Constable Steven Gravel. He's stationed at Fort McLeod. My father, Cletis Dawson."

Dawson stood and extended a hairy hand. "What can we do for the Mounted Police, constable?"

Steven removed his hat and tucked it under his arm. "I'd like to talk to you about procuring beef for the fort."

He watched Dawson's eyes light up. Obviously, here was the man who had waved the magic wand and produced this miracle in the middle of nowhere, a man who knew a good thing when he heard it.

"Have a seat, Constable Gravel." Dawson pointed to a leather-upholstered chair in front of his desk. He rifled through papers, then looked up. "Emily!"

"Yes, Pa?" she answered from somewhere in the house.

"Call Willow to come in here."

"Yes, Pa." He heard the door open and heard Emily's lilting voice call her sister. A far-away answer came and the door closed.

"She'll be right here," Emily said, poking her head around the door frame. She disappeared and Steven heard her steps recede to the back of the house.

"What kind of numbers did you have in mind?" Dawson asked, leaning forward.

Steven mentally calculated the number of buffalo they took every month. What a luxury it would be to have beef readily available. "We'd like to maintain a herd of about two hundred and fifty at Fort McLeod and another fifty or so at Wood Mountain, to the east."

Emily appeared again at the door, this time in dry clothes, her hair combed and restyled, bearing a napkin-draped tray with a slice of fresh bread and a cup of tea.

How long had it been since he'd had a cup of real tea? Did she have a magic wand of her own to have produced this treat so quickly?

She set the tray on a small table at his side, bending close. The scent of roses swirled around her.

Dim memories rose from some dark depths within him. Soft skin. Warm hands. The scent of passion in a darkened room.

Hesitantly, he glanced up at her, hoping his most recent thoughts didn't show in his eyes. She met his gaze for a moment, then colored a delicious shade of peach. Long lashes quivered, delicate dark circles on those same smooth cheeks.

She pulled away and swished out of the room, leaving Steven amazed that his heart still throbbed out its steady, plodding beat. Where was the rush of excitement? Where were the sweaty palms? The pounding pulse? The tightness in the pit of his stomach? Aside from the fact she'd stirred up old ghosts, Emily Dawson had had no effect whatsoever on his body, a reality that concerned him. Had he been too long without a woman, or had he just gone too long without wanting one?

Before he had time to fully contemplate his lack of arousal, a whirlwind swept in the front door in a flurry of dress, hair, and goat.

Chapter Three

A gangly young girl stopped dead in the middle of the foyer, a long sweep of lace torn off her dress and dragging behind her. Once a modest shade of blue, the garment was now streaked with dirt and stains. Hair disheveled and missing one shoe, she lunged for the little brown-and-white nanny goat that skated across the polished parlor floor on delicate little hooves.

Cletis Dawson rose from his chair like Neptune from the deep and planted both his hands on his desk. "Elizabeth Dawson, what in hell are you doing?"

Libby made a dive for the nanny, belly-flopped onto the hardwood floor with a painful "oof," then jerked her head up and peered at her father from between handfuls of brown hair. "Wilbur said he was going to roast Bell."

The corners of Cletis's mouth jerked in a suppressed grin. "And what has Bell done this time to earn her the place of honor at this banquet?"

Libby shoved back the curtain of hair and widened her eyes when she saw Steven. "She . . . she . . . she ate Wilbur's hat. But it was his *old* hat, Pa."

Just at that moment, Willow slid around the corner and scooped the offending Bell into her arms just as a broom hit the wooden floor, *smack*, right in front of her feet.

"Get that . . . goat out of my house!" Emily wielded the broom again, poised this time to swat Bell right out into the middle of the yard.

Willow had apparently lost her hat in the chase, and a cloud of dark, shiny hair swirled around her, covering her shoulders and sliding down her back. Steven blinked to dissolve the vision of that same hair spread across a white, lace-edged pillowcase.

Clutching a bleating, squirming Bell to her chest, Willow glared at her sister with dark, mysterious eyes. "I'm taking her outside. She was scared because Wilbur was chasing her. Somehow the door opened and she ran inside by accident." Willow turned without a glance toward the parlor. "And it's not your house. It's Pa's."

Emily froze and turned a stricken face toward the parlor, as if just remembering Steven was there. Willow followed her sister's gaze, but there was no embarrassment in her eyes, only amusement edged with defiance.

"Constable Gravel and I would like to discuss some cattle prices with you," Cletis said, his remark obviously directed at Willow.

Still unruffled, she handed the bleating nanny to Libby and sauntered into the parlor as if the scene just played out had never happened.

She moved to a small desk on the other side of

the room—an oak secretary with a lace-edged doily peeping over the top—and opened it. Neat stacks of papers filled the compartments. She pulled a chair to the desk, sat down, and pulled toward her a paper filled with neat columns. Once the paper was in her hand, she swiveled in the chair to face them.

"Constable Gravel, how much beef are you interested in?"

"About three hundred head. Delivered to Fort McLeod."

She lifted the mane of dark hair, twisted it on top of her head, and stuck a pencil through the coil. The image was like a fine work of art: long, slim fingers moving in symmetry; shiny, black strands of hair sliding against each other as those same fingers quickly tamed them into a neat bun; the graceful line of her neck as she bent her head ever so slightly to secure the hair.

His arousal was immediate and intense. Steven shifted in his chair and tried to refocus his thoughts on cattle prices.

"We can't deliver the beef, constable. We run a short crew during the winter months. Perhaps your men could come and herd the cattle to Fort McLeod." Her hands returned to the papers. "I'd be willing to cut off a few cents per head if you agree."

"Of course. I think we can arrange that."

"These are shorthorn cattle available. I have a few Herefords, but I'm using them as breeding stock now."

"Shorthorns are fine."

She turned her back, lifted a quill from an ink-well, and began to scratch figures onto the paper. All the while, Cletis sat back in his chair, a slight smile on his face. Looking between the two of them, Steven wondered at this unusual business relationship.

"This is my price." Willow handed him a piece of paper with a final figure underlined twice. Gazing at the elegant flourishes and loops, Steven had no idea whether the price was good or bad.

"Is this market price?" he ventured, hoping she wouldn't think him a complete idiot.

"A little better than the Chicago stockyard price," she said after a short pause. "I'm allowing for the fact you're with the Mounted Police, and I've cut off a few cents per head as we agreed."

"Uh-huh." Steven continued to stare at the paper, hoping some revelation would suddenly appear in his mind.

"Constable, have you bought cattle before?" She turned and hung one arm off the back of her chair, making him feel even more at a loss by her nonchalance.

"No, I admit that I have not. In fact, I have no idea if this price is acceptable or outright gouging."

Fire snapped in her eyes, but the pleasant little smile on her face never changed. "That's a fair price. You might get a little better or a little worse someplace else, but our cattle are some of the finest in the Territories. We know that and charge accordingly. They are pasture grazed, then kept in a feedlot to increase weight gain just before they are herded to market. And then, we allow enough time on our trail drives for the cattle to graze at their leisure and maintain their weight."

She was a vixen, a sharp-tongued shrew destined to make some man's life a living misery. And yet, beneath that self-confident gaze that both ruffled and excited lay a wispy vulnerability that surfaced only occasionally, making a man want to brave the serpent's tongue and further investigate that hidden quality. But he was not that man, Steven decided over the protestations of his baser desires.

"I believe this price is acceptable. I'll arrange with my commander to have the cash sent up from Benton and we'll return to pick up the cattle in a few weeks." Steven pocketed the piece of paper and rose.

"I'll bring the cattle in and lot-feed them until you and your men arrive."

"Constable, you are welcome to stay for supper." The invitation was given in a voice edged in desperation as Cletis lurched up from his chair.

Steven shook his head. "I have to get back to the fort and discuss this with my commander. It's imperative that we get our request for payment in the correct hands as soon as possible."

Cletis forged on. "Saturday, then. Please come. Bring your commander and as many of your men as you would like. We should become acquainted if we are to develop a long business relationship."

Steven glanced first at Willow's unreadable face, then to Emily's eager one, framed in the doorway. He supposed they had few callers, and even a few winter-weary Mounted Policemen would be preferable to no one. A visit would be fun—a nice break to the long winter, and a needed diversion for the men. "Saturday it is, then."

He picked up his hat and started for the door. Emily moved to open the door for him, and the scent of roses moved with her, enveloping them both. She curved her lips into a soft smile.

"Good-bye," he said and nodded to her.

"Good-bye, Constable. I'll be looking forward to

Saturday." There was an invitation in her voice, a sweetness that should appeal to any man.

Steven strode across the porch and stopped when he saw that Buck had been fed, groomed, and returned to the hitching post at the front of the house. Willow moved up beside him, pulling on an oilskin coat against the rising north wind.

"Thank you for seeing to Buck."

She nodded. "He's a fine horse, from good stock." She finished buttoning her coat. "He's got a small stone bruise on his left front foot. I'd rest him a day or two when you get back."

Steven stepped down from the porch and lifted Buck's foot. Sure enough, a small, purplish bruise stained the soft frog of his newly cleaned hoof.

"Don't believe me?" she asked.

Steven looked up at her, then put Buck's foot back down with a pat to his withers. "Of course I do, I just don't take any chances with Buck. He must have done this coming down off that ridge." He pointed at the rise of land that had kept Cletis Dawson's ranch a secret until now.

Willow glanced up at the sky. "I could lend you a horse, but I wouldn't recommend riding out into what's coming." She pointed up at scudding gray clouds. "We can put you up for the night. You can ride out in the morning. I'll put a poultice on his foot overnight."

At best, the ride back to Fort McLeod would take the better part of a day. In a blizzard, it might take two. Then there was Buck to consider.

"Yes, please stay," Emily said from the doorway.

"I'll show you part of my place before this storm hits," Cletis said.

Before he could give an answer, Willow took Buck's reins and led him back toward the barn.

Steven watched them go, nursing a nugget of irritation. She was the most presumptuous female he'd ever encountered, and would probably be a millstone around her father's neck for the rest of her life. No man in his right mind would get involved with Willow Dawson.

"I guess my answer is yes, then," Steven answered.

Tiny bits of ice driven by a chilly wind stung Steven's face. He pulled up the collar of his buffalo-hide coat and noticed that Cletis paid the snow little heed, his attention consumed by the land that stretched out before them. Rolling hills, snow now creating abstract patterns on their treeless sides, filled the horizon. To the west, the backbone of the Rockies etched an erratic horizon. A large herd of cattle grazed on long, yellowed grass, the wind ruffling their hair.

"It's all mine, as far as you can see." He swept the horizon with his arm, unabashed pride in his voice. "And I started it all with a bunch of stolen cattle."

Steven cocked an eyebrow. "You're sure you want to tell me this?"

Cletis laughed. "That was near onto twelve years ago and nobody missed those scrubs. I was a buffalo hunter. Skint a many of 'em and traded their hides to the Blackfeet, Assiniboins, Saulteaux. The land was black with 'em back then. A man couldn't even ride through 'em without pushing a few out of the way. The girls' Ma was Blackfoot and she was heavy with Libby when I decided that weren't no life for young'uns."

Even with the wind buffeting his cheeks, Cletis's face softened noticeably at the mention of his wife.

"There's a ranch a hundred miles or so to the south; some titled bloke from England owns the place. A group of his cows took to hiding in a little depression on the backside of his range with every storm. I already had this land picked out and the house started, so one day I just rounded 'em up, brought 'em here, and that was the beginning of the Dawson Cattle Company. Come spring, he probably thought he'd had a bad wolf year."

Steven laughed and shook his head.

"You a married man?" Cletis asked without taking his eyes off the horizon.

"No, I'm not."

"You got plans when you serve out your time in the Mounties?"

Steven glanced at Cletis from the corner of his eye. The conversation was beginning to feel like an interview. "No. I'll probably be a career man. Hadn't thought much about it, really."

"Nothing'll make you feel more like a man than looking over your own land. You claim it, tame it, then bury your bones in it. Nothing like that, except watching your daughters come into the world." Cletis smiled. "Family's a common man's fortune, constable. Most of us don't leave much else behind."

Cletis turned his horse into the wind. The snow had thickened and now blew sideways, the larger flakes rapidly accumulating on dried blades of grass.

"Could be a deep one," Cletis shouted over his shoulder.

The lights of the house appeared through the snow, beckoning yellow squares, beacons to safety and comfort. They veered past to ride straight into the barn. The cavernous interior muted the fury of the storm, and as he swung down from the saddle, Steven wondered how Cletis had managed to raise such a structure with only three daughters and a few ranch hands to help him.

Their horses stabled, they plodded their way to the house and stamped off their snow-encrusted boots before stepping inside. Warm, moist heat rolled out to welcome them, carrying with it the aroma of roasting meat and baking bread. Wood smoke, faint but sharp, mingled with the supper smells, blending to create a definition of home perceived only by the nose.

"Supper's almost ready." Emily emerged from the kitchen, a lacy apron tied around her middle protecting a pink-sprigged dress that highlighted the color in her cheeks.

Cletis wagged two fingers and strode toward the parlor. He rounded his desk, opened a glass-fronted liquor cabinet, and lifted out a bottle. "Would you like a drink of legal whiskey, constable?"

Real liquor. Smooth. Aged. Bottled under supposedly clean conditions. After four years of seeking out and destroying illegal whiskey, made and bottled under every condition conceivable, the thought seemed a rare luxury.

Cletis took down two sparkling glasses from the same cabinet and filled each with the amber liquid. Taking one for himself, he handed the other to Steven, then held his up in salute. "To rising cattle prices," he said with a smile.

Steven clicked his glass against Cletis's and downed part of the liquor. Expecting a searing in his throat, he was pleasantly surprised when the liquor slid down smoothly, filling him with a pleasant warmth.

Emily appeared at the door and announced that supper was ready. From the shadows by the fireplace, Willow appeared, rising from a high-backed wing chair turned toward the hearth. Startled, Steven tried to hide his surprise as she stretched like a lazy cat and stepped around the chair to join them.

A sly smile crossed her lips as she lifted her father's glass from his hand and took a drink of the liquor. Cletis knitted his brows and glanced toward the open parlor door. "You know your sister'll give me hell if she finds out."

The tip of a pink tongue swept her lips and she handed him back the glass. Without a word or a backward glance, she sauntered out the door.

Supper was served in a fashion Steven had not experienced for many years. Food steamed from china bowls, and water sparkled in crystal glasses. A fine cloth of linen lay over the table with matching napkins folded at each place. Still puzzled by the incongruity of Cletis Dawson's life, Steven slid into his assigned chair.

"How long have you been in the Mounted Police, constable?" Emily asked as she started a dish of potatoes around the table.

"Five years. I signed up in seventy-three."

"You were one of the original force, then?"

"Yes, I was."

Emily smiled sweetly from her place at her father's side. "How romantic."

Steven chuckled. "I'm afraid there was very little romance attached to those first two years. Fort McLeod was our first outpost in the Territories. It was little better than a collection of mud huts that first winter. Roofs poured mud when it rained. Men were sick and the snow was deep. We chased whiskey traders in every conceivable weather and condition."

"But I understand you routed the whiskey trade in short time."

Steven nodded. "Yes, with the cooperation of the Blackfeet, who were already tired of illegal whiskey ruining the lives of their people."

"And Fort McLeod has grown into a small town since the establishment of the fort," Cletis said as he devoured a forkful of potatoes.

"You can buy almost anything in Fort McLeod that you can buy in Ottawa," Steven replied.

"I understand there are cattle ranches springing up all over the Alberta Territory, that titled Englishmen are coming here to make their fortunes," Willow commented.

Steven noticed from the edge of his vision that her two sisters exchanged knowing glances.

"I'm afraid I know almost nothing about cattle, Miss Dawson."

"I read that some of the successful American ranchers have discovered that fattening cattle in feed lots and then driving them hard to market cost them profits in weight loss, so they've adopted a new practice of allowing the cattle to set their own pace to allow adequate grazing—a practice we're already using."

Her comments drew silence and a scolding look from Emily; then all eyes turned toward Steven. Clear and intelligent, Willow's eyes challenged him to offer an opinion on the future of western Canada, a subject she'd obviously thought much about, and he immediately felt at a loss. The future was a time he avoided thinking about until it became the present.

Shreds of information began to coalesce in his mind, bits and pieces he'd heard on visits to Benton and from traders at Fort McLeod. "Cattle has an optimistic future here in the west. The land is good, the grass tall. We have markets in the United States and in the East. More and more settlers arrive every day, now that the problem of illegal whiskey is past. It seems the next logical step."

He knew immediately he'd failed her test, even though he had no idea what she'd wanted him to say. She watched him for a moment, then glanced down at her plate.

"What did you do before you became a Mounted Policeman?" Emily slid easily into the conversation, changing the subject to something even more uncomfortable.

Always dreading the inevitable question, Steven drew in a breath. "I was a professional clown."

"You mean like a clown in a circus?" Libby leaned forward, her eyes sparkling.

"Yep, just like that."

"How wonderful," Emily said, clasping her hands together. "You must have delightful stories you could tell us."

"Is there any money in that sort of work?" Willow asked, and the conversation suffered a dramatic pause.

"Willow, that's rude!" Emily chided, and Willow threw her a frown.

"It's a perfectly good question." Willow turned back toward him expectantly.

Unnerved in ways he couldn't begin to explain, Steven met Willow's honest stare. "No, there's not much money in it. But, I enjoyed working with people, children in particular. I was very good at it, and following my talent seemed the natural thing to do."

He held her gaze, refusing to look away first, refusing to bow to her unfathomable attempt to embarrass him. She blinked, and he noticed that her lashes were dark and curly. The corners of her mouth tipped up slightly in a hint of a smile. "Yes, constable, that does seem like the natural thing to do."

Emily bolted up from her chair, setting the china to rattling. "I have dessert all ready in the kitchen." She hurried away in a flurry of skirts and returned in record time with a serving tray filled with plates of pie. She brushed across Steven's shoulder as she set the rose-entwined china plate in front of him, then hurried on to serve her father.

"Our Em is a mighty fine cook," Cletis said with a mouthful of pie and a pride-filled glance at Emily.

"She is indeed." And indeed she was, Steven thought. He hadn't tasted such decadence since leaving Ottawa and his mother's blueberry concoctions.

Steven glanced down the table. Emily consumed her treat with dainty bites, employing a napkin after every forkful.

He could do worse, Steven thought. Maybe this discontent eating away at his insides was curable. Maybe he was yearning for home and hearth. Maybe he wanted someone to hold in the night, welcoming arms at the end of a day, someone to represent the future. His years with the Mounted Police had fulfilled his dream of excitement and adventure. But now, with the illegal whiskey trade practically abolished and any misunderstandings with the Indians under control, no imminent danger loomed on his horizon.

The once-shining dream of conquering the Western Territories began to tarnish when placed alongside the prospect of sleeping in a barracks with twenty other men, eating in a mess hall, and riding lonely, cold patrols for another twenty years. His second term would be up in late summer. Maybe he should look for a wife, buy a small ranch, settle down. Emily looked up at that moment and smiled warmly, as if reading his thoughts.

Aware of movement to his right, he slanted a glance to where Libby sat, her chin planted in her palms, openly staring at him with her elbows on the table.

He turned full toward her and she batted her eyelashes at him in imitation of one hopelessly love-struck. Quickly, he covered his mouth with his napkin to hide a laugh. Glancing around the table, he realized no one else had seen her flirtation. When he looked back at her, she smiled innocently, making him wonder if he'd imagined it.

After supper, Emily shooed Libby off to bed, Willow disappeared, and Steven spent the rest of the evening discussing politics with Cletis in the parlor. As the fire died down to embers, Cletis stood and stretched.

"Time for bed," he announced, and Emily appeared from the kitchen as if on cue.

"I've made up the guest room for you, constable, and laid a fire," Emily said, gazing up at him.

"I wouldn't want to put you to any trouble," he countered halfheartedly.

"It was no trouble. I love to have guests." She led him up the stairs to the second story and swung open a door. Had he not known better, Steven would have sworn he was in a hotel in Ottawa.

A tall, carved bed frame squatted in the center of the room, guarding the shiny hardwood floor beneath its carved feet. A quilt covered its expanse and draped the sides to touch the floor. A fire burned softly on the hearth, and a lamp cast a comfortable glow over it all.

"If there's anything you need, I'm just across the hall," Emily said and paused before him. He looked down into her face and the thought to kiss her crossed his mind. How would her lips taste? Would they grow soft and pliant beneath his mouth? Would she mold her body to his if he took her in his arms?

"Sleep well, Constable Gravel," she said, then swept away, closing the door behind her.

He admired the room for a moment, then turned down the lamp wick. The cool, white light of reflected moonglow quickly filled the room, chased from one small corner by the fire. Shedding his jacket and pants, Steven stretched his arms over his head and arched his back. Called to the window by a provocative moonbeam, he moved to stare out across the yard, now covered by a soft snowfall. Snow was still falling, in fact—large, feathery flakes floating down past the window glass, sometimes pausing suspended for a moment on an errant breath of wind.

Movement below caught his eye. A bundled figure moved across the expanse between the house and the barn. Head bowed and hands shoved in pants pockets, the figure wore a broad hat, the crown encrusted with snow.

Then, as Steven watched, the figure stopped and abruptly fell backward in the snow, spread-eagled beneath the cold gaze of the moon. Arms moved up and down; legs moved side to side. Snow angels. Someone was making snow angels.

He peered closer, enchanted. Hat flung aside, the figure sat up and glanced around furtively, dark hair spilling across her shoulders.

Willow.

She scrambled to her feet, moved over a short distance, and flopped back in the snow again, repeating the process until a choir of heavenly beings came to life side by side. She then stood, shook off the snow, and held her arms out to her sides. Head flung back, she offered her face to the falling flakes as she whirled around, her buffalo coat flying out behind her.

Palms against the cold glass, Steven leaned his forehead against the window frame, watching the snow nymph below him. Instinctively, he sensed he was watching a very private moment, a bit of time she stole for herself. And in this private moment, she lay open her soul to the heavens above and allowed herself to indulge in whimsy uncharacteristic of the face she presented to the world.

All thoughts of kissing Emily Dawson fled his mind.

Chapter Four

"Do a trick for me."

"I beg your pardon?" Steven halted his fork halfway to his mouth.

"Elizabeth May! Has this whole family abandoned their manners?" Emily's face was first stricken, then angry as she glared at Libby's effort at feigned innocence.

Willow stifled an outright laugh and winked at Libby.

"It's all right." Steven held up a hand, put down his fork, and reached into his pocket. He drew out three small blue balls and turned his chair toward Libby.

"Watch carefully now." He grinned and long fingers manipulated the balls across the back of his hand, under his palm, and back between his fingers with lightning speed.

Willow wondered if he knew how his face changed when he smiled at Libby's glee, true joy filling his beautiful gray eyes. It was evident that he loved children.

Libby clapped her hands and begged for more. Emily gazed at the pair with a misty expression that Willow knew meant trouble. Folding her napkin, she shoved back her chair, an odd pressure gathering in her chest. "I'm going out to check on the calf and then I'm riding down to the lower pasture."

Her father turned and pinned her with the expression she'd expected. "Andy'll do that."

Suddenly anxious to be out of the house, Willow shook her head. "Wilbur's laid up with his leg and Andy's mucking out the barn."

"What's wrong with Wilbur's leg?"

Libby turned terrified eyes toward Willow, and Steven's cool gaze soon followed. "He tripped over Bell and went down hard on his knee."

Cletis rolled his eyes toward the post-and-beam ceiling. "Is there no end to the mischief one little goat can cause?"

"Please, Daddy. Bell didn't mean it."

Cletis smiled. "I never thought it was Bell's intention to undermine my entire ranch, but she's doing a damn good job at it."

"You won't sell her to the Blackfeet, will you?"

Steven's gaze darted to her father, and a slight furrow shadowed his brows. Did he really think them capable of crushing a child's world?

"Of course not, Libby, but see if you can keep Bell out of trouble for one day. Just one day." He held up a beefy finger.

Steven pocketed the balls. "If you're riding out to look at the herd, I'd like to ride out with you, if you don't mind." Steven carefully laid his napkin by the side of his plate. "Emily, those were the best pancakes I've had in a long time. Someday I'll take you to Fort McLeod and let you teach Constable Jackson how to cook them like that."

Emily colored prettily and smiled. "Why, thank you. I'd be glad to write down the recipe."

Suddenly irritated with the politeness piling up around her like soiled hay, Willow strode to the back door and slipped into her oilskin coat, balancing the plate she'd filled and covered with a clean napkin. Steven slid into the narrow space alongside her and lifted his heavy buffalo coat clear of the coatrack.

"Don't leave my linens out there." Emily's voice carried to her even after she closed the door behind them.

The brilliance of the fresh snowfall blinded her, and she squinted against the whiteness for a moment before stepping into the drifts and wading a path to the bunkhouse. Steven followed and they stomped up onto the covered porch.

"Wilbur? You all right?" she called, jerking open the door without warning.

Her answer was a muffled snore and a grunt from somewhere in the darkened room. "Yeah. I'm all right." The ropes of a bed frame creaked. "Come on back."

Walking past the table filled with dirty dishes, Willow stopped in front of Wilbur's bunk. His head in one hand, the other hand massaged his knee through a pair of worn brown pants.

"Brought you some of Emily's pancakes."

He raised his head and reached for the plate. "Miss Emily made pancakes?"

"We had company."

Wilbur leaned to look beyond her, and Steven stepped into sight.

"Constable Steven Gravel of the Northwest

Mounted Police," he said extending a hand. "I'm attached to Fort McLeod. We're interested in buying some of your cattle."

Wilbur turned bloodshot eyes to Willow. "We ain't got nobody to drive 'em up there."

"The Mounties have offered to drive them themselves."

"You boys know anything about drivin' cattle?"

Unperturbed, Steven shook his head. "No, but we'll learn on the way."

"Somebody's gotta go and show 'em at least a thing or two."

Willow swallowed, fighting down the uneasiness that erupted whenever Steven stepped close. "I'll go along."

"No. You ain't going, Willow. I've told you before, this ain't a fittin' job for you."

"I do it as well as you, you old cripple."

Wilbur grinned and Willow's heart warmed. "There ain't no argument there, missy. It just ain't a fittin' thing. You oughta be in the house knitting some of them frilly things Miss Emily knits."

The words ran down Willow's spine like the irritating squeak of an unoiled barn door. "You leave the knitting to Emily and the cowpunching to me."

"What's your Pa say about this?" Wilbur stood, teetered a minute, then tested his knee with a few short, hopping steps.

"I haven't told him. Constable Gravel hasn't even presented my price to his superiors yet."

"Did you figure up the bill?"

"Of course I did."

"Watch out you've got your shirt when she's through with you, young fella," Wilbur said to Steven with a grin. "She's a slick one with a pencil."

"I can see that," Steven responded.

"You want me to bring you some hot towels for that knee?" Willow asked.

Wilbur shook his head. "No, I'm gonna eat these pancakes first, then I'll soak 'er." He cleared a place on the table by shoving aside plates and cups, then he sat down, careful of the extended limb. "You going out to the herd?"

"Yeah. I thought I'd ride down to the lower pasture."

"See that they ain't all piled up in that coulee to the west." He stuffed a forkful of pancakes into his mouth and closed his eyes briefly. "Hmmm."

"I'll chase them out if they are." She swung around and headed to the door.

"Show him them Hereford of your'n. Good meat cattle."

"I'll show him, but I'm not selling them yet," she called back over her shoulder.

They made a path to the barn and swung open one of the double doors. The familiar scent of horse and hay poured out, and Willow felt at ease for the first time since she'd opened her eyes that morning.

Steven clamped his bottom lip between his teeth and whistled softly. Buck answered with a nicker from his borrowed stall deep in the barn. Grinning as if he'd invented the trick, Steven sauntered toward the depths of the barn. *Arrogant ass,* she thought, watching him walk away, but something within her quickly took in the smooth line of his spine and the way his jacket hugged his narrow hips.

She stepped into a nearby stall and ran a hand down Pat's smooth neck. He dipped his head and searched her pockets for the hidden bit of apple he eventually found. Chomping with delight, he stood still as she saddled him. Deeper in the barn, interspersed with bits of murmured conversation, she heard the jingle of Steven's tack.

He rode up behind her, already in the saddle as she checked her cinch one last time and lowered her stirrup. From the corner of her eye she noted that he sat a horse well, truly the picture of authority.

"The Herefords Wilbur mentioned are grazing to the south of where we're going." She swung up into the saddle and Pat hurried toward the door, pushing past Steven's horse. "They gain weight quickly on pasture and their meat is tender. We've recently added them to our herd." She shoved open the barn door with her foot and Pat trotted out into the snow.

As before, the brilliance of the day blinded her for a moment, and she clamped down on Pat with her knees as he danced sideways, stirring the dry snow into a second flight.

Together, they rode past the house and onto the open prairie. An occasional tree broke the serenity of the white blanket that softened the rolls of the distant hills.

"Do you enjoy the business end of ranching?" he asked suddenly, startling her with his directness.

"Why shouldn't I?" she countered with a glance in his direction.

"No reason you shouldn't. It's unusual to find a woman so interested in cattle prices and grazing practices."

His slight smile was maddening and intriguing at the same time. "What would you have me doing? Crocheting doilies?"

"I think you should do whatever you do best.

I'm just nosy, I guess, as to why you chose riding the range over tending the kitchen stove."

"Emily does all the stove tending one family needs. Somebody has to help Pa. I was always good with figures and I love to be outside. After Ma died, we just sort of settled into these roles and been this way ever since."

Suddenly seized with the urge to bite her tongue, Willow wondered why she was telling him all this. He'd get his cattle and they'd never see him again. If she was lucky. But a tendril of suspicion was growing within her. Emily wanted and needed a husband. Steven was the only eligible man for miles, and she could see the gleam of an idea in her father's eye. Nope, she'd not be rid of Constable Gravel soon. In fact, he could become her brother-in-law. That possibility struck a chord within her she could not define or dismiss from her mind. Sadness, envy, all wrapped around a core of relief, permeated her like a creeping morning fog, knocking out of balance her carefully figured world.

"Your mother was Blackfoot, your father said."

"Yes, she was." She slanted him a glance. No displeasure crossed his face—none of the disgust she'd often seen in the faces of traders and merchants.

"She must have been some woman to settle down an old buffalo hunter like your father."

"She was," Willow replied without hesitation.

"He must have loved her very much to build all this for her."

"Well, Pa loved Ma. That's a fact. Married her right off when most men kept Blackfeet women as squaws." She smiled and at the same time cursed her flapping tongue.

"A friend of mine, a fellow policeman, recently married Sitting Bull's niece."

"For sure? One of the refugee Sioux?"

"Yep."

"How did his fellow officers take the news?"

Steven turned toward her, fixing her with his gray gaze. "They were a little surprised—more at the fact he married at all than that he married Dancing Bird."

Perhaps he would do as a brother-in-law after all.

They rode over a rise and spread before them was the snow-filled coulee Wilbur had warned them about. Sure enough, the snow was churned into a muddy mire and the cattle were huddled against a bluff at the west end, muddy and bedraggled.

Willow lifted her rope from the saddle horn and urged Pat into the thick of the herd. Reluctant to leave their safe haven, they resisted her pokes and prods and began to move to the clear end only after she smacked a few soundly on the rump with her coiled rope.

"Get out of here before the wolves have you for supper." Pat, ears pricked forward, dodged and ducked from side to side, preventing stragglers from returning to the coulee.

When the herd was moving forward together, Pat urged them forward faster until they moved along at a lope, bawling their indignation.

"They bunch up in these coulees in a storm, then don't have sense enough to leave. A wolf pack can pick off five or six before they get the idea they better get out in the open."

Wind had sculpted the snow into soft curves and dips as the horses cantered along. Feeling the sharp cold biting her cheeks, Willow wondered if she'd ever love anything more than a snowy gallop. She sneaked a glance at Steven; his horse was keeping pace with hers. His heavy coat had blown open, revealing the striking scarlet of his jacket and the tight fit of his pants over his thighs. Muscles rippled beneath the fabric as his knees tightened and flexed with his horse's gait. He was a natural born horseman, one of that rare breed born to spend their lives on the back of a horse. Maybe this was why he'd left such an odd profession to come west. Perhaps fate had whispered in his ear. Perhaps the same whisper of destiny had sent him to Emily, intending him to take over the ranch when Pa was no longer able.

"They're fine cattle," he shouted over the wind, nodding his head in the direction of the galloping herd.

"I know," she shouted back.

Willow pulled Pat down to a walk, and the cattle soon stopped their flight and looked back over their shoulders with disgust.

"Pa and I'll bring a wagon-load of hay out tomorrow if the snow doesn't melt soon."

Steven folded his hands over his saddle horn. "I'll give your price to my commander, and if he agrees, I'll be back with the men to move them inside of a week."

Even as she nodded, the tiny dark flecks in his eyes gave birth to a herd of butterflies in her stomach.

"Looks like a fair deal." Major James McLeod looked over the pricing for the cattle, then over the edge of the paper at Steven. "It's signed 'Willow Dawson.'"

"Yes sir."

"Is it Mrs. or Miss?"

Behind him, Steven heard Braden chuckle. Commissioner James McLeod had become suspicious of every eligible woman in the Northwest Territories, especially since Braden and his wife, Dancing Bird, had created a major diplomatic crisis with their love affair.

"It's Miss."

"She runs the ranch?" McLeod looked up, glowering beneath heavy, dark eyebrows.

"No, she manages the business of the ranch."

McLeod looked back down at the estimate and sighed. "Before I send a patrol to this ranch, how many sisters does she have?"

"Two, sir."

"Any of them marriageable age?"

"One. Emily."

McLeod cleared his throat. Headquarters in Ottawa was still reluctant to grant their men permission to marry, as they had since the formation of the Northwest Mounted Police in 1873. Feeling life in the Territories too much to ask of a wife and family, Ottawa preferred the men remain single, a preference that had endured with the same success as a straw hut against a windstorm. Two of the original contingent of men had married, and more had left the service when their initial three years were up to pursue the desires of their hearts. To McLeod and other commanders of outposts fell the task of carrying out this doomed requirement.

"Take this signed agreement back to Mr. Dawson." McLeod scrawled a note and his signature on the bottom of the document. "Go on ahead and select the cattle. I'll send Constables Flynn,

McGavin and Jackson with the payment and to help you trail the cattle back here in about three days."

McLeod threaded his fingers together and stared at Steven. "Do you have any intentions you'd like to declare before you leave?"

Steven leaned forward, puzzled. "Sir?"

"Do you intend to marry one of these sisters?" Braden's chuckle matured into a guffaw.

"Absolutely not, sir," Steven said. "The thought hadn't crossed my mind." *Liar*, he thought and wondered if his face gave him away.

"Are you sure, Constable?"

"Yes sir. Quite sure."

"You fellas move on this sort of thing pretty quickly, and I don't like surprises."

"I assure you, sir. I have no intentions in that direction."

"Famous last words," McLeod mumbled to the scrawled papers. "I'll expect you back in two weeks, three at the most. We wouldn't want you away for Christmas."

Steven stood, turned, and strode from the room, a disquieting feeling riding him all the way out the door.

"Is there a guilty secret you'd like ta tell me, Steven?" Braden teased with a huge grin.

"Nope." Steven seated his Stetson firmly on his head and headed for the barracks.

By noon the next day, he was on his way back to the Dawson ranch. As he topped the ridge and looked down on the meandering spread of corrals and buildings, he was struck again with the longing for a home. A family. Roots that would grow strong and deep. He again called Emily's face to mind. The silky smoothness of her skin, the gentle line of her jaw, the soft peach color that stained her cheeks. For his trouble, all he experienced was a warm feeling of familiarity.

Unbidden into his musings rose Willow's face. The shiny darkness of her hair. The red pout of her lips. The inviting curves of her body, boldly evident beneath the men's clothes she wore. And his traitorous body responded with quickening pulse and a tightening in the pit of his stomach.

He nudged Buck down the incline of the ridge and wondered, as the rattling rocks announced his descent, if his self-destructive streak was hereditary.

Libby danced out onto the porch, fluffing the cream lace-looped skirts of her green dress. She hooked a porch column with one hand and swung around it.

"Why'd you come back so soon?" she asked, adjusting her skirts. "Did you come to court Emily?"

Steven swung down from Buck's back and knew he was facing an imposing adversary. "No, I came to make a deal with your father for the cattle."

Libby shook her head solemnly. "Pa won't talk money with you. You gotta see Willow 'bout that."

"Then I'll make a deal with Willow."

Libby pressed a finger to her lips, stepped forward, and glanced around furtively. "This is a secret, so you can't tell nobody," she whispered.

Steven moved forward and lowered his head. "All right. What is it?"

"Willow'll get a man out of his pants." She nodded over the garbled sentence with a confident expression.

"What?"

She thought a moment; then her face brightened. "Pa says Willow'll *trade* a man out of his pants."

"She will, will she?"

"Yep." She nodded knowingly. "She ain't never made a bad trade yet."

"Well, I'll watch myself, then." He stepped up onto the porch.

"She ain't here."

"Where is she?"

Libby jerked her head toward the barn. "Out yonder with the calf. He's bad sick and Willow won't let me go out there."

"Very sick."

"That's what I said." She pursed her lips. "You sound like Emily."

Steven shook his head and walked toward the barn, leading Buck through the muddy patches of remaining snow. The barn door was ajar and he pushed it open quietly and stepped inside. From deep within the dark interior, he heard a soft voice crooning words he could not distinguish. Dropping Buck's reins to the ground, he walked quietly to where a soft yellow glow illuminated a small corner.

The voice grew clearer and the anguish in it more evident. A soft sigh roughened with tears replaced words, and he peeped over the top stall railing. Willow sat in the hay, the brown calf spread across her lap, its head lolled to the side. Large brown eyes stared upward, unseeing. Head bent, one hand on her forehead, Willow sobbed, her small shoulders trembling with the effort.

The urge to step into the stall and take her into his arms was almost overwhelming, but Steven remained unseen, mystified by yet another glimpse into the heart of this chameleon in men's pants.

She ran a palm down the calf's narrow face, across its nose, and back up to scratch its soft, blunt ears. So this was the calf she'd pulled from the storm. From the collection of bottles and jars strewn around her, she'd made a valiant effort to save it.

Gently, she slid the calf off her lap, brushing her hand over the eyes to close them. Steven stepped back into the dark and quickly padded down the length of the barn back to Buck's side. He picked up the reins, stepped to the barn door and banged it shut.

"Hello?" he called.

"Constable Gravel?" she answered.

"Yes, I've returned with authorization for the cattle."

"I'll be right there." No trace of tears remained in her voice. And when she emerged from the twilight of the barn, her face bore no signs of sorrow. Apparently, Willow Dawson kept a close rein on her heart.

He searched her eyes for some trace of what he'd witnessed. Except for a slight redness that shadowed her deep, brown eyes, the last few seconds could have been his imagination. What had happened, he wondered, to have given her the ability to so completely disguise what was in her heart?

"Commissioner McLeod has agreed to your price, and my men will arrive in a day or two to drive them back to the fort."

"Wilbur's still laid up, but Andy and I'll cut out the ones you want . . . that is if we don't get any more snow."

"I'd like to help you, if you don't mind."

She cocked her head to the side, floppy hat all but hiding half her face. "Don't trust me, Constable Gravel?"

"Of course I do; I'd just like to know more about the cattle business."

She seemed about to say more; then she stepped forward to take Buck's reins. Her hand brushed his and a bolt of awareness shot up his arm, across his chest, and straight to the pit of his stomach, where it grew into moist, heavy desire. Wondering if she'd felt the same thing, he peered into her face. She stood looking down at the point where their skin touched, but none of what he was feeling showed on her face. She looked up slowly, her expression neutral. "Do you want me to feed and water him?"

"Sure. Thank you. Is your father in the house?"

She nodded. "In the parlor."

He turned away, strode through the door, and left her in the dark holding the worn leather reins. She let out her breath and watched her steady grip dissolve into trembles. She flopped down on a nearby keg of nails and took a deep breath. Unable to resist a silly notion, she looked down at the straw-strewn barn floor to see if she really had melted into a puddle. Never, in all her years, had she experienced such emotions from a mere touch—or anything else.

Watching the door swing closed behind him, she wondered what devastation his hands could wreak if he touched her in other places, other ways. She shook her head to clear it of the images, and Buck nudged her hat off.

"All right. I'll feed you." Sweeping her hat up and teetering on jelly-filled legs, she led Buck to an empty stall.

Chapter Five

Libby had him treed. Yep, *treed* would be the word he'd use.

Steven fidgeted on the sofa and glanced around the room—anywhere away from the worshipful adoration in Libby's eyes. She'd plied him with Emily's sweets and tea and now sat staring at him as only first, intense love can. Part of him wanted to panic, and the other part to laugh, but he dared not do either. Her adoration of him was real and bottomless, and he'd do nothing to break her fragile heart. Perhaps tomorrow a new calf or a new kitten would steal her love from him. Whoever established that the male was the aggressor in matters of love had never met the Dawson sisters.

"Would you like some more tea, constable?" Libby asked, her eyes brightening.

"No, Libby. I'm fine."

"More cake, then?"

"No. But the cake was delicious."

"Libby, leave Constable Gravel alone. I dare say he is quite full." Emily swept in and bent low to retrieve the china dishes upon which Libby had served him.

"Please, call me Steven," he said, breathing in Emily's sweet scent that swirled around him, tantalizing and teasing.

"Of course, Steven." Then she sailed gracefully away. He didn't miss the slight frown Libby threw her receding back.

And they're territorial even at thirteen, he added to his bank of knowledge about women.

But in that reservoir of knowledge was no reference that would fit Willow. Across the room she sat at her desk, poring over papers, her quill pen held at the ready. At Emily's words she glanced up and cocked an eyebrow at him, as if she knew exactly what was going on and was enjoying his discomfort immensely.

"I think I shall go up to bed," Emily announced from the doorway. "Can I get anyone anything before I go?"

"No, thank you," Steven answered. Cletis responded with a soft snore from his chair by the fire, and no one else commented.

"Libby, it's time for bed."

Libby threw her a loathing-filled glance, as only a sister can do, and dragged herself off the sofa. With a mumbled "Good night," she scuffed behind Emily up the stairs.

"I think I'll go to bed, too," Steven said; being alone with Willow's quiet intensity was suddenly unnerving.

Willow looked up again. "We'll head out early and ride down to the south pasture. Wilbur's knee's still giving him trouble, but Andy's going with us."

"Should we wait until my patrol arrives?"

She shook her head. "Shorthorns are easy to handle. We can bring them in ourselves." She paused and fixed him with one of her bone-jarring direct stares. "That is, if you still want to help."

"Of course."

The moment passed and she directed her attention back to the papers in front of her. "Good, then. I'll see you in the morning."

In his guest room, Steven tossed and turned beneath the soft quilts. His path in life, once so straight and sure in his mind, now suddenly twisted and curved, and he wondered how and why that had happened. He rolled onto his side and pillowed his cheek on his arm, praying for sleep to still his racing thoughts, taunting devils that threatened to make him reconsider his choices. His life was planned, set in stone, signed in long-dried ink on a forgotten paper. Orders from superiors would direct his days, and never again would he have to make a heart-wrenching decision.

He flopped over onto his back and stared at the patterns of moonlight playing above his bed. Only days ago, he hadn't given a thought to life outside the force, and now dissatisfaction chewed at his soul.

Sighing, he raised one knee and locked his fingers behind his head. Visions of Emily floated through his mind, and he wondered if his attraction to her was for herself or what she represented. Stability. Home. Family. She was sweet and kind, gentle and pleasant. Everything a man could want in a wife. Then why didn't his heart pound when he touched her hand? And why didn't desire rush into his veins when she entered a room. Why didn't her presence affect him like Willow's did?

He sat up on the side of the bed and stared at his own reflection mirrored in the window. Willow was both a curiosity to be pursued and trouble to be avoided. And as much as he hated to admit it, something about Willow Dawson terrified him right down to his wool socks.

He rose and padded across the floor to poke at the fire that needed no attention. Poker in hand, he sat down in a chair and stared into the small flames he had aggravated into life. Deciding a visit to the outhouse was in order, he slipped on his uniform pants, pulled on his heavy buffalo coat, and eased open his bedroom door.

Soft moonlight spilled in through a long window at the end of the hall and painted a lengthened pattern on the polished wooden floor. Steven stared down at the shadow, then glanced to the window, where a figure stood looking out across the yard. Dark hair hung down her back, nearly touching the buttons on the back of her droopy one-piece suit of winter underwear. Even the bagginess of the material didn't hide the enticing lines of a feminine figure.

Willow.

Entranced, Steven watched her, taking in the long line of her spine and the way her hips flared softly to blend into long legs. Both hands pressed against the glass, she looked like some caged night creature longing for freedom. When he walked up behind her, she turned, unruffled by his sudden presence or her lack of clothes.

"I couldn't sleep," he babbled, feeling like a fool for stating the obvious.

A small smile said she thought him a fool, too. "Wolves." She turned back to the window and nodded toward the moonlit yard, completely unaware that every mound and curve of her body was visible beneath the soft knit material. "Once in a while they try to get into the barn, but I fixed it so they couldn't. I like to watch them in the moonlight."

Steven understood completely. Soft, gray shadows, slipping along just inside the eye's perception of reality. Long-legged stalkers whose plaintive howls brought gooseflesh to a man's arms, finding and touching some primeval urge within.

"I do, too."

"Do you see many on your patrols?"

He moved up beside her and she sidled over to allow him space at the window. Hip touching hip, Steven struggled for words. "Sometimes up near the tree line or following a buffalo herd."

"They're the perfect animal, you know. They cull the weak and consume the dead. They never take more game than they and their family can eat."

The pounding heart he had despaired of ever feeling again was hammering away at his ribs, and he remained, their bodies touching, to see what she would do.

If she felt the same wild emotions as he, she didn't let on. "You love this place, don't you?"

She turned toward him, her face filled with amazement. As if seeing him for the first time, her eyes searched his. "Yes, I do. I love the wind on my face and the cold that nips at my ears. In the summer, I love the way the grasshoppers spring up in front of my horse, and the warm sun on my back."

For a brief moment, she'd given him a glimpse inside her world, something he instinctively knew she bestowed on few people. "I love the open spaces, too," seemed a feeble response to such a gift.

Reluctant to give up the tender thread holding them here together, he continued to stare into her dark-brown eyes. She didn't look away, nor did she seem to disapprove that he was unintentionally leaning toward her. Instead, she watched him the way a predator watches game—alert, yet detached. No emotional involvement. He leaned closer, the urge to kiss her overwhelming his good sense. She met his eyes fearlessly, and not a flicker of doubt passed over her face as he neared. Her lips parted slightly, and as his eyes slid closed, her voice broke through the haze of desire rapidly consuming him.

"What are you doing?"

Steven opened his eyes and stared into hers. "I . . . guess I'm kissing you."

She stared back, not with anger or fear, but with curiosity. "Why?"

Why had never been an issue when he kissed a woman before. "Because I want to," was the only answer he could come up with.

He expected a sudden lash of temper to set him right and dispel this stubborn notion to taste her lips.

The tip of a pink tongue flittered across her bottom lip, the only sign his closeness affected her at all. His knees trembled, and he wanted more of her than he could have here in the upstairs hall.

"All right," she agreed in the same matter-of-fact tone with which she agreed to cattle prices.

Steven pulled slightly away. "Are you sure?"

"Yes."

Suddenly self conscious, Steven leaned forward again, closed his eyes, and expected to feel the sting of her palm against his cheek. Instead, he felt the softness of her lips. She went rigid for a second, then relaxed against him with a soft sigh that stirred the hair at his temple. Encouraged, he slid an arm around her waist to pull her closer. Expecting resistance, he was pleasantly surprised when she willingly relaxed against his chest, her curves molding to his. His fingers bunched the soft fabric of her undershirt, feeling her silky skin slide beneath his touch. As if she'd been kissed for years, she combed her fingers through the back of his hair. Searing, demanding passion poured through him.

Her lips moved beneath his with such confidence that he briefly wondered if she was, indeed, an innocent. He hadn't kissed a woman since he'd kissed his Catherine good-bye minutes before she died, and the reluctance he'd anticipated at ever doing this again surprisingly forgot to materialize.

She was as aroused as he, her breaths shallow and fast, warm against his cheeks. Seemingly oblivious to the intimate way his body was responding to her, she continued to run her fingers through his hair and kiss him in a way he'd only imagined when he looked at her. The sound of a door softly closing intruded and they sprang apart.

Across the adequate space now between them, her chest rose and fell in harmony with his own as she fearlessly met his eyes. Despite their intimacy, asking her about her reaction suddenly seemed inappropriate, adding one more enigma to his growing list.

"Well, I should be going along. I was headed . . . outside," he said, feeling as stupid as the words sounded. The earth had just moved and he was suggesting he should just shuffle off to the outhouse.

She only nodded her agreement.

He wanted to take her back to bed with him, tumble her into the soft quilts and peel away the layers of her personality until he found the woman who'd just seduced him to complete arousal with a chaste kiss.

Reluctantly, he turned and started back down the hall; then he stopped and swiveled around. She stood in the moonlight, her hair an unruly cloud around her shoulders, watching him go.

"Have you ever been kissed before?" he asked softly.

She shook her head slowly after a moment's hesitation, sending her hair sliding across her shoulders in a manner that begged attention.

"You're a quick learner," he muttered, dragging himself down the stairs and out the door, where he stepped into the frigid night, closed the door behind him, and leaned against it for good measure.

Sunrise was only a sincere promise in the east when Willow slipped out of the house, stuffing her hair up under her hat. Sleep had been fleeting and she'd tied her covers in a knot with her twisting and tumbling.

The shadows of night still claimed the yard, and she paused to allow her eyes to adjust to the dim light. Far away the howl of a wolf raised the hair on the back of her neck. Delicious apprehension slithered through her. She glanced back at the house and up to the window where he'd kissed her, and her body tingled again at the memory.

Why she'd allowed such a thing to happen had chased away her peaceful sleep. She'd never kissed a man, never wanted to, and had, in fact, dreaded with knee-trembling fear ever being placed in such a position. And yet when he'd leaned forward, she'd known exactly what he wanted and what her response would be. His arm around her waist had brought a sense of security she'd never admitted she wanted. And now that she knew such warmth existed, she'd want it again and again, despite the fear of intimacy whispering in her head. Weakness for a man would derail all her carefully laid plans and stir to life fears better forgotten.

Now able to see in the dim light, she walked to the barn and swung open the door. The pungent odor of hay and horse swept out. She inhaled and some of her reason returned. Sucking air between her teeth, she whistled softly and Pat answered with a soft whicker.

She opened his stall door and led him out by the halter. When she passed Buck's stall, he pricked his ears forward and watched her in expectation. She reached into her pocket and withdrew a piece of apple. Holding it in the palm of her hand, she offered the treat to the buckskin, who greedily snatched it away.

Steven's tack hung on a peg by the stall. Willow reached out her hand to touch the saddle, hesitated, then smoothed her fingers across the leather anyway. Well-oiled and cared for, the saddle said much about the man. He obviously realized the value of good leather and a good horse. Buck was well groomed and plump. She touched the saddle-bags, the lumps of his possessions inside tempting her to explore.

She pulled her hand away, paused, then opened the flap of the nearest bag. Burning with embarrassment, she allowed the demon of curiosity to tempt her into disobedience.

A soft white shirt, folded carefully, came out first. Below it was a scruffy wig of buffalo hide dyed a hideous red. She lifted the wig out, chuckled silently, and dove back in. Underneath it were a series of small balls, a deck of cards, and a small square of metal. In the soft lantern light, she couldn't make out what the square was, so she lifted it out of the bag's bottom and held it underneath the lantern.

A woman's face smiled at her from the polished silver frame. Quite lovely, she had a delicate quality that reminded Willow of Emily. Her eyes were soft and gentle, as if someone she loved stood just beyond the edge of the picture. Willow turned the frame over and on the back of the picture were the words "For my love, Steven. Catherine."

The reality of her invasion suddenly dawned and Willow shoved the picture back into the saddlebag. Quickly, she repacked what she'd taken out and buckled the leather flap.

Was the smiling woman his wife? A woman he'd promised to marry waiting for him somewhere? He'd not mentioned either, though she'd not have expected him to tell her such a personal thing.

Disturbed, she saddled Pat and led him outside. The soft, yellow glow of a lantern from the kitchen window said Emily was up, making preparations for breakfast. Willow swung into the saddle and rode to the house, stopping just beneath the window. Inside, Emily moved about in her nightclothes and wrapper. A woman so willing to devote her life to a man and his comforts deserved a chance to do both. So why had Steven chosen to kiss her, a rough cowhand?

As Willow spied through the window, Emily stopped kneading a pile of dough on the table and gazed out the window. The sun peeped above the edge of the prairie, spilling yellow light across the sleeping land. Willow felt she could offer Steven nothing except rough hands, sun-tortured skin, and the inability to love a man the way he needed to be loved. Emily could offer him a gracious home and a family. The thought brought a twist to her heart that she hurriedly dismissed. She'd have to make sure Emily got that chance.

For a man long past his prime, Cletis Dawson sat a horse with an ease many men wished for. Steven watched as he easily maneuvered in and out of the cattle, using only his knees to guide his horse, slapping his leather-covered leg with a coiled rope.

"They're easy cattle to manage," Cletis called across the distance. "Not so apt to bolt and run in all directions."

The morning was cold but pleasant, with no biting wind or hint of snow. The shorthorns grazed contentedly on brown grass, their sleek brown-and-white coats in abrupt contrast to the winter-dulled landscape. Reluctant to give up their grazing, the cattle snatched a few more mouthfuls of grass before beginning a slow movement toward the north, where the holding pens waited.

Across the sea of cattle, Willow dipped in and out of the herd on her beloved Pat. Like her father, she rode with the confidence of one who spent many hours on horseback. She hadn't said a word to Steven since sunup, and the willing woman he'd kissed in the moonlight seemed to have vanished.

Suddenly, a young bull made a plunge for freedom, veering away from the herd and galloping back toward the grazing they'd just left. Willow heeled her horse into a slow canter, quickly gaining on the fugitive. As she rocked easily with the horse's gait, she dropped the reins and uncoiled her rope. Pat drew alongside the bull and Willow's rope flew in a wide, slow loop that settled around the bull's neck. She tightened the noose and snubbed the rope around her saddlehorn. Pat slowed to a walk and pulled backward on the taut line. After a moment's resistance, the young bull stopped, shook his head, and allowed himself to be led closer to Pat's side.

Amazed, Steven pulled Buck to a stop to watch.

"Ain't she something?" Cletis said, riding up to his side. "Always did have a way with the cattle."

"She does that."

"Strong willed, that one. Got it from me, I reckon. Pity she won't never make a wife. She'd be a help to a man."

Steven turned. "What do you mean?"

Cletis turned his horse to follow the slowly moving herd.

"Can't hardly call this cattle punching," Cletis said with a grin. "Ain't nothing like that first bunch I brought here. Thought I'd never get 'em here in one piece, they fought me so bad."

"This is a beautiful spread, Mr. Dawson. You're a lucky man."

"Luck has a way of gettin' her revenge, though. I got no sons to leave it to."

"But you have three beautiful daughters. That should bring you some sons-in-law."

The sparkle in Cletis's eyes told him he should have kept his mouth shut. "And therein lies the problem. Only men come through here are cow hands I wouldn't trust with Nelly here, much less my daughters."

"Settlers are moving into the area every day, especially now since the Sioux have moved farther south and none of the anticipated trouble came to pass. There should be ample opportunity for them to meet young men."

"Wouldn't trust my land nor my girls to just any man. Gotta be an honest fellow who'll treat 'em good. Somebody who likes young'uns—an educated fellow but one that ain't afraid of hard work." Cletis grinned at him with raised eyebrows and Steven felt a noose tighten around his neck.

"Now, Mr. Dawson, I hope I haven't led you—"

"Come court my Emily. You ain't gotta make no promises to her. She's a good cook, good housekeeper. She looks fragile, but I can guarantee she ain't. She's every bit as hardy as her Ma, just gets her coloring and such from me."

Taken aback, Steven stared at Cletis's waggling eyebrows.

"I'll throw in fifty extra head."

Steven hauled Buck to a stop. "You'd sell your daughter for fifty head of cattle?"

Cletis's smile faded. "Oh, all right. Forget the cattle. It was a desperate thought, anyway. I ain't sayin' you gotta marry her; just pay her some attention for a time." He gazed off at the house, the roof just now visible over a gentle rise of land. "She's yearning for a family of her own. She's ripe. Emily ain't never learned to love the loneliness like me and Willow."

"Mr. Dawson, this hardly seems right."

"She ain't got to know we've even talked. Just take her for a walk or two. Why, we're almost neighbors with you bein' only a day's ride away. Who knows? You might get to like her."

"I already like her, Mr. Dawson. That's not the point. The point is I'd be deceiving her, allowing her to think I'm courting her when I'm—" He stopped. There was no explanation for what Cletis was asking him to do.

"She'll see it however you handle it, Constable." Cletis smiled. "I got a soft place in my heart for my girls. Spoiled 'em rotten, I did, after their Ma died. Can't blame a father for wantin' to make his children happy."

Steven looked down at his gloves and the scarlet sleeves of his jacket. They'd talk. He'd tell her about the East and she'd probably tell him about apple preserves. Even as the thought passed through his mind, he realized that a discussion about apple preserves might not be so bad.

"All right, Mr. Dawson. But I'm going to be honest with her. I'll not let her think this is other than a friendship."

Cletis smiled. "That's all I'm asking."

They rode on toward the house in silence, but Steven found his thoughts coming back time and again to Cletis's comments about Willow.

"What about Willow? What does she want?"

Cletis looked startled. "Willow?" He shook his head. "No need of even looking for a man for her. None could suit her. She's happy here with the horses and the cattle. Destined for spinsterhood, that one. Runs in the blood, just like my sister Carrie. Weren't never a man good enough. I got plans to leave her a little spread she can work most of her life. By then maybe she'll have enough money to move to town." Sadness rimmed his eyes. "Who knows? Maybe town'll come to her."

The starkness of the life just described clamped a cold hand around Steven's heart. No family, no children. No hopes for either. He wanted to curse at Cletis and ask him why he couldn't see beneath that hard exterior she carried before her like a warrior's shield—see that for some reason she'd hidden away her heart and her hopes.

"Nope, Willow ain't the marryin' kind. Won't no man ever lasso her."

By twilight, they'd rounded up about three hundred head of cattle and they were all in the holding pens feeding on hay. Short days brought long nights. The sun slid behind the horizon early and draped a mantle of deep purple over the day.

"Willow and Andy'll finish here," Cletis said as the last shorthorns hurried through the holding pen gate. "You and me'll go on to the barn."

Steven glanced back at Willow's horse, dodging in and out of the cattle milling around in the pens. Occasionally, she'd lean down from the saddle and slap one on the rump. Lowing mournfully, the chastised cow would move to another part of the pen when urged with a coiled rope and Pat's body. Something about how she worked these beasts was lyrical, in perfect harmony with her surroundings. And as the last light of day faded and shut her out of his vision, Steven wondered briefly if he could be the man to prove Cletis Dawson wrong.

Chapter Six

Pinions flying, the patrol from Fort McLeod rode over the ridge behind the Dawson ranch, silhouetted against an orange sunset. His mouth full of nails, Steven glanced up from where he was repairing a gnawed hitching rail when the clattering of loose rocks announced their arrival. Three abreast and resplendent in their scarlet, they rode into the yard. Steven smiled, always amazed at the sense of authority the scarlet uniform imparted to anyone who wore it.

Stationed in the porch rocker, Libby had held forth the whole time he'd hammered away at the rickety hitching rail. Plying him with questions about a dozen unrelated things, she'd flirted outrageously. But when Commissioner McLeod led his patrol to a stop in front of the house, her attention swung to a young man who dismounted, wobbled uncertainly on stiff legs for a moment, then straightened and lifted his chin.

Constable William Jackson, cook extraordinaire.

And probably way underage, although no one could prove he'd lied when he listed his age as eighteen. More like fifteen, was the general consensus among the men. William spoke little about his past and was stubbornly silent about his family, so the men of Fort McLeod ignored his suspected lie and accepted him into their midst. Early on he exhibited a unique talent toward culinary matters, and McLeod had made him the fort cook with prayerful thanks that a way had been provided to keep the youngster safe and make him useful at the same time.

Steven spit the nails into his hand and smiled at James McLeod as he dismounted and nodded in his direction.

McLeod returned the smile and said to Libby, "Good afternoon, young lady. I'm James McLeod. Is your father home?"

Eyes wide, she faltered but a second before she gathered her feminine wiles and smiled devastatingly. "Of course. Please wait here." Ruffles flouncing, she rose from the porch swing and hurried inside.

"Do they have you earning your keep, lad?" Big Ben McGavin stepped out from behind McLeod wearing a characteristically wide grin.

"They run a short crew in the winter. Thought I'd help out where I could."

Ben was a bear of a man with more experiences that most ordinary men accumulated in a lifetime. Before he came to the Mounties he'd been a trapper, a buffalo hunter, a shopkeeper in Ottawa, and, for a brief time, an undertaker.

"And a fine job your doin', too," Ben said with a devilish glint in his eye as he ran his hand down the uneven nailing. "You'd never make a fittin' coffin."

Steven was about to shoot back a comment when the door scraped open and Emily and Libby emerged. Wringing a dishtowel in her hands, Emily swiped at a streak of flour on her blue dress, then faced the men with a smile. "Please, gentlemen, come inside. My father is in the parlor, and I was just about ready to serve supper. You and your men will stay, won't you, Commissioner McLeod?"

William hurried up the steps, the mention of food all the encouragement the lad needed. Besides being an excellent cook, William was an enthusiastic eater, his lanky frame belying the amount of food he could consume.

"Begging your pardon, ma'am." He skidded to a stop and sheepishly tipped his hat to Emily. "I'm William, Constable William Jackson." Even as he greeted Emily, his eyes slid to Libby. Eyelashes batting, she adopted her sweetest, most demure expression, carefully hiding the hellion that lay beneath.

"I'm very pleased to meet you, William," Emily said. "Please go inside where it's warm and help yourself to some treats."

With a last quizzical glance at Libby, he strode inside, his uniform a little too large, as if he'd shrunk one size all over.

"Are the cattle ready to be moved?" McLeod asked, stepping in Steven's direction.

Steven nodded. "They're in the holding pens waiting. Were you able to arrange for payment?"

McLeod walked over to his horse and lifted off his saddlebags. "A rider brought payment up from Benton yesterday."

Steven put down his hammer and followed Mc-

Leod and McGavin into the house. Now thoroughly
strewn with Christmas decorations, the house
smelled like an evergreen forest and shimmered
with color and sparkle. Mouth full of pastry, William stood in the foyer gazing up with wide eyes
at the suspended golden balls and elegant bows.

"Commissioner McLeod," Cletis said, emerging
from his parlor. "Your cattle are ready for you to
take."

"This is Constable William Jackson," McLeod
said, and William turned and nodded, his cheeks
bulging with food.

"And Constable Ben McGavin."

Ben stepped forward, and Cletis looked shocked
for a second before he gripped the big beefy hand
so like his own. Except for the difference in clothing, the two men could have been twins. Tall and
broad-shouldered, each man had a full beard,
shaggy hair, and glittering blue eyes.

Ben glanced at the parlor walls, where a huge
stuffed buffalo head kept vigil over all business
dealings there. "Magnificent beasts, aren't they?"

Cletis glanced over his shoulder, then back to
McGavin. "Yep, worthy opponents, the bison. Did
you ever hunt 'em?"

Ben nodded. "Killed many of 'em for their hides
back in those days." He shook his head. "Pity there
ain't many left. I can remember when you coulda'
walked across the Cypress Hills on their backs. Ever
hunt down in the Dakotas?"

Cletis grinned. "Many a season. There was a herd
that'd gather in the Blackfoot Valley. Tall thick
grass."

"South of Mud Creek? Below the old Indian
camp?"

"That's the place."

McLeod and Steven watched in amazement while an instant camaraderie developed between the two men as they recounted past glories.

"We should get the herd on the trail before another blizzard catches us," McLeod finally said, interrupting their reminiscing.

"Of course, of course," Cletis said, scurrying back into the parlor to his desk. "Willow ain't here. She usually handles all the business, but she left this contract and bill of sale." Cletis handed McLeod the two papers filled in an elegant, looping hand.

As McLeod sat down in a chair to read the document, Steven looked out the window, where the last ribbons of day faded into dull sunset that foretold weather approaching, and wondered where Willow had gone. She'd ridden out early and hadn't returned since. Strangely, no one seemed worried about her absence.

"I think this is all in order." McLeod signed the contract and handed it and the saddlebag of money to Cletis, who quickly counted it and added his name to the bottom of the document. Then he handed the contract back to McLeod.

"Supper is served," Emily said from the doorway, having amazingly changed her clothes and neatened her hair in the short span of minutes.

Miraculously, she'd prepared a huge meal for them all. Roasted turkey lay golden and plump on a china platter. Bowls of vegetables and jars of preserves dotted the lace-spread table. A plate of warm, soft bread sat at one end.

"My compliments, Miss Dawson," McLeod said in his rich, deep voice. "You set a fine table."

Emily colored and bowed her head. "Thank you,

Commissioner. All I ask is that you bring a hearty appetite to the table.''

"That I can provide," McLeod said with a chuckle. An imposing figure with his dark hair and beard, McLeod was known throughout the Northwest Mounted Police for his wisdom, gentle ways, and deep devotion to his wife, Mary. A devoted family man, McLeod obviously missed an elegant meal and the sight of a bit of lace.

The table was crowded with extra chairs brought in from other rooms. The conversation was lively and the food delicious. But throughout the meal, Steven was aware of Willow's absence and the fact that no one else seemed to notice.

"We have a large party on Christmas Day. Why don't you and your family join us, Mr. Dawson?" McLeod asked, dabbing at the corners of his mouth with a napkin. "A rather large village has grown up around Fort McLeod. Traders carry almost everything you could get in Benton, and it's half the distance away."

Steven nearly choked on his forkful of turkey dressing. He slanted a glance first at Ben, who raised his great, bushy eyebrows and then his shoulders. McLeod was actually inviting Cletis Dawson— and his daughters—into the midst of unmarried, lonely men. Had Emily's culinary wiles gone to his head? Or had he just lost his mind? Steven glanced at McLeod, who was smiling congenially at Emily.

"Why, that's a fine offer," Cletis declared with a resounding slap to the top of the dining table. "What do you think, girls?"

"Where's Willow?" Libby suddenly asked.

Cletis frowned and glanced around the table. "Emily, where's your sister?"

Emily looked ruffled for a moment before gaining her composure. "Well . . . I thought she came in with everyone else. She'll be along, I'm sure. I'll save her a plate." Steven's heart twisted for Willow. Strong and confident, yet as invisible to her family as the stout beams that kept a roof over their heads and held up the weight of winter snow.

Like a lonely shadow, like the wolves she so admired, she silently slipped in and out of their lives.

"I'm sure she'll be along," Emily repeated, "and I, for one, would love to come to your Christmas party."

"It's settled, then," McLeod said with uncharacteristic gaiety. "You'll be my guests."

"You and your men will stay tonight, of course, and leave first thing in the morning. We have a guest room where you can stay, Commissioner. We can put your men in the barn. Plenty of hay, and the barn's tight against the wind."

"That's very kind of you, Mr. Dawson, but I stay where my men stay. I'll take you up on that offer."

Arms crossed behind his head, Steven lay on his back and stared up into the darkness of the hayloft. Cletis was right. Not a shaft of light penetrated the interior. The hay beneath his blanket crackled with every flinch. Beside him, Ben snored softly, and further down, William mumbled in a dream. Steven smiled and wondered if the lad was dreaming of Libby.

A shaft of moonlight temporarily disturbed the darkness as someone below opened the barn door and slipped inside. The soft shuffle of horses hooves stopped, and the jingle of tack said Willow had come home.

Steven rose from his bed and crawled to the ladder. He descended and dropped onto the dirt floor near the front of the barn. She'd chosen not to light a lantern and unsaddled Pat by touch.

"Hello?" he said softly and heard her gasp. "Willow?"

"Yes," she answered, her voice slightly breathless.

He moved to her side and lit the lantern hanging on a post.

"What are you doing here?" she asked, looking up into his face.

"Commissioner McLeod and the patrol are here, upstairs in the hayloft. They've come to get the cattle."

She turned back to the saddle and dragged it off Pat's sweaty back. "So, you'll be leaving tomorrow?"

"Yes. First light."

She remained silent as she hung the saddle and bridle in the tack room and returned to wipe down Pat with a handful of dry hay.

"We missed you at dinner."

She paused in her long, languid strokes. "I can't imagine that's true. There's must have been quite a crowd around Emily's table."

"Yes, there was."

She returned to wiping down Pat. "Emily'll save me a plate. She always does."

"Do you miss many meals like this?"

She stopped again and turned toward him. "Now and again. I don't like a crowd. Besides, I had work to do."

"I'd like to call on you . . . sometime."

She looked at him as if he'd lost his mind, and

he wondered if he had. "Fort McLeod is a day's ride away."

"I know that."

"You'd ride all this way to call on me?"

"Yes."

"You've got the wrong sister, Constable. Emily is the one who wants a husband." She began to stroke Pat's back again, but with less interest, Steven noticed.

"You don't want to get married?"

"And sell myself into slavery? No, I don't."

His interest now thoroughly piqued, Steven pursued. "Why do you consider marriage slavery?"

She threw him an over-the-shoulder glance that said he was on the same intellectual level as Bell. "Isn't it? For a woman, at least?"

"No, I wouldn't consider it that at all."

"What do you know about it?"

"I was married once."

She turned, horrified. "Did you leave a wife behind in the East?"

"No. She died several years ago."

Her face relaxed in relief and she quickly turned away.

"Do you have children?" Her hand, so attentive to Pat's back, slowed in its strokes and then stopped altogether, the handful of hay clutched tightly . . . waiting.

"Did. A son. He died at birth."

"Along with your wife?" Her voice had grown smaller, weaker, and he thought he saw the bits of hay tremble in the dim light as she kept her back to him.

"Yes."

"I'm sorry." Still she didn't turn around. "Look, I have to finish here and get into bed."

"I understand." Steven turned and walked back to the bottom of the ladder. "May I call on you?"

She stood where he'd left her, one hand on Pat's withers the other on his rump, staring straight ahead into the dark.

"No."

Dawn came innocent and pink, forecasting good weather, and Steven's hopes lightened. Perhaps the weather would hold and they would not have to fight driving snow and cold on their way back to Fort McLeod. When he led Buck out of the barn and into the early light, he noticed that Pat was already saddled and waiting in front of the house, a bedroll tied behind his saddle. Hopes for an uncomplicated trip died and Steven's head began to ache between his eyes.

Cletis came out, pulling on his coat. "I hope the cattle are what you expected, Commissioner," he said, shaking McLeod's hand. "I'm sendin' Willow along to help you fellows with the drive."

McLeod frowned. "This is a long ride, Mr. Dawson, through unsettled country—hardly the return trip a woman would want to make alone."

Cletis laughed. "Willow ain't no ordinary woman, Commissioner. She's cut her teeth on this country and there's more things out there afraid of her than the other way around. You ain't got to give her any special considerations. She can look after herself."

Willow stepped out on the porch, pulling on a pair of gloves as Emily hurried out and pressed a wrapped package into her hands. Cletis might be nonchalant about his daughter's adventures, but her sister, apparently, was not.

"Please take care," Emily said. "I wish you'd reconsider this."

Willow took the package and gave Emily a slight smile. "This is my job, Em. Just like cooking is yours." She indicated the cloth-bound package.

"I'm sure the commissioner and his men can handle the herd."

Willow shook her head. "I told Constable Gravel from the first I'd accompany the herd, and I mean to keep my word." The discussion closed, Willow stepped off the porch and climbed into the saddle.

Commissioner McLeod threw Steven a glance, then turned back to Cletis. "We shall see you at Christmas, then?"

"Yes sir. We'll be there a day or two ahead so's Emily can do some shopping."

McLeod touched the brim of his hat and turned his horse away from the house.

Pat trotted over to the holding pens and Willow leaned down and opened the gate. Andy, astride a dun mare, joined her and together they rode into the pen and urged the cattle through the gate.

"Flank them," she called to the constables. "They're not going to run. Just guide them toward the south. We'll have to ride around this ridge." She pointed toward the hill behind the house.

Like brown spring runoff, the herd sauntered out of the gate and strolled in the direction the riders guided them. When the last cow trotted out, Willow shut the gate behind her.

"I wish you'd let me go with you," Andy said, a pout in his voice.

"Somebody's got to stay behind and look after things, especially with Wilbur's knee like it is."

"Still and all, you gotta make a long ride back

by yourself. I don't know what I'd do iffen somethin' were to happen to you."

Steven suppressed a smile. So, he wasn't the only one who appreciated Willow. Willow swatted good-naturedly at the boy with her coiled rope. "You just stay out of trouble and keep the cattle out of mischief. I'll be back in a day or two and I'll tell you all about Fort McLeod."

She turned Pat after the herd and heeled the mustang into a trot. Having lingered behind, Steven fell in beside her. "Are you sure this is a good idea? It is a long trip back."

Willow turned in her saddle. "You're the third person who's said that to me in the last fifteen minutes. I've been doing this since I could sit a horse. I'm not worried. Don't you be." With that she urged Pat to the front of the herd and rode up beside McLeod. Immediately, she engaged him in conversation, darting off only once or twice to chase a reluctant cow, leaving Steven to trail behind.

The first night's camp was in a coulee, sheltered from the north wind by a rise of land. Grass, long and brown, crowded the narrow banks of a stream, freed from ice by the chinook gracing them with tolerable temperatures. The cattle eagerly snatched at the long grass, content to eat their fill.

The day had progressed without incident. Any fugitives Willow had quickly brought under control. She circulated among the constables, offering nuggets of information about cattle and the cattle business in general. All except Steven. She avoided him like bad water.

For supper, all ate pemmican except Willow, and

she shared with them the gifts Emily had pressed into her hand on the front porch.

"Your sister is some cook," Ben said, licking a finger and smacking his lips over a bit of pie. "And you're some cow herder." His praise was accompanied by a wide, infectious smile that Willow willingly caught. She smiled back and held out the paper package again.

"Do you want some more? There's plenty."

"She sure is a thoughtful lady," he said as he selected another small piece.

Steven held up a hand when she offered him the same choice. "No, I might get spoiled and then pemmican wouldn't taste nearly as good."

Willow smiled, surprising him. She'd barely acknowledged him all day. "Emily likes to spoil people. She'll be glad to hear that."

She closed the paper and excused herself from the ring of men around the fire. Steven waited, giving her some time to herself; then he made an excuse to check on Buck.

He found her exactly where he expected, beside a bend in the river where a gnarled willow bent its short limbs protectively over the gurgling stream. The landscape beyond was open, moonlit prairie. One shoulder leaned against the trunk and arms crossed, she stared out across the openness.

"I think the drive today went well," he began lamely.

She pivoted just enough to see him. "Yes, it went well."

"Have you ever been to Fort McLeod?"

"No. Pa does most of his business in Benton."

"I dare say there's more businesses in Fort McLeod than any place besides Benton."

"Why did you kiss me that night?"

Her question knocked his knees out from underneath him. He hadn't expected so direct a question, and he had no ready answer. In fact, he had no answer at all. How could he explain?

He looked down at the muddy ground and prayed for golden words to make her understand. "I like you and I wanted to show you how much."

"Well, that's not quite all the truth, is it, constable?"

Steven laughed and looked back up into her face. "No, I guess it isn't. Why did you kiss me back?"

Her confidence faltered for a moment and indecision flashed through her eyes. Then she shrugged her shoulders. "I wanted to know how it felt to kiss a man. Especially one that wanted me. And you obviously did. At least at the moment."

The heat of embarrassment scorched Steven's cheeks and he was grateful for the cover of night. "There was more to it than that. You're a beautiful woman who looked like she needed kissing."

Willow looked back toward the dark-blue shadows gliding across the ground, cast there by clouds passing over a three-quarter moon. "I'm neither, Constable. And I'm not interested in a husband. I've got my own plans and there's no room for a man in them. I'm sorry if my actions led you to believe otherwise."

Her words, so bitter, so hard, twisted within him. Was her father correct in his assessment of her? Was she destined for spinsterhood by her own choice?

"What *are* your plans?"

She turned again, toward him and away from the moonlight. "I don't consider that any of your business, Constable, but I don't mind telling you, since you've asked. Pa's promised me land of my own. I intend to breed and raise Herefords and eventually black Angus. With the west filling up with people, the market should be high and stable. I figure I can run them down to Calgary for sale.''

Ambitious plans, but lonely. He studied the pride and defiance in her face and wondered again what had made her reject any hopes of love.

"What about a family?"

"I told you there's no room for a man—now or ever."

He should walk away, he told himself; run away, far away from Willow Dawson. She was as stubborn and immovable as the Rockies and he'd have no luck changing her mind now that it was made up. But he liked a challenge, so he took a step closer.

"That's not what your lips said that night in the window."

"I was just curious. Now I know."

"Know what, Willow?" he said, stepping closer still.

"Know what it feels like to be kissed." The first hint of hesitation registered on her face. At least Steven hoped it wasn't a trick of the moon.

"You kissed me back. And you liked it. I could tell." He stopped when the toes of his boots touched hers. She raised her face to look into his.

"Maybe I did. That doesn't mean I want to do it again."

"Don't you?" Steven slid his arms around her, knowing he was pushing his luck, risking their fragile relationship, risking their reputations should they be discovered.

"No," she said, her eyes now wide with alarm as he leaned closer.

"I think you mean yes." His lips touched hers and her eyes slid shut. She sighed against him as he pulled her close, molded her against him, enveloped her in his embrace. But she didn't quite yield as she'd done that night, didn't fall into the embrace as before. She allowed his kiss and returned it, but with a reserve that hadn't been there before.

When Steven raised his head, she looked up at him with fear-filled, adamant eyes. "I'm not the one you want, Steven," she whispered, her voice slipping. "I'll never be a wife. I don't know how to do those things and have no desire to learn. Emily needs you. *We* need you. Pa wants somebody to take over the ranch. I'd like it if it was you."

Taken aback, Steven released her and took a step backward. "You want me to marry Emily?"

"Yes. I'd have part of the ranch and you and Emily would have the other part. Don't you see?"

She couldn't see past dollar signs, couldn't let down her defenses for even one second. Something, somewhere had made her this way. But it was some other man's job to find out, not his. He'd pursue her no further.

Without an answer to her question, he turned on his heel and walked back to the fire, thoroughly confused.

Chapter Seven

They made the trip to Fort McLeod in three days, blessed by good weather. The whitewashed stockade walls had never looked so good as the large main gates swung open and red-suited men hurried out.

Holding pens waited on the other side of the river, and the cattle willingly swung in that direction, poured into the enclosure, and began to eat the waiting hay. Willow rode into the pen and moved the cattle to the back until all were inside; then she slipped back through the gate and stopped Pat at McLeod's side.

McLeod sat with his hands folded over the saddle horn, leaning slightly forward to relieve a tired backside.

"Thank you for your help, Miss Dawson. You will stay as our guest for a day to two before you start back?"

"She sure as hell will."

All turned to see Maggie Fraser striding toward them, Baby Mary firmly clutched in her arms. "Don't let that woman out of here."

"Maggie Hayes!" Willow slid out of the saddle and strode toward Maggie, a smile on her face.

They stopped toe to toe. Steven glanced at James McLeod, who paled as the two women embraced. "These two know each other?" he asked.

"It's Maggie Fraser now. And this is Mary."

Willow touched Mary's fuzzy head and smiled. "She's beautiful, Maggie. You're married?"

Maggie shifted the baby to her other arm. "Yep, married one of these Mounties. His name's Colin."

And so, the chameleon changed her color again. Willow's face softened as she smiled at Mary's tiny, exploring hand that grabbed at her long, black braids. She caught the tiny hand in hers and kissed the fat fingers. "Aren't you beautiful?" Then Willow raised her eyes to Maggie's face. "It's so good to see you again."

James McLeod shook his head. Colin and Maggie's courtship had caused him many a sleepless night and more than one pounding headache in that first year. The daughter of one of the notorious whiskey traders the Mounted Police had been formed to eradicate, Maggie had quickly captured the heart of Fort McLeod's surgeon.

"Where's your father?" Willow asked.

Maggie's smile faded. "He died that first winter."

"I'm sorry. Here. Want me to take her?" Willow held out her arms and Maggie placed the infant in them.

She stared down at the sleeping baby with an expression of such longing, Steven's chest tightened. He wanted to see her look at their children like that, see her gaze down at a dark-haired son with almond skin and his mother's eyes.

When he dragged his gaze away, Maggie Fraser was staring straight at him with an impish smile plastered across her face.

"Welcome back, Steven. Colin's a-waitin' fer you. He's got another birthin' tale to tell you."

Despite her rough manners and blunt language, Steven loved Maggie Fraser. And he wasn't alone. She'd stolen the heart of nearly every man at Fort McLeod that first miserable winter when leaky roofs and deep snow sapped men's will and energies. She and her father had led them a merry chase, keeping their wits and humor finely honed. In the end, Maggie won, becoming Colin's wife and causing ripples all the way back to Northwest Mounted Police Headquarters in Ottawa.

"All these were yours?" Maggie asked Willow, nodding toward the pen of milling beasts.

"Yep."

"You and your Pa've done all right, then?"

Willow nodded and extricated her hair from Mary's steely grip. "We've done well so far. I've got bigger plans, though."

Maggie raised her eyebrows again. "Yeah?" she said, glancing at Steven. "Come home with me and meet Colin. You can stay with us for a day or two and tell me all about it." She grabbed Pat's reins, and the two women, child, and horse set off toward the stockaded fort.

Steven glanced away from McLeod's glowering, all-knowing stare. "I'll see to the cattle."

"Her head popped out first. I swear, it was the damndest thing I'd ever seen. I made Colin put me a mirror right up there." Maggie pointed to a beam that extended the width of the room. "He turned plumb pale the day I asked him fer it." She grinned at her husband, who lounged in his chair by the fireplace, ankles crossed and arms folded over his chest.

"My reaction was nothing compared to Abraham's when I asked if I could borrow the mirror behind his bar," Colin countered. "Of course, he had to know why I wanted it. I was so tired by that time, I couldn't think of a plausible lie. He's never looked at me the same since."

Companionable chuckles floated around the room and Steven joined in. Colin had invited him for supper and he'd accepted, even though he knew Willow would be there also. Now, watching the two women renew an old friendship, he couldn't help but smile and think how alike they were. Both true daughters of the Territories— tough and practical. And both survivors of change and hardship.

While Cletis roamed the plains in search of buffalo, he'd often crossed paths with George Hayes and his traveling bootleg operation, Maggie had explained over her supper of rabbit and potatoes. They'd even spent a summer camped together, Cletis supplying the meat and George supplying the spirits, and the young girls had become fast friends until life separated them. From his seat by the fireplace, Steven watched the two tell stories and take turns spoiling Mary.

"So, what's between the two of you?" Colin asked as Steven pulled a chair to the hearth, leaving the table to the women and Mary.

Steven shook his head. "Absolutely nothing."

"You say that as if you wish it were different."

"She's made her position very clear. She wants to be the largest rancher in the Alberta Territory. No husband to get in the way. Or anyone else, for that matter."

"So, you've discussed this?"

A sudden burst of laughter drew Steven's attention back to the table. Maggie rose, with Mary asleep in her arms, and disappeared into the bedroom with Willow on her heels.

"No, actually she warned me off before I could even begin a discussion."

"And you're not satisfied with her explanation?"

Maggie reemerged, a brown earthen jug in her hands, Willow following close behind.

"Anybody want some?" Maggie asked, sloshing the jug side to side.

Willow grinned and nodded. "Sure," she said as she reclaimed her seat.

"Do I want to know where you got that?" Colin asked, seeming completely unsurprised that his wife possessed a gallon of illegal whiskey.

"Nope," she replied shortly as she sat back down at the plank table and poured out two equal measures for Willow and herself.

"Steven?" Maggie nudged the jug.

"No. Thank you." Steven held up his hands.

Maggie and Willow touched cups and both downed the concoction quickly. Steven threw a glance to Colin, who shrugged his shoulders and smiled. Laughter again floated through the room and stirred to life Steven's banked discontent. Small reminders of Colin and Maggie's life together lay strewn about the room. One of Mary's blankets lay across the arm of a rocking chair. Colin's medical bag sat by the door. Above, a nail held two coats, a small brown oilcloth one overspread by Steven's dark-blue cloak, a jarring intimacy to a man suddenly attuned to such.

Colin Fraser was an enviable man. He was now surgeon for Fort McLeod since the headquarters had moved to Fort Walsh, taking along Surgeon Kittson. He was desperately in love with his wife and had a beautiful, healthy daughter. He'd managed to capture the best of two worlds: a family and a job he loved.

Tinkling laughter drew Steven's attention back to the table and the two women seated there. Willow was as dark as Maggie was light, her black hair gleaming under the soft lamplight. She leaned forward laughing, her defenses completely abandoned as she swapped tales with Maggie. Was this the real Willow, this carefree woman with sparkling eyes and tousled hair? Was this the way she'd been before? Before something made her as hard and cold as the prairies she loved? His heart did a curious little thump and he felt Colin's gaze on him.

"But you fell in love with her anyway, didn't you?" Colin's voice was barely above a whisper.

Steven turned, knowing that lying to someone who knew him as well as Colin Fraser did was useless. "Yes, I did."

Colin turned to look at his wife and a smile crept across his face. "So, she's reluctant to give up her independence. Maggie was, too, but we managed to work out an agreement between us and we both got what we wanted."

Steven shook his head as a burst of laughter erupted.

"What she wants and what I want are two very different things," Steven said. "She wants me to marry her sister."

"I see," Colin said slowly. "And how do you feel about the sister?"

"Therein lies the problem."

"Don't tell me you're in love with the sister, too?"

"No, of course not." He paused, knowing his next words would bring a twist of pain. "I'm not going to reenlist when my time's up."

"What?"

"I want a home. Children. A life other than the force."

Another burst of laughter interrupted their conversation. Colin chuckled as Maggie caught his eye and waved.

"That stuff's going to go right to her head. I'm proud to say she can't hold her liquor like she once could."

Willow, too, was feeling the effects of the liquor, turning and smiling broadly at Steven, her face soft and happy. The bottom of his stomach clenched.

The evening wore on until both women were happily, thoroughly drunk. Laughing and winking at Steven, Colin coaxed Maggie out of her chair and into the bedroom. Giggles and whispers came from the dark room as Colin closed the door behind them.

"I'm suppos' ta sleep in the corner." Willow pointed to her bedroll, still rolled up beside the hearth. Bracing her hands on the table, she lurched to her feet. "I'll be right back."

She took wobbly steps toward the door, but Steven stepped into her path. "Whoa. Where are you going?"

She looked up at him, her eyes red and watery. "I have to go . . . to the woods," she said, covering her mouth to stifle the giggle that bubbled out.

"To the woods. Isn't that a funny way of sayin' I gotta go pee?"

"Yes, that's hilarious." Steven looped her arm across his shoulder, opened the door, and looked around. All he needed was to be seen outside with a drunk woman in pants. Worse would be a drunken Willow Dawson staggering around Fort McLeod on her own.

No one was in sight. He took a breath and tried to relax. And then he froze. There was no cover for her intended task within the stockade walls of the fort. He was sure the only chamber pot in Colin's house was in the bedroom . . . with Colin and Maggie. He paused, considering his options.

"Whatsa matter?" she asked, tugging him forward. "I gotta go."

"We're inside the fort, Willow. There's no place for you to 'go'."

"Well . . . we better find someplace quick." She poked a finger at his nose, missed, and stabbed his cheek. Giggling, she lunged forward, nearly dragging him off the porch with the momentum of her body.

The back wall of the hospital nearly rested against the stockade wall, allowing only a few feet passage between the two. If they could make it across the open area, he could take her there. No one was likely to happen by.

Giving thanks for a waning moon and floating clouds, he helped her across the open area and into the shadowy recess of the hospital wall.

"Now, don't peek," she cautioned with one finger and disappeared into the dark.

Steven turned his back. From the shadows, he

heard a soft curse and hoped she'd managed to get her pants down in time. What would he do about that type of disaster? But true to Willow's style, she emerged with all her clothes dry and intact.

"Thank you," she said, attempting to muster some dignity, and he thought for a moment that the cold night air might have helped sober her. He changed his mind when she stood staring at him for several long minutes, her face lost to the darkness. "You know when I told you I wanted you to kiss me so I'd know what it was like?"

"Yes?" he answered cautiously.

"Well, I wanna know . . . something else," she hiccuped."

"What's that?"

"I wanna know what it feels like to make love." She held up a finger. "Just one time. You're a genna . . . genna . . . gentleman and you won't tell." She swayed toward him and he lunged to catch her before she pitched face-first into a lingering puddle.

"Willow, you've had a lot to drink—"

" 'Course I have or I wouldn't be sayin' this, silly." She batted at her nose with her sleeve and missed, her voice rising with every word. "Why do you think I got drunk?"

Steven glanced around. Somebody, even the dead in the little cemetery by the river, had surely heard her. "Sssh. Somebody'll hear."

"Let 'em," she said even louder. "I want you to make love to me. Right now." She pointed at the ground and stamped a foot.

"It isn't quite that easy, Willow. Let me help you

back to Maggie's house. You'll feel better in the morning." *Or maybe not.*

"I don't want to go back to Maggie's. She's just too happy with the baby and Colin . . ." She let her words drift off and swayed on her feet. "I can't ever have that."

He took her shoulders in his hands, knowing he was treading on dangerous ground even touching her. She was trembling from the cold. "Let me take you home."

She raised her eyes, dark and terrified. "There was so much blood, Steven. Everything was red with it. It was on the floor and the bed and all over her. And the baby, he was all red and blue and white and he was so still. He didn't even cry." Tears were pouring down her cheeks now. "She wanted just one more baby, she said, 'cause Libby was getting so big."

Steven pulled her against him, trying to sort out the jumbled words. She wrapped her arms around his waist and lay her head on his chest. "And I knew right then I couldn't ever have a baby. Seeing her lying there'd be all I'd think of the whole time I was carrying it. But then I started thinking that I'd go my whole life and never know how it felt to be loved. And Ma and Pa loved each other so much. Pa was so sad for so long."

She raised her head and a gliding moonbeam caught her face. "But if we do it just one time, I won't get pregnant, will I?"

Her poor, tortured heart. *"Willow—"*

"Kiss me. I wanna know what you feel like . . . when you're all . . . roused up." She breathed the last words into his face, her body close and warm and tempting.

He knew he shouldn't. This wasn't his Willow, wearing her cool dignity like a knight's armor. This was a lonely woman begging for intimacy, a concoction of distilled grain having let her desire out for a quick run. But, this Willow he very much wanted to kiss . . . and make love to, God help him.

Steven lowered his lips to her eager ones and tasted the whiskey lingering there. He planned to take one kiss to comfort her and then step away, but his traitorous body had other ideas.

Her fingers spider-walked up his chest, across his shoulders, and into his hair, sending shivers to pool in the small of his back. She spread her hands in his hair and drew his head down closer. Her lips moved beneath his, hinting at other sensuous dances. Caution dimmed and desire took its place within Steven. He barely noticed when she linked her fingers behind his neck.

She tightened her grip, jumped, and wrapped her legs around his waist. The extra weight drove him backward, slamming his back against the rough stockade wall. Instinctively, he grabbed for her and caught her backside in both hands. Off balance, he was at her mercy. Quickly, he moved his hands to her back and scuffled his feet backwards to better support them both. All the while, she continued to kiss him, as if nothing had happened, effectively destroying the last of his good sense.

"Make love to me, Steven," she begged, her breath soft against his mouth. "Please."

"Willow, this isn't right—"

"I don't care what's right. I want to know what it feels like to be loved and held and . . ." Her words drifted off and she returned to torturing his lips.

Tumbled under her wave of passion, Steven clasped her to him, wanting her to know what she'd done to his body and his control.

"You want me, too."

"Yes," he whispered, the words marching out of his brain. "Yes, God, Willow, I want you."

He buried his face in her shoulder, nipping at the soft skin revealed by the neck of her shirt. She tasted as he'd imagined. Sweet. Smoky. And something else that bypassed his brain and went straight to the pit of his stomach. Erotic possibilities began to form in his mind. The hayloft would be quiet and deserted; only the horses below would know. Her body would be soft and warm as it surrounded his, and she would sigh his name as he made love to her. Afterward, she would smile at him and promise her heart to his.

"I'm gonna throw up."

The words threw cold water over his vivid daydreams. She loosed her arms from around his neck and slid to stand on her own. She paused, looked up at him for a moment, then staggered over to the stockade wall and emptied her stomach.

Steven moved behind her, caught her forehead in the palm of his hand, and held her heaving body tight against his aching one.

"I'm so sorry," she murmured as he pulled a handkerchief from his inside pocket and offered it to her.

With trembling hands, she wiped her mouth and stuck the bit of cloth in her pocket. "I never could drink more than a shot or two at the time. I don't know what made me try tonight."

"It's all right." He pulled her toward him and she lay her head against his chest.

"You're so good to me," she murmured into his red serge. "Why can't I love you?"

Willow awoke on the floor of Colin's examination room with a horrible taste in her mouth and vague, embarrassing memories. She was carefully rolled in her blanket, a pillow stuffed with soft summer hay beneath her head.

She sat up, then waited while the room spun and her head pounded. Shoving her hair back with both hands, she sorted through her memories of last night. She'd kissed Steven, begged him to make love to her, and then she'd thrown up. A fresh headache rolled into her brain. Oh, God. She hadn't thrown up on him, had she? Had they made love?

Running a cool hand over her face, she tried to narrow her concentration despite the drum chorus in her head.

She'd held him, kissed him . . . and enjoyed it. He'd returned her kisses . . . with enthusiasm. A small smile spread across her aching face, quickly followed by a frown as a vivid image flashed through her mind. Dear Lord, they hadn't, had they? His back was against a wall, and her legs were . . .

Willow threw back her blanket and scrambled to her feet. What on earth had possessed her to do such a thing? She looked down and found that she wore her long, baggy underwear and her shirt. Where were her pants? Holding her head with both hands, she scanned the floor and found them peeping out from underneath the end of her bedroll.

Hopping on one foot, she managed to get the tangled garment and her boots on and then rolled up her blankets. She caught up her hat from a nail by the door and plopped it onto her head as she eased open the door. There was barely enough light to see as she slipped out of the warm house and into the bitterly cold morning. Her bedroll tucked under her arm, she hurried to the barn, praying she wouldn't run into Steven on the way.

Pat huffed his quiet greeting when she rubbed his velvety nose and quickly saddled him. She rode through the front gates of Fort McLeod with no more notice than a genteel nod from the sentry. Once outside the walls, she drew a deep breath of relief and shoved away her mind's nagging question of why.

But her curiosity turned on her, traitor that it was, and sought an answer anyway, sneaking into her peaceful thoughts. Why had she cornered Steven, acted like a trollop when she knew, down to the center of her soul, that the last thing she wanted in life was to be responsible for another human being?

Men turned into husbands and husbands produced babies. She had nothing against babies, as long as they were somebody else's. Babies meant sleepless nights and loss of freedom and . . . She pushed the rest of the thought away. Had she told Steven? Somehow she remembered telling someone, and recently, of the blood and the fear, images that drifted through her thoughts like wisps of morning fog. His eyes had been dark and compassionate, wells of desire and a dungeon for her heart.

She heeled Pat, who grunted in surprise and changed to a rolling lope. The sooner she put distance between herself and Fort McLeod, the better off she'd be, she told herself. A glance to the sky said she was in for a long, cold, snowy ride, but she didn't care. Soon she'd be home on familiar territory where she was safe and secure and temptation was very far away.

Chapter Eight

"You're coming with us and that's all there is to it." Emily crossed her arms over her red-and-white pinafore and planted herself in the doorway of Willow's bedroom.

Willow jammed her hands on her hips and shifted her weight with a sigh.

"It won't be Christmas if you don't come, Willow." Libby's bottom lip rolled out in an exaggerated pout and huge tears glistened in her eyes. "We ain't never been apart at Christmas. Ever."

Willow narrowed her eyes at Libby, the little wheedler. But despite her best glare, Libby's pout seemed genuine, a fact that began to nibble away at Willow's resolve.

"I can't leave you here all alone for the holidays," Pa chimed in from the hallway.

She was surrounded and outgunned. She didn't stand a chance.

"Somebody has to look after the cattle."

"Andy can do that. They don't need much looking after, anyway. They're cows, Willow, not children," Pa countered.

"Well, then, somebody's got to look after Wilbur."

"His knee's much better, and besides, I'm leaving him one of my potions to soak it in. It'll be good as new when we get back." Emily stepped to Willow's bed and plucked a dress from the pile that spilled over the quilt and onto the floor.

Willow swung her gaze to Libby. "Well, what's your reason?"

Libby knitted her smooth brows together briefly. "I ain't got no particular reason, I reckon. I just want you to come 'cause Em ain't no fun."

"Elizabeth Dawson, do you know how many perfectly good English words you just slew? You see," Emily swung her attack to Pa, "this is all the more reason she should spend more time in the company of people other than cowhands."

"That's why you gotta come, Willow. This is how she'll be the whole time lessen you're there."

Willow crossed her arms. "Why would it be different if I'm there?"

" 'Cause then she'll pick on you and not me."

"Spoken like a true Dawson. Straight to the point." Willow turned her attention back to Emily. She could never deny Emily anything. Damn it. In the end, she knew she'd lose. But she wouldn't go down without a fight, and Fort McLeod was the last place she wanted to spend three days.

Emily fluffed out the ruffles on her emerald green dress, folded it onto itself and laid it in the bottom of an open trunk at her feet. "Constable McGavin says that Baron Von Roth will be there for the Christmas party."

Willow stepped forward. "You've seen Ben McGavin?"

Emily stopped creasing the skirt of the dress and looked up. "Of course I have. He came by today."

"Why did he come here?" Suspicious, Willow laid a hand on Emily's arm.

She turned an innocent face. "He said that we're on his patrol now, that he'd be by often."

"He did, huh?"

Emily held up a white dress edged in embroidered pink rosettes and smiled.

"Oh, no. I'm not taking that," Willow said, shaking her head.

"It's a lovely dress and it took me weeks to embroider those roses." She ran a finger over the delicate work, then turned and held the dress against Willow's chest. "It's lovely with your coloring, too."

"I didn't ask you to make this dress." Willow stepped backward and Emily threw her a frown. "Why, of course you didn't. You'd never ask for a dress like this. But I thought you'd look lovely in it."

Willow sighed. Emily had just fired the final volley—straight into the center of Willow's abiding guilt where Emily was concerned. She gave of herself so unselfishly for them all. How could Willow deny her a family trip to Fort McLeod, a chance to be a young, beautiful woman instead of their housekeeper and cook? Even if it meant facing Steven again.

"All right, I'll go. But I won't wear that dress."

Emily carefully folded the garment and placed it in the trunk. "Perhaps you'll change your mind."

Willow stalked down the stairs and heard her father clunking down behind her with a deliberate tread. He stopped her with a hand to her arm before she could make her escape out the front door.

"You've made your sister very happy," he said, a gentle smile in his eyes. "It wouldn't have been the same without you; you know that."

Willow smiled back. "Who's this Baron Von Roth she's talking about?"

Cletis continued into the parlor and sat in his desk chair with a grunt. He rummaged in a pile of old newspapers, then pulled one out and slid it across the polished desktop. "Some titled English bloke that's interested in ranching. He's bought himself a big spread down near the border."

Willow picked up the paper and read the description of the baron's arrival in Alberta, his subsequent land purchase, and his plans to raise new breeds of cattle.

Perhaps this could be an interesting trip after all.

H. T. Smith had seen an opportunity back in 1874 and built a two-story hotel amid the village of tents and shacks that had sprung up around Fort McLeod. Now, the Emporium regally ruled the main street of Fort McLeod. Offering elegant quarters and dining, it attracted a wide variety of clientele, from titled Englishmen to cowhands with flush pockets.

"How wonderful," Emily said, tilting her head back to look up at the elegant gold script letters that scrolled across an elaborate false front. Bundled to the chin in a quilt and seated on the wagon seat, she turned to smile at Libby's face as she, too, stared at the hotel and gripped the sides of the wagon bed.

"Hrummph," Willow said and shifted uneasily in the saddle. The ride had been cold and damp and every jarred bone in her body ached. She'd insisted on riding Pat, assuring herself some measure of independence during this jaunt. Now all she wanted was a bath and a soft bed.

"Do you suppose they dress for dinner in the restaurant?"

"I hope to hell they don't go in naked."

Three sets of eyes turned to glare at Willow. "All right. I'm sorry. It's just a hotel on a muddy street, for God's sakes. I'm going to find the livery."

Cletis pointed to the other side of the Emporium, where a sign reading "WILLIS LIVERY" swung in the increasing wind. Willow poked Pat in the sides and rode him into the generous barn whose door stood open to customers.

A sandy-haired boy, barely older than Libby, rose from his seat on a nail barrel and took Pat's reins as Willow swung down. She paid him, gave him instructions for Pat's care, and then, with a final pat to Pat's nose, hoisted her saddle to her shoulder and started for the door.

"Ma'am?"

She turned.

"Ma'am, we can keep that for you. Right here in this locked room." He took a key from his pants pocket, unlocked a door, and swung it open to reveal a collection of saddles and harness, all neatly installed on smooth, wooden saddle trees.

Reluctantly Willow handed over her saddle and pressed a few more coins in the boy's hand. With her saddlebags thrown over her shoulder, she stepped out into the gathering storm now tossing snowflakes about wildly.

She walked the short distance to the hotel, stepped inside, and gazed about in amazement. She'd expected a decent, modest place, but instead the inside was decorated more ornately than even Emily could imagine. A huge chandelier hung from the high ceiling, dozens of candles waiting to be lit. Her booted feet sank into a soft red-and-tan rug that covered a polished wooden floor.

"Pa." Willow caught his arm as he stood at the desk, counting out money to the suited young man on the other side. "We can't afford this," she whispered.

"Of course we can." Cletis handed the money to the young clerk, who recorded the transaction with a waving quill. "My girls don't get to town very often. They deserve the best."

Willow turned again to stare at potted palms and polished brass that seemed to be everywhere. Such surroundings dictated certain behavior. And that was what frightened her most.

"Could you have someone take this message to the fort?" Pa was saying as he signed his name with a flourish and pushed the paper back across the desk.

"Yes, sir, Mr. Dawson. Right away."

"What was that?" Willow questioned, suspicion beginning to nibble at her like a mouse.

Emily stood at her father's side, her quilt neatly folded over her arm, wearing a satisfied smile. Libby watched them all, eyes wide—a sure sign of impending disaster.

"What are you all up to?"

"I've sent a message to Fort McLeod requesting

Constables Gravel and McGavin join us for dinner, along with Commissioner McLeod."

Willow swallowed, too tired to care if the fear showed in her face. Emily hooked her arm with hers and started for the stairs. "I assure you, you will survive this, Willow. It's no worse than facing a pack of wolves."

"I'm not wearing the pink rosebuds." Willow shoved back her mane of wet hair and glared across the four-poster bed that served as a battleground between her and Emily.

Lips pressed tightly together, Emily held the dress up like a warrior's shield. "It's very appropriate for this occasion."

"I don't care how appropriate it is, Em, I look like a fool wearing that . . . that dress." She pointed at the pink-and-white confection, her stomach doing a little flip at the image of herself sweeping down the stairs dressed in a cloud of white.

"This is why I brought it."

"Ah ha. You do have something planned. Something I'm not going to like, and I'll have no part in it." Willow flopped down and the bed gave enticingly beneath her. Wrapped in a towel, she stared longingly at the steaming hip tub she'd been hurried out of. Libby was there now, her feet hanging off the end, shooting the soap into the air by squeezing it out of her clenched hands time and again. How she'd have loved to soak until the water chilled.

She turned to look over her shoulder at Emily, who stood staring at the dress. "You wear the dress, Em, if you like it so much. I brought other clothes."

"I'm not going to dinner with you in pants. You

just can't run about in pants here in Fort McLeod. This is not the open range or the prairie. You're old enough to realize you cannot do just as you wish whenever you wish. The world simply does not work that way."

What did Emily know of the world? Willow wanted to ask. She'd barely been beyond the boundaries of the ranch, spending her time buried in books and the newspapers Pa brought back from Benton. What did Emily know of her? They were as different as two sisters could possibly be, different in every way. And yet there was a bond between them, a thread of silk—thin and yet strong—that drew them together.

"I'll wear the blue dress," Willow capitulated. "The plain blue one with the tiny edging."

"But that's a plain housedress," Emily began. "All right, the blue one it is," she added, quickly accepting Willow's concession.

Willow fell back on the bed and closed her eyes, listening to Emily rustle in the trunk. Material swished as Emily lifted a garment out and clucked beneath her breath, probably at the wrinkles ridging the fabric.

"I'll iron it if you want," Willow offered, sleep beckoning her.

"Absolutely not. You scorch something every time you iron."

Willow put an arm over her eyes and gave in to the softness of the feather bed and the lingering lethargy from her bath.

"You can't lie about like that, half covered."

"Hmmm."

"At least put on your wrapper."

"Didn't bring it."

Emily's rustling stopped. "You didn't bring your wrapper? What clothes did you bring?"

"A couple pairs of pants and a shirt or two."

There was a long, silent pause. "Then it's fortunate I repacked your bags for you."

Willow shot straight up, her longing for a nap forgotten. "What do you mean you 'repacked my bags'?"

Emily swished away toward an ironing board that had been brought up soon after their arrival. "I put in a few things you might need that you didn't think of."

"You didn't—"

"Take out all your horrid pants and shirts? No, I didn't. I know you better than that. You'd be miserable and this is Christmas. No, as I said, I put in a few things." Emily pointed to a lone trunk sitting away from the others.

Willow stood, clasping the towel around her, and padded over to the trunk that she hadn't noticed until now. She eased back the lid to reveal neatly folded clothes. The first garment she lifted out was a jacket made of mottled brown material, its varicolored threads woven in and out to create a repeating pattern. The garment was plain—no frills or flounces—and beautifully sewn.

"It's yours," Emily answered Willow's unanswered question. "So are the rest of the things in there."

"You made all these? For me?"

Emily smiled. "Do you think the only thing I do is cook and clean?"

"This must have taken you weeks, months." Willow ruffled through the stack.

"Quite months. I stored them all and added new

ones when I went to Benton with Pa and bought the material.''

Willow turned. "But why?''

Emily hurried back from the fireplace with a flatiron, a piece of towel wrapped around the handle. The appealing scent of warm cotton rose as she applied the iron to the muted blue of Willow's dress.

"I knew that someday you would need those things. You always get what you go after and one day you'll own your own ranch. You can't live forever in men's clothes. You'll have to go on trips and will need to dress like a successful woman.''

Amazed, Willow slid to sit on the soft carpet. "You've already thought of all that?''

Emily looked up, a lock of her hair curling on her forehead, loosened from her neat bun by the heat of the iron and the water she sprinkled on the fabric. "Whether you believe it or not, people are often judged by the cut of their clothes. I know that grates against all you believe, but it is true. Else, there wouldn't be so many articles in the paper and in magazines pertaining to fashion.''

Willow stared up at Emily, humming and stirring her way through life while her brain churned along like a fine, practical machine. Willow had always considered herself the practical one in the family, but these days Emily was constantly amazing her.

"Libby, get out of that tub. You're wrinkling. And mop up all that water you sloshed out.''

With a splash and muttered discontent, Libby obediently rose and wrapped herself in a towel.

"Girls?'' Pa's voice boomed at the door. "Our guests will be arriving at about seven. They're to meet us in the dining room.''

"Yes, Pa.''

Emily answered without a flicker of panic while Willow's heart pounded. Seeing Steven again face to face was bad enough, but for him to see her laced and gussetted was humiliation doubled.

Soft yellow light warmed the elegant dining room as the tinkling of china and silverware sang harmony to the pleasant hum of conversation. Shades of green and gold swirled through the carpet to accent the rich red of the heavy drapes that covered long windows.

"Stop gawking at me, Libby," Willow hissed through her teeth. Hands folded demurely in her lap, Willow felt like every eye in the room was trained on her and the ridiculous picture she must make.

"I ain't . . . haven't ever seen you look like this," Libby replied, awe in her voice.

"Well, remember this well, because you won't see me like this again anytime soon."

"You look lovely, Willow. Stop fidgeting."

"Is any of this supposed to feel good?"

From across the table, Emily looked down and smoothed the skirt of her dress. "It's just because you're not used to wearing these clothes. I find mine very comfortable."

"Even your corset?"

Emily frowned and shook her head, sending her carefully done curls bouncing. "Don't say that in public."

"Doesn't everybody know I've got one on?" Willow shot back.

"Of course, but it's not discussed."

"Nobody's got enough breath to discuss it if

they're wearing one." Willow shifted and felt the stays of the undergarment dig into her skin.

"The dress doesn't look right without it," Emily whispered across the table.

"I don't care. I'm going upstairs and take it off this minute." She'd planted her hands on the table to stand when a stir caught her attention.

Diners already seated near the door craned their necks, smiled and whispered. More heads turned and Willow followed their gaze. Steven and Ben stepped into the room and conversation stopped. In their ceremonial uniforms, they were a sight, Willow had to admit as her heart slammed against her already constricted ribs.

Gleaming white helmets sprouting white, fluffy plumes were quickly swept off their heads and put underneath their arms as they spoke with the head-waiter. Sparkling sabers rattled against their legs, tapping against black, shiny boots. Steven ran a hand across his carefully combed brown waves and Ben smiled at him. Their scarlet jackets were freshly brushed and the brass buttons shined. They pulled off their white gloves, tossed them into the up-turned helmets, and, at the waiter's direction, shifted their gazes in Willow's direction.

Steven's eyes met hers, awareness slamming into her. She swallowed and bit her bottom lip, remembering suddenly and vividly the sensation of his lips pressed there. He started forward, moving easily between tables and chairs, greeting interested diners with a nod and a smile and an occasional exchanged word.

"Good evening, Mr. Dawson," he said as he stopped at their table and directed his gaze to her father. "Commissioner McLeod sends his regrets. He's fighting a fever."

Cletis stood and offered his hand, which Steven eagerly shook. "Nothing serious, I hope?"

Steven shook his head and the lamplight revealed shards of colors in his hair. "Just a cold, he thinks."

"Sit down, constables." Cletis swept an arm at the empty chairs—one between Emily and Willow and one between himself and Emily. Steven chose to sit at Cletis's side, a choice Willow rejoiced in—at least she thought so.

Ben settled into the chair at Willow's side, and the waiter hurried over to take both men's helmets for safekeeping.

"You're a lovely sight this evening," Ben said in his gentle, booming voice that caused diners to look up and smile.

"Thank you." She turned toward Ben. "You look very nice, too."

Ben grinned and leaned toward her. "Ain't we a fine bunch, preening over our Sunday clothes like roosters."

His unexpected comment caught Willow off guard and she whooped with laughter—until Emily's stricken look killed her mirth. She looked down to compose herself and caught the sly, teasing look Ben slid her that said they were both naughty children.

She felt Steven's gaze on her before she finally looked up to meet his eyes. The corners of his mouth turned up slightly and his eyes were gentle, giving birth to a firestorm in her belly. "You look very nice, Willow. That color suits you."

There was no hint in his voice or his manner that said their brief encounter weeks ago was anything but an event best forgotten. "Thank you." Had she suddenly grown incapable of making any other comment? But then, the art of polite drivel had always evaded her.

"You're wearing your hair differently."

"Emily did it for me," she muttered, touching her upswept hair, remembering Emily's struggle to make the unruly locks behave.

"Emily is very talented." He graced her sister with a dazzling smile, and the first talons of jealousy gripped Willow.

For the remainder of the meal, conversation flowed around Willow. They talked of politics, plans for the Mounted Police, and recent events in the papers. She knew nothing of the subjects and wanted to know even less. Steven and Emily seemed to have developed a true camaraderie, and Libby kept Ben laughing with tales of Bell's latest escapades. She was marooned on a sea of small talk and, by the time dessert arrived, just wanted the evening to be over.

Ben made his excuses first, thanking Cletis for the meal and saying he had sentry duty tonight. Promising to see them at the Christmas party, he gathered his helmet and gloves and swept out, his wide body barely able fit between the tables and chairs.

Steven lingered longer, directing most of his comments to Emily and Cletis. Willow had long since lost her appetite and amused herself by drawing patterns in the icing dragged off her uneaten piece of chocolate cake.

Steven's comments cut through her misery and she lifted her eyes.

"With your permission, Mr. Dawson, I'd like to ask Emily to take a walk with me. I'd like to show her a bit of the town of Fort McLeod. I regret I have a patrol to ride tomorrow."

Cletis glanced out the window, where snow was blowing sideways past the gold-letter-encrusted windows. "It's kicking up a bit out there."

"We won't be long, I assure you."

Cletis nodded and Willow's heart plunged all the way down into the toes of her delicate, uncomfortable slippers. Wasn't this what she'd wanted all along, she asked herself? Hadn't she decided Steven would make a good brother-in-law? Someone to share the responsibilities of the ranch with? Someone to make Emily happy and give her the home and family she so craved.

She'd thought so, but her heart had other ideas and had fallen in love without her permission.

Stupid. Stupid. Stupid, she chided herself. How could she have been so stupid and so blind to have let him sneak inside her carefully fortified heart?

Steven rose and pulled Emily's chair out for her. Their waiter hastily brought Steven's helmet and Emily's wrap. Gently Steven laid the shawl across her shoulders. The same hands that had held Willow in forbidden places, had pressed her against his body, ready and eager for her, now rested on the round of her sister's shoulders.

With a hand on the center of Emily's back and no look back, he guided her through the dining room, the lobby, and out into the snowy night.

"I'm going on up to bed," Willow said, suddenly pushing back her chair. Unfamiliar, confusing feelings surged through her, making her wish for solitude.

"Libby, go with your sister. I'm going to stay down here for a bit," her father said, eyeing the bar.

Willow gratefully mounted the spiral staircase, holding her skirts up so as not to trip.

"I think Constable Gravel likes Emily," Libby said as they stepped up onto the second floor landing.

"You think so?"

"Yep. He talked to her all evening. Do you think they'll get married and live with us so I can play with their babies?"

Libby's jumbled question brought another wave of reality slamming home. The sweet domestic picture she'd once envisioned for them all could now never be. She had to get out—and soon.

Libby went straight to bed and was asleep in minutes, a small lump under the layers of quilts. Willow turned out all the lamps and drew a peaceful breath as the silver-white reflection of starlight off snow filled the room. She unfastened her dress, dropped it to the floor, then clawed loose the offending corset. Clad only in thin pantalets and chemise, she walked into the moonlight-stenciled path on the floor and stared at the snow-covered landscape beyond the second-floor window. Resting her cheek against the cold glass, she imagined a breathless ride with only the moon and stars for company and wished she knew her own heart.

Chapter Nine

"You're in love with Willow, aren't you?"

Steven shoved his hands deeper into his pockets. There was no use denying it. If he wanted the answers he was pursuing, he had to be honest—to Emily and to himself. No matter if the subject matter wasn't exactly appropriate between a single man and woman. "Miserably, yes."

Emily laughed softly. "That seems to be most people's opinion of my sister, unfortunately." She stepped over a drift and Steven caught her elbow to steady her. They were passing a Millinery shop and Emily paused before the window to gaze at the bits of straw and lace inside. Wind had blown the sidewalks nearly bare of drifting snow.

"And what does Willow say?" she continued.

"She doesn't know." Steven stepped to her side and looked inside the shop, amazed that women could find such bits of fluff fascinating.

"Oh, she knows. Willow's very intuitive where

people are concerned. Animals. People. Birds. Fish. They all get equal consideration and on an equal level."

Steven smiled at Emily's assessment of her sister. Obviously, she knew Willow's wild heart very well. "I haven't told her yet."

"You don't have to, Constable. A woman knows these things. Even Willow, though you'd barely get her to admit she's a woman."

"So it's written all over my face. Is that it?"

Emily turned from the window and smiled. "Only to some of us. But you hide it very well, I will admit. Until you look at her." Emily laughed. "Don't look so shocked. Men are no different than women in affairs of the heart. They just think so."

Someone, someday would be a lucky man to snare Emily Dawson. Her clear head would keep some man on his toes. Steven smiled back, genuinely liking her. "So what do you suggest I do?"

"Tell her. Oh, she'll object at first. Stomp around and declare that she's going to live her life as a hermit surrounded by cows and dogs and whatever other creatures she can lure into her own house, as she likes to put it. But she'll come around eventually. I've seen changes in her since you came along."

Emily started up the sidewalk again. "But that's not what you really brought me here to ask, is it?"

Did all the Dawson women share some strange intuitive power? "No, it isn't."

"Then out with it, constable."

"Please, call me Steven."

Emily threw him a quizzical glance. "All right, Steven. This must be a serious question. You look just as miserable as you profess."

"I suppose I shouldn't ask you this. I mean, it's

very . . . personal." He looked down at his ice-flecked boots and wondered if he should abandon the conversation now, before he was totally immersed in embarrassment.

"Despite the opinion of my family, I do not have delicate sensibilities. I'm sure you won't astound me."

"Why is Willow afraid of childbirth?"

Emily stopped and pivoted toward Steven. For several minutes she stared at him, her face blanching. "What did she tell you?"

Steven glanced toward a small cafe, the lights still glowing. Without a word he took Emily's arm and led her inside. He ordered two cups of tea and seated her at a small table near the back. When the tea arrived, Emily cupped her hands around the warmth.

"Most of what she said made no sense. Something about her mother and a baby. She said there was a lot of blood."

When Emily continued to stare into her tea, he thought he might have trod on ground too personal. "I'm sorry. Perhaps I have no right to ask."

"No, if you intend to marry my sister, you have every right to know." She raised her face and visibly took a deep breath. "Ma conceived again when Libby was two. She wanted to give Pa a son. But things did not go well. I can barely remember it myself," she said with a shake of her head. "I was only seven. Ma was in labor for a long, long time. I can remember her screaming." She smiled sadly. "I hid under my bed and covered my ears. Willow, as the oldest, had to help."

Emily took a sip of her tea and her hands shook as, with a rattle, she set the cup back into its saucer. "Pa finally sent for Ma's people. Her brother is a

Blackfoot medicine man. Pa must have been very frightened to have trusted her fate to 'Injun medicine,' as he called it. I suspect that no one could have saved her by the time Uncle Lame Deer arrived. She was weak and had lost so much blood.''

Emily paused, tears filling her eyes. "It puddled on the floor of the bedroom, a bright, quivering puddle.'' She cleared her throat. "Our brother, Aaron, was born dead. There were twins. The second . . . wasn't quite right.''

Steven's mouth went dry as his own memories intruded and blended with the picture Emily was painting. "Willow saw all of this?''

Emily nodded. "Oh, yes. She brought Uncle the things he needed, clothes and thread and such. Uncle said it was the work of evil spirits, because Ma did not believe in the Blackfoot way any longer.''

Swallowing back bitter bile, Steven tightened his own grip on his cup to hide the quivering of his hands. Catherine's death had been long and painful and terrifying. Willow's terror must have been double his own.

"Pa told us that wasn't true, that that was just what Uncle believed. Willow could never quite accept Pa's explanation. She had nightmares for years. Willow being Willow, I don't think she ever quite accepted that explanation. She's always felt close to Ma's people. But since that day Pa has blamed all of Ma's family for her death. He won't let any of us near them, although Willow sneaks away to see them. She brings Libby and me things—moccasins, beads, soft buckskin—which we hide from Pa. She says she's traded for them someplace, but I think she wants us to remember who we are and this is her way of assuring it.''

"She believes the same thing will happen to her?"

"If a man and woman are blessed, marriage usually brings children. She intends to cut off all possibilities—if you let her." She looked pointedly at him. "Don't let her, Steven, if you really love her. Pa's content to shrug his shoulders and say Willow's not the marrying kind. He refuses to admit she still carries those scars, because then he'd have to remember his own pain. Willow's a strong woman and he's content to let her bear her burden. He sees her as a daughter. I see her as a woman. She wants the same thing any woman wants—a home and family—but she won't open that part of herself to anyone but you. I'm convinced of it."

Her hand gripped his tightly. "Fight for her, even if you have to fight against her. Please don't let her condemn herself to a lonely existence. Because she will and convince herself that's what she wants. You know how stubborn she is."

They left the cafe as the snow turned into large, drifting flakes and the wind died to a whisper. When they reached the front of the hotel, Steven reached to open the door, but Emily caught his arm. "Libby and I wouldn't have a home if it weren't for Willow."

She clutched the serge of his coat in her hand as if she were desperate for him to know this sister she obviously adored.

"We each played to our own strengths after Ma's death. Mine was cooking, sewing, and taking care of everyone else. Pa sent me and Libby to live with his sister, Carrie, in Benton for a while. Willow wouldn't leave him and refused to go. She was his salvation, I see now. While I learned to bake a perfect cake and sew a straight seam, Willow learned to herd cows and judge the weather. Now, he relies on her almost completely where business is concerned. But she can't devote her life to his dream. She has to have one of her own—to take the place of the nightmares."

Emily smiled and cupped his cheek. "And I think you're the man to give her that dream—maybe the only man who can see through to her heart."

Steven bent and kissed her cheek. "How about applying some of those intuitive powers to your sister and sway her to my way of thinking?"

Steven shifted in the saddle, cold despite Buck's warm back underneath. Emily's confession had kept him up all night, staring at the ceiling and wishing Willow were in his arms. A thousand times he'd imagined Willow as a child, huddled next to her mother's bed, watching blood pool around her feet. And in the darkness, the tears that filled his ears and dampened his pillow went unnoticed to all save him and the creaking heater that kept him company.

Below, the Blackfoot village lay peaceful and serene, a layer of low smoke snaking its way among the lodges. They knew nothing of the white man's Christmas, nothing of the celebrations and decorations. Steven found peculiar comfort in that. Although he was deeply spiritual, he'd found since Catherine's death that the overwhelming joy of the season was difficult to fit into a life that was lonely and miserable.

He pulled a brown woolen scarf across his face. His patrol today was short; given the impending celebration tomorrow, his only responsibility to visit Lame Deer's village, as he often did, keeping a close eye on the whiskey trade. But today, he hoped for more personal answers.

Steven heeled Buck down the small hump of land and rode into the village, a crowd of children and dogs following along behind. He doled out bits of rock candy until he reached a large teepee, its sides adorned with cavorting stick figures.

"Constable Gravel," Lame Deer said, ducking to step out of his lodge, "you come this time when food is ready."

Steven looked at Lame Deer differently now, but he couldn't settle in his mind if the Blackfoot was healer or butcher. He had come to find out the answer. He swung down and looped Buck's reins around a convenient stub of wood. "What's for dinner today, Lame Deer?"

A wide grin stretched the Blackfoot's weathered face. Streaks of gray marred his dark hair and harsh winters had dimmed his laughing eyes, but now Steven saw traces of Willow in those eyes. "No dog today. I killed deer yesterday."

"You're sure that's what's in the stew? Deer?" Steven teased.

"Lame Deer would not lie to the great police."

Steven ducked to enter the home. "You better not be lying," he replied with a grin, enjoying the banter between them.

The Christmas decorations were absent and the fireplace was a ring of rocks on bare ground, but the poignant coziness of family huddled against a cold winter's afternoon was the same.

Faces turned. Large-eyed children peeped around the legs of a woman with long, dark hair, obviously with child.

Lame Deer spoke softly to the woman and she quickly dipped two bowls of food from a skin

paunch bubbling by the fire. She nodded to the
children and they scattered outside.

"You sit there." Lame Deer pointed to a fur
drawn close to the fire.

Steven folded his legs and sat down, then
accepted the bowl of food with a smile and a nod.
The woman looked away quickly.

Steven dipped his fingers into the fragrant, thick
mixture and tasted a chunk of the meat. "Well,
it's not dog. But it's not deer, either, is it?"

Lame Deer smiled. "Mounted Policeman is
wise."

"Whose cattle did you steal?"

Lame Deer arranged his face into a proper
expression of shock. "I did not steal; I trade."

Suspicion uncurled. "Who did you trade with?"
Steven fished another piece of beef out of the rich
broth and savored the tender flavor.

"Trade with niece."

"You mean Willow Dawson."

Lame Deer stopped eating and stared. "Yes, Willow. You know her?"

"Yes, I know her." Steven lifted another portion
to his mouth. "Can you tell me what happened to
her mother?"

Slowly, Lame Deer set down his bowl and leaned
back. "Who sends you here to ask this?"

Steven set his bowl down, too. "No one. I want
to marry her and I need to know what happened."

Lame Deer studied him. "She will never take a
husband."

"So she says. But her sister thinks otherwise."

"You think you can change her mind?"

"Yes, I think I can."

"She wants no man."

"She wants me."

Lame Deer smiled, the lines around his eyes bunching into dark furrows. "You are a brave man."

Then he sobered and spoke to his wife. She wrapped a fur around her shoulders and ducked out of the lodge, leaving the men alone. The wind buffeted the skin sides, making them flap against the lodge poles with little *puff puffs*.

"Pretty Water was very sick. Baby could not come out. She was sick long time before Cletis Dawson come for me."

"Cletis came for you?"

Lame Deer nodded. "He ride hard all day. By the time I get there, I know sister will not live. She is only waiting for baby before she go."

"So you tried to deliver the baby?"

Lame Deer nodded. "We give medicine sometimes to hurry births. I give this medicine to her." He leaned forward and met Steven's eyes. "I already knew she will not live. Much blood. I tried to save son . . . for her. You understand?"

Steven nodded. "And Cletis blames you for her death?"

"He blames himself more. He wanted son. Pretty Water was young." He shrugged thin shoulders. "This is way of nature."

What a luxury to be able to place such complete faith on the rising of the sun and all her presence wrought. To meet unexplainable disasters with the knowledge that everything was part of one big plan.

And so Cletis clung to Willow, his firstborn. How odd his choice had not been Libby or Emily. And then Steven realized an underlying current that seemed to have pulled everyone into its flow: Willow looked like her mother.

* * *

Willow awoke with a headache and a heavy heart. She cracked open one eye to stare back at the low, dark clouds that peeked in the hotel window. Gray and dismal, the morning did little to lift her sagging spirits.

She swung her feet over the edge of the bed and sat up. The chorus of anvils pounding in her head grew to a crescendo and she flopped back on the bed with an arm across her eyes.

"Willow? Are you all right?" Libby's small voice asked as the bed gave under her weight.

"Yes, I've got a headache; that's all."

"You want me to get Emily?"

"No," Willow shot back, then reconsidered the harshness of her answer. She moved her arm and stared into Libby's questioning face. "No, don't disturb her. I just need some fresh air is all."

She sat up again, waited for the pounding to subside, then pulled on her pants and shirt. A brisk ride was what she needed, to ease her headache and clear her mind. She could think best when the wind was whipping past her and the landscape was speeding by as a soft blur.

She splashed water on her face and drew a comb through her hair before tying it back with a bit of leather. Libby had crawled into Willow's spacious bed, abandoning her trundle, and lay almost unnoticeable amid the piles of quilts. Grabbing her oilskin coat off a chair, Willow slipped quietly out the door, closing it softly behind her.

The rattle of silverware and the enticing smell of cooking food said breakfast was being served. As she crept past the dining room door, she spotted an entourage of diners that brought her up short.

The man in the center of the group, dressed in an elegant deep-red coat, was undeniably the rumored Baron Von Roth. She watched, fascinated, as his jewel-encrusted fingers lifted a delicate china cup to his lips. Dark-haired and handsome, he leaned forward until his lips nearly touched the ear of the woman at his side. Stunningly blond, she smiled softly, affection glowing in her eyes, and answered, her lips inches from his.

Three men completed their party, all graying and suited, almost copies of each other. With understanding smiles on their faces, they watched the couple while devouring their breakfast with relish.

The obvious affection between the couple, the sweet way they leaned into each other, all served to resurrect the painful memories of last night and fan back to life the flames of urgency.

Willow strode into the dining room, leaving her self-doubts and probably her good sense outside.

"Baron Von Roth? I'm Willow Dawson." She stuck out her hand and waited.

The baron looked up, a smile in his eyes. Slowly, he reached across his partner and clasped her hand. "I'm pleased to meet you. Is it 'Miss' Dawson?" His voice was flavored with a subtle accent she couldn't define. It didn't sound like an England-born voice or a Canadian. Something more exotic. German, maybe.

"Yes. It's Miss. My father and I have a ranch southwest of here and, if you have some time during your visit, I would like to discuss the introduction of black Angus into our herd." The words tumbled out, as if they had tiny legs of their own, spilling from her in a hurried jumble.

The baron smiled. "What breed are you running presently?"

"Shorthorns and a small herd of polled Herefords. The shorthorns endure our winters very well on native grass."

The woman at his side looked up with gentle eyes. "Do you help your father with the cattle?" she asked in the same sultry accent.

"Yes. I . . . like the outdoors," she offered, a feeble explanation, she judged, for her peculiar lifestyle. How could she explain her life to a woman so obviously pampered and privileged?

"This is my wife, Anna," the baron said, covering his wife's delicate hand with his. "We have come here on our . . . wedding trip. I have heard much about Fort McLeod, and Anna wanted to see it."

How odd that a woman so obviously protected would want to spend her wedding trip in a poor frontier outpost when she could probably have chosen from all of Europe.

"This afternoon, four o'clock, in the parlor. My wife and I would like very much to speak with you," he continued, smiling. "We will take tea."

"Yes. Four o'clock," Willow said, backing away, her courage faltering.

She turned and strode out of the dining room, stopping in the lobby to draw a deep breath that set her head to pounding again. Excitement rippled through her. Here was the one man who could advise her on introducing a new breed, one sought after in the East. Perhaps he could provide her with enough information to set her plan in motion.

"Tea with the Baron and his wife? How did you ever get the nerve to approach them?" Emily asked, sending a stream of dresses flying from the trunks to scatter across the bed. "The white one with pink embroidery. I knew it would come in handy."

"No," Willow said.

Emily turned and looked over her shoulder. "You're not—"

"I'll wear the brown riding dress. This is business."

"But a riding dress isn't appropriate—"

"That's the way I want it, Emily."

Eyes narrowed, Emily rose from her kneeling position in front of the trunks. "Is something wrong?" she asked, searching Willow's face with her blue, probing eyes.

"You know I don't like frills and feathers, Em. This is a business meeting. I want him to take me seriously."

"What are you going to speak to him about?" she persisted.

An edge of dread crept up Willow's back as the conversation careened into dangerous territory. They'd had this argument many times, she and Emily. Emily felt the only life worth living was as a wife and mother and that everyone should feel the same. She couldn't understand, couldn't fathom why Willow would want to spend hers alone on her own land, answering to no one except God and the whims of the weather.

"He's introducing black Angus into his herd of cattle. I'd like to do the same."

"There's more to this than cattle, isn't there?"

"No."

"You're going to leave us, aren't you?"

Willow met Emily's eyes and almost lied when she read the pain there. But she could never fool Emily. "It's time, Em. I'm almost twenty."

She'd expected an outburst, a frantic argument, but Emily simply dropped her hands from where they'd clasped Willow's forearms and walked to the fireplace. Willow could have walked away, out the door, and at least postponed another confrontation, but she stayed, sensing Emily needed to say what was spinning in her mind. Willow knew she owed her that much.

"I don't remember it like you do," Emily murmured softly. "In fact, I have no memories of her at all, except what you and Pa have told me." She turned. "It must have been awful for you."

Her words brought the vivid pictures slamming back, like a punch to her midsection. Funny how those images had never dimmed. They were as horrid and terrifying as the day her nine-year-old brain had recorded them.

"You can't let that rule the rest of your life, Willow. Men and women make babies just like cows and horses do. Sometimes things go wrong, but most of the time they don't," she said in her every-thing-will-be-all-right voice. "You should know that. You work with the animals every day. Look how many successful births we have every season and how few we lose. The same is true with people."

Above all else, Willow had wanted to avoid this conversation this morning. She wasn't ready, or willing, to take out her fears and examine them closely. Nor was she eager to admit these frailties to Emily. Not now, when jealousy gnawed away at her, forcing her to see flaws in and harbor resentment against the sister she adored.

"Em, I don't want to talk about this today."

"We have to talk about this some time."

"Just not today."

Emily stepped to the bed and lifted the brown

riding skirt from underneath the pile of clothes. "Promise me we'll talk about this one day soon."

"Yes." Willow took the skirt and jacket from her and sidestepped toward their adjoining door, eager to be away from Emily, away from the possibility of more heartfelt discussions. She needed all her senses about her to talk to the Baron and his wife.

"Promise me like you mean it," Emily pursued.

"I said I would."

Willow had almost reached the door when Emily's voice stopped her cold in her tracks.

"I would imagine fear makes a poor lover."

At the stroke of four, Willow stepped into the parlor of the hotel, her heart in her throat. True to his word, Baron Von Roth and his wife were ensconced on a sofa, a small tea service in front of them.

"You are just in time, Miss Dawson," he said in his peculiar accent, standing to welcome her. Anna lifted another delicate cup and poured it full of tea.

Willow slid into a chair at their side and took the cup from her, praying her hands wouldn't tremble.

"So, tell us about yourself and your interest in black Angus cattle."

Willow took a sip of the liquid that seared her throat, then set the cup back into its saucer with a soft clatter.

"My family owns a ranch southwest of here. My father established it on his own, and I would like to help him build it into a very successful enterprise."

"You have a husband?" the baron asked.

"No."

"Brothers?"

Willow chafed at the implication, then shook her head. "No, I have two sisters."

"Your father has no sons or sons-in-law to help him?"

Willow ignored the niggle of irritation that ran through her. She'd encountered this sort of disbelief before. "We have hands that return every year to help with the spring roundup and work around the ranch through the summer. When they're not around, my father and I manage the herd."

The baron smiled a warm smile that crinkled the corners of his eyes. "So, you are a cowhand, too?"

"Yes, and I handle most of the business of the ranch." Willow took another sip of tea and decided it was time for her to take the lead. "Baron—"

"Please, call me George. I grow so tired of being called 'Baron.' Makes me sound like an old man," he said with a wave of his hand and a devastating smile.

She paused and glanced at his wife. She nodded and smiled serenely. "And my name is Anna." She pronounced the short, common name with an elegance, rounding the syllables until it came out "Ahnna."

"George, I'm interested in incorporating black Angus into my herd because they fetch higher prices both here on the western market in Calgary and on the eastern markets in Chicago. Even though the shorthorns are hardier against our winters, more and more ranchers are seeing the benefit of confining and lot-feeding the cattle during the winter months. I believe the Angus could be handled this way."

George and his wife exchanged smiling glances. "You know a lot about cattle and markets. Where did you get such information here?"

"I've been to Benton with my Pa many times. I listen to the men talk. I read the papers and books and magazines that Pa brings back. I accompany him when I can and talk to other ranchers."

"I should not be talking to you," he said with a frown and a wave of his ring-laden finger. "You are my competition."

"I beg your pardon?"

"I have come to make deal with Mounted Police to sell them cattle, and Commissioner McLeod tells me they have already made deal with Dawson Cattle Company. That is you, no?"

The sudden shift in conversation was unnerving, but Willow took a breath and replied, "Yes, I believe my cattle are on tomorrow's menu. I just delivered three hundred head to the outpost."

He studied her for a several seconds, then burst into laughter. Patrons in the hotel lobby paused and stared into the parlor.

"You are very unusual woman. What do you want to know about Angus cattle?" He slipped to the edge of the sofa and laced his fingers together. "I will tell you whatever you want."

For the next half hour, Willow plied him with questions. Had he seen a substantial difference between the Herefords, the shorthorns, and the Angus in grazing habits? Did he pen up his herd and feed them through the winter? Was the price for Angus higher on the eastern markets? Patiently, he answered every question.

"I will send you books," he offered finally, leaning back. "I have many books, new books at home. I will have rider bring them to you." He planted his palms on his knees and rose. "It is almost time for dinner."

"Do you get lonely there on your ranch, so far

from other people?" Anna's dark eyes watched her, measuring her reply. Perhaps she asked the question because she, herself, knew the bite of solitude.

"No. I love the prairie, the wind. I intend to start my own ranch soon with land Pa's promised me."

"By yourself?"

Willow nodded, shoving away the tendril of doubt that Steven's touch had created. "Yes, by myself."

Anna exchanged a glance with her husband. "I will send you books, too, books to keep you company there on your ranch."

"That's very kind of you. They would be on loan, of course."

Anna nodded. "If you wish." Then her expression brightened. "In the spring, you must come for a visit to our ranch." She turned a delighted face toward George. "They must all come. It would be a celebration after the long winter and many spring births."

"An excellent idea. Please say you and your family will come. I will send an invitation when I send your books."

"We would be honored," she accepted, thinking Emily would be beside herself for months in anticipation, something to help her while away the long, dark winter days ahead.

"You will be at the Christmas celebration tomorrow? At Fort McLeod?"

"Yes," Willow answered as she stood. "My family and I will be there."

"And the dance tonight?"

Willow swallowed and tried not to look surprised. "No. I hadn't planned on attending."

"You must come," Anna said with clasped hands.

"It is in the dining hall of the fort. I understand that it is quite festive."

"Perhaps I will," Willow said, knowing that to argue that she didn't know how to dance was fruitless and would result in an offer of hurried instruction.

"Until tonight, then," George said, and, with a hand on her elbow, led his wife out of the parlor and up the staircase.

Chapter Ten

The whine of the fiddle bows sawed as much against Willow's nerves as they did against the strings. A waltz, lovely and haunting, filled the dining hall, and lanterns softened the edges of the rough-hewn walls. Her back against the wall, she watched George and Anna glide across the plank floor, as elegant and graceful as if they were dancing on a marble floor in some elegant hall. Eyes on each other, they twirled and swooped, the whole floor their stage as everyone gave way to their perfection.

With the last dying note, George kissed his wife on her temple and turned to thank the crowd. Applause crackled and then voices filled the space the music had left.

Willow watched couples pair off for another waltz and fidgeted in her hated corset. The day after tomorrow they'd be on their way home, and she could return to being herself instead of some trussed-up imitation. Losing one's identity, if even for a short time, was unnerving, she decided. Shifting her weight, she glanced down at the blue slippers Emily had coerced her into wearing. Even though they perfectly matched the dress Emily had also insisted that she wear, they were of little value for anything except covering up her toes.

"May I have this dance?"

Willow looked up into Steven's gray eyes. In his ceremonial uniform he seemed larger, taller, looming over her. He bent close to be heard over the music, and the tiny flecks of black in his irises were mesmerizing. She longed to shut her eyes for a moment, to block out what she saw in his gaze, to scold her mind into obedience. But he might take the action as flirting, and so she met his eyes directly. "Yes, you may," she answered without knowing why she agreed to be swept around the room held in his arms.

She followed him out onto the floor, now clogged with couples. He put an arm loosely around her waist, his hand resting on the small of her back. The other hand found her fingers and entwined with them. They started a discreet distance apart, but the crowd soon pushed them closer together.

His movements were fluid and graceful as he waltzed her around the floor, and she was reminded of seeing him on horseback the first time, his thighs flexing, rippling, his motions graceful and smooth.

She was painfully aware of every place their bodies touched. Hands. Chests. Hips. His arm around her waist brought her in closer to him as they danced through the crowd. She'd have thought the layers of petticoats Emily had thrown over her head would have insulated her from the ridges and planes of his body. But she felt every one. Intimately so. Her cheeks heated as foggy and yet potent memories of a dark night and a hard body resurfaced. Their bodies pressed together, him helpless beneath her, pinned against a rough wall.

"Are you enjoying the dance?" he whispered in her ear, his breath warm.

"Yes," she lied. At this moment, she'd rather be any place else except in his arms. At least that was what her mind said. Her heart was perfectly happy nestled against his.

"Where's Emily?" she asked.

"She's dancing with Ben," he said in her ear and raised his head to nod across the room.

Willow strained to see above the crowd; then she spotted Emily's blond curls. Big Ben McGavin was stumping around the room in imitation of a waltz, holding Emily in his arms as if she were a fragile china whatnot that would break into a thousand pieces at any moment. He frowned with the effort, but Emily . . . Emily looked ecstatic. She gazed up at him with such . . . sweetness.

Willow frowned and looked up into Steven's face. "Ben and Emily?"

He grinned at her. "I think so."

"But I thought . . ."

"You thought I was interested in Emily."

"Aren't you?"

His steps slowed until they were standing still in the center of the room while the music ended and bodies halted beside them. "It's not Emily I'm interested in," he said, lowering his face until his lips nearly brushed her ear.

And then he was gone, releasing her and disappearing into the sea of red coats at the other end of the room. Willow attempted to follow, pushing her way through the uniformed men who either stepped aside or bid her a soft "Pardon me" as she passed. But Steven had vanished, a feat as improbable as the way he'd just made her heart thump.

"What's wrong?" Emily stepped into her field of vision, her too-sharp eyes taking in Willow's confusion.

"Nothing," she said, attempting a smile. "Are you having a good time?" She glanced pointedly at Ben, looming over Emily's shoulder.

"Yes, Ben is a wonderful host," she replied, her cheeks pinking slightly.

"Let me get you both something to eat," Ben offered, then pivoted and plowed a path to the refreshment table.

Emily had never looked so alive. Her cheeks were pink, her eyes bright, and she fairly twittered as she related her every step with Ben.

A sweep of cold air slithered across the floor and a rush of excited voices lured the guests toward the front of the room. The wall of broad backs prevented Willow from getting a clear view of the visitor who swept into the room. Assuming it must be Santa come to deliver presents to the kids, Willow laughed when a head of riotous red hair and a bulbous nose appeared briefly in a part in the crowd.

"Santa's running a little late," the familiar voice said, "so he sent me on ahead."

"Is that Steven?" Libby whispered at Willow's elbow.

"Constable Gravel, young lady," Emily corrected. "It is Steven, isn't it?"

"Yes, it's Steven." Willow wedged herself through

the crowd, dragging Libby behind her. She emerged in the front row of partygoers and pulled Libby around in front of her. Libby's amazed expression as she looked back over her shoulder said it all. Except for the slightly rough voice, she'd have never known the outrageous character before them was Constable Steven Gravel.

A red-and-white striped shirt hugged his body, shaping the muscles in his arms down to his wrists. Huge, baggy red overalls billowed around him, several sizes too large. Floppy red shoes, obviously a homemade version, flapped around on the floor to the delight of the wide-eyed children clustered in front of him. A white, pasty substance covered his face except for two bright red circles painted on his cheeks and an exaggerated red mouth.

He pulled up a straight-backed chair, sat down, and leaned toward the children. Some buried their faces in their mothers' skirts, and the bolder ones inched forward to stand in front of him.

"Who asked Santa for candy this Christmas?"

A weak chorus of "me" went up, and he cupped a hand behind one ear. "I couldn't hear that. Did somebody say 'me'?" He cocked his head to one side, exaggerating a quizzical expression on his face.

"Me!" they chorused louder.

Steven slapped his hands on his knees. "That's better. Now, my name is Bubbles. I want to know all of yourrrr names." He elongated the word and swept a pointing finger across the children.

"Billy. Mary. Susie." One by one they gave their names, some shouted, some murmured into folds of skirt fabric.

"Why's your name Bubbles?" a little boy pressed shyly against his father's trouser legs asked.

Steven slapped one knee. "I'm glad you asked that." Then he grabbed the end of his nose, pinched it, and a tinny *honk* echoed through the room.

Children and adults roared with laughter. All except the little boy. He stepped forward, grabbed Steven's nose and yanked it hard. Nothing happened. Frowning, the child squeezed again. Still no sound.

"It ain't working," he said with a scowl.

Steven squeezed his nose and the honk echoed again, followed by more laughter. Then, he slowly drew a small horn from his pocket. He squeezed its rubber bulb to produce the honk, grinned at the boy, and handed it to him. Beaming, the child stepped back to huddle against his father, a smile stretching his face.

"Now, back to the candy. Who wanted candy?"

A loud chorus went up this time, and Steven made colorfully wrapped chunks of candy magically appear in his palms. He leaned forward and snatched a piece or two from behind ears, out of pigtails, and from beneath collars.

"Me! Me!" The children clamored, their hesitancy forgotten, shoving each other to stand in front of Steven. When everyone had been treated, Steven straightened and stepped toward Libby. "I think there's one more thing." He reached behind Libby's ear and produced a bright-red rose, carefully folded and shaped from a scrap of red fabric and speared on a bit of wire.

Libby gasped and took the flower with trembling hands. "How'd you do that?" she asked, rubbing the flower against her cheek.

"Magic," he replied, then shifted his gaze to Willow.

Introducing Ballad,
A LINE OF HISTORICAL ROMANCES

As a lover of historical romance, you'll adore Ballad Romances. Written by today's most popular romance authors, every book in the Ballad line is not only an individual story, but part of a two to six book series as well. You can look forward to 4 new titles each month – each taking place at a different time and place in history.

But don't take our word for how wonderful these stories are! Accept our introductory shipment of 4 Ballad Romance novels – a $23.96 value – ABSOLUTELY FREE – and see for yourself!

Once you've experienced your first 4 Ballad Romances, we're sure you'll want to continue receiving these wonderful historical romance novels each month – without ever having to leave your home – using our convenient and inexpensive home subscription service. Here's what you get for joining:

- *4 BRAND NEW Ballad Romances delivered to your door each month*

- *30% off the cover price with your home subscription.*

- *A FREE monthly newsletter filled with author interviews, book previews, special offers, and more!*

- *No risk or obligation...you're free to cancel whenever you wish... no questions asked.*

To start your membership, simply complete and return the card provided. You'll receive your Introductory Shipment of 4 FREE Ballad Romances. Then, each month, as long as your account is in good standing, you will receive the 4 newest Ballad Romances. Each shipment will be yours to examine for 10 days. If you decide to keep the books, you'll pay the preferred home subscriber's price – a savings of 30% off the cover price! (plus shipping & handling) If you want us to stop sending books, just say the word it's that simple

assion-
dventure-
xcitement-
omance-
allad!

A $23.96 value – **FREE** No obligation to buy anything – ever.
4 FREE BOOKS are waiting for you! Just mail in the certificate below!

Get 4 Ballad Historical Romance Novels FREE! ❖

BOOK CERTIFICATE

Yes! Please send me 4 Ballad Romances ABSOLUTELY FREE! After my introductory shipment, I will receive 4 new Ballad Romances each month to preview FREE for 10 days (as long as my account is in good standing). If I decide to keep the books, I will pay the money-saving preferred publisher's price plus shipping and handling. That's 30% off the cover price. I may return the shipment within 10 days and owe nothing, and I may cancel my subscription at any time. The 4 FREE books will be mine to keep in any case.

Name _____

Address _____ Apt. _____

City _____ State _____ Zip _____

Telephone (___) _____

Signature _____

(If under 18, parent or guardian must sign)

All orders subject to approval by Zebra Home Subscription Service.
Terms and prices subject to change. Offer valid only in the U.S.

DN121A

Passion...
Adventure...
Excitement...
Romance...

Get 4
Ballad
Historical
Romance
Novels
FREE!

ll..l..lll...ll..ll.l.l.l..lll..l.ll..llll..l

BALLAD ROMANCES
Zebra Home Subscription Service, Inc.
P.O. Box 5214
Clifton NJ 07015-5214

She'd have known his eyes anywhere, despite the layers of makeup on his face. He watched her for several seconds and the room grew quiet. Then he passed his hands in front of each other and produced a bouquet of bobbing red-and-white fabric roses. He bowed, offered them to her, and looked up at her with a sideways grin. "Roses in winter."

Willow took them from his hand, intentionally brushing the top of his hand with her fingers and shivering with the thrill it gave her. She stared down at the bobbing flowers, stunned by the care and time each flower had taken to produce.

He shifted his attention to Emily, touched her shoulder, and produced a long, flowing snow white scarf, which he draped around her neck. But his eyes shifted back to Willow, the slate gray depths now darkened, a meaning in their intensity.

He cupped a hand behind his ear and cocked his head at a silly angle toward the door. "Do I hear sleigh bells?"

The children's chatter ceased and their eyes widened with anticipation. The door burst open and a burly, red Santa bustled inside, his beard sprinkling flour onto his red fur-edged jacket. Willow glanced behind her. Ben was gone.

With a mighty "Ho-ho-ho," he launched into his act, effectively stealing the stage from Steven, who stepped into the crowd at Willow's side to watch.

"He's wonderful," she whispered to Emily.

"Yes, he is, isn't he?" she replied, an unusual softness to her voice.

Willow turned to see Emily intently watching Santa, a child perched on each knee, one with his fingers entwined in the plentiful beard, the other yanking at the rabbit fur that decorated the neck of his coat.

"He's very good with children," Emily mused, mostly to herself.

Willow turned and found Steven watching her. "Would you like to walk outside for a moment?" he asked.

Leaving Emily and Libby riveted on Ben's performance, Willow slipped quietly out behind Steven.

The crisp air was a welcome change from the stuffiness inside the crowded hall. Steven stepped to the side of the porch and pulled off the red wig, then raked his fingers through his hair.

"You were very good," Willow said, hoping she didn't sound as awed as she felt.

He chuckled and smoothed down his tumbled waves. "There's always something freeing about hiding behind dear old Bubbles for a short time."

"Where did you get these flowers?" She held up the bobbing bouquet. "They're lovely."

Steven's face sobered and Willow shivered. "I made them. At night in the barracks."

"Didn't your roommates think you were a little odd, making fabric roses."

He laughed and drew a handkerchief out of his pocket and rubbed at the paste on his face. "Actually, during the winter any distraction, is a good distraction and I had plenty of volunteers."

Willow laughed. "What a picture you all must have made, sitting around the stove folding roses."

"They asked me who they were for."

She sobered, anticipating words she didn't want to hear. "And what did you say?"

A pause lay between them for several seconds. Inside, the tinkle of childish laughter harmonized with the chuckles of their parents. Staring down at the flowers, Willow couldn't force herself to look up at him for fear of what she'd see in his eyes. He was about to say something that would change her life forever. She felt it as sure as she felt the approach of a summer storm.

The door opened and a couple hurried out, their children in tow. Dark figures against the splotchy and churned snowfall, they huddled together in a comfortable intimacy.

"I told them—"

"Don't."

"What do you mean 'don't'?"

"Don't say what you were about to say."

He moved out of the shadows then, crossing the porch to stand beside her. "What do you think I was about to say, Willow?"

His tone demanded that she look up, so she dragged her gaze up to meet his eyes. "I don't know. I just know . . ."

"I told them they were for the woman I'd like to marry. When she's ready and if she'll have me."

Shocked all the way down to the thin soles of her hated slippers, Willow blinked and wondered if she'd heard him correctly. "Is Bubbles proposing?"

"No. Steven is testing the water."

"Steven—"

He held up a hand, then stepped closer. She thought for a moment he would take her into his embrace. "I don't want an answer." He dropped his hand back to his side. "I'm not ready to ask the question yet. I just want you to think about what I've said."

"Steven . . ." she tried again.

"No. No discussion tonight. Just . . . think about it."

The door to the mess hall swung open and partygoers poured out, bundled against the Christmas Eve chill. He backed away from her and graciously accepted the compliments that came his way.

Emily stepped to her side, bearing her wrap. "Pa's anxious to get back to the hotel. I would imagine the bar still being open has something to do with that urgency," she said as she draped the soft knitted shawl over Willow's shoulders.

Willow caught Steven's eye over the heads of the crowd for only a brief second before Cletis drove up with the wagon. But in that second, he reaffirmed his words and his determination, and an odd and unanticipated happiness moved into her thoughts.

"Bull's-eye for the lady!"

Willow lowered her rifle, the acrid scent of gunpowder burning her nose. Cletis grinned and pointed at the dark target marked on a piece of hide with charcoal where she'd drilled a hole straight through the center.

"She's a crack shot," he said, pride filling his voice.

Despite a blustery wind, a small crowd had gathered around a stack of hay and the target pinned to it.

"Could I have a try?" Emily stepped to the front of the crowd, elegantly feminine in her sweeping skirts. A titter of amusement rippled through the crowd.

Willow glanced at her father and handed Emily the Enfield.

"Somebody should stand behind her. It'll knock

her right off her feet," a voice in the crowd cautioned.

Willow met Emily's eyes and smiled. Ben, standing a few feet behind, knitted his eyebrows together in consternation.

Emily positioned the heavy gun on her shoulder, sighted down the barrel and slowly squeezed the trigger. The report was sharp and loud, and when the smoke cleared, Emily stood firm, the gun still leveled at the target. A second neat hole was punched through the dark center of the target.

Not a word was said for a few seconds; then Ben slapped his thighs and guffawed. "Well, I'll be."

Emily lowered the gun, smiling her genteel smile, and handed the weapon back to her sister. "Pa always said that might come in handy." With a wink to Willow, Emily stepped to Ben's side and resumed her place as observer.

"Where'd you learn to do that, Em?" Libby asked, her eyes huge and amazed.

Willow looked at Emily, a thousand memories passing between them. Days when the wind blew cold and bitter and they huddled together, wrapped in a buffalo fur, their short legs spraddled across a fat mare's back.

Bundled against winter's fury, they'd followed behind their parents as they searched for shelter, back in the days before Libby was born and before Cletis Dawson stole a herd of cattle to make his children a home.

"Pa taught her," Willow answered, focused on Emily's smile. "And she was always better than me."

Ben gazed down at Emily, his face open and tender, and Willow realized with a jolt that Emily had found what she was seeking. Ben adored her and Willow knew without being told that Emily returned his love in her own quiet way. Soon, she'd leave them to follow Ben, and their lives would never be the same.

Young Constable Jackson slipped into their midst. With a length of cloth tied around his waist as a makeshift apron, he clanged a spoon against a pot. "Dinner is served," he proclaimed, his voice slipping into an embarrassing squawk on the last word.

The crowd chuckled and began a slow drift toward the mess hall.

Boughs of greenery, gleaned from the surrounding hills, hung in fragrant loops along the walls, adding their sharp tang to the delicious smells of roasted meat and baked pastries. William and his legion of helpers paraded out their masterpieces on large, steaming platters. When every chair was filled, James McLeod rose, a tin cup in his hand.

"Here's to another successful year for the Northwest Mounted Police and Fort McLeod."

Cups clinked together and voices chimed in to echo his words.

"The whiskey trade is all but abolished and settlers are coming to join us here in Alberta Territory. This we have accomplished without undue bloodshed. Our neighbors, the Blackfeet, have peacefully accepted our presence. Congratulate yourselves, gentlemen, and thank God for our successes."

Another swell of agreement met his words, and he spoke a quick prayer blessing all the souls who served in the Mounted Police and the guests who now joined them around the humble, rough table. Then he declared the commencement of the Christmas feast.

The comforting hum of conversation accompa-

river. Lonely wooden crosses dotted the snow-flecked ground, barren sentinels to lives that once were. Steven drew a deep breath as he looked out over the little cemetery. He'd helped dig most of the graves and had known well the majority of the men lowered into them.

He glanced sideways at Willow, her face solemn and unreadable, and yet he could imagine what was running through her thoughts. "Death is part of life, Willow, just as love and joy and birth are."

She stood with her back to him, to the crosses, staring across the water and into the woods beyond. She crossed her arms as he spoke, in a sort of defense against his words, he guessed. He moved up behind her and laid his hands on her shoulders. "We can't bring back the ones we lose. We can only do as they'd wish—continue living."

She turned around and looked into his eyes, meeting his gaze fully. A swirl of desire in the pit of his stomach threatened to rob Steven of his carefully thought-out words.

"I told you once I lost my wife in childbirth."

A flash of compassion passed through her dark eyes. "I'm sorry. You must have loved her very much."

"More than life itself," he replied, and she winced slightly at the frankness of his words.

"Catherine was a generous, loving woman who wouldn't have wanted me to stop feeling because she died." Willow's eyes still held his, waiting. "Just as your mother wouldn't have wanted you to live a life of loneliness because of her."

Willow turned away then; his words were striking the chord he'd hoped to strum. "My mother's death has nothing to do with my choices. I've always wanted my own land, my own home, to do in as I wish." She hunched her shoulders against the wind that whipped her riding skirt against her legs.

"I thought you weren't afraid of anything."

She pivoted around, her arms still firmly crossed over her chest. "I'm not a fool, Steven. Of course I'm afraid sometimes. Everybody is, of some things."

"Then why are you afraid to marry, afraid of the pleasure you might find in my arms and in my bed?"

Her eyes widened in alarm. At least he had her attention. Part of him expected to see her fleeing across the snowy ground, and the other part expected her palm to leave a red splotch on his cheek. Instead, her eyes narrowed and grew cold.

"I don't know what you're talking about."

"You know exactly what I'm talking about."

"I don't think we should be having this conversation. It's not proper."

She started to walk past him, but he grabbed her arm. "You hide behind what's 'proper' when it suits you and thumb your nose at convention the rest of the time."

She wrenched her arm away, pure anger flashing in her eyes.

"Let me go. What makes you think I ever think of you in that . . . way? You're the most arrogant— I'd never even entertain the idea of . . . you and me . . ."

"Your kiss said otherwise. We're adults, you and I, and we both know what happened between us and what it meant." He eased his grip on her arm. "I love you, Willow, and that's a fact as certain as the seasons and the weather."

His caution and common sense scuttled away to that dark place it sometimes hid, and his heart assumed dominance over thought and body. Steven dropped to one knee, the cold dampness of the sodden ground soaking through his pants. He wanted her more fiercely than he'd ever wanted anything in his life. And despite his careful words of last night, despite his promise to himself to give her time to come to love him as he loved her, he suddenly realized he couldn't survive another minute without her heart promised to his. "Marry me, Willow. Marry me and let me chase away your nightmares."

Chapter Eleven

"Steven, get up!" Willow wrenched her hand out of his grasp and stumbled backward a step or two. "You're making fools out of both of us!" She threw an anxious glance toward the fort gates, visible from where they stood. Fortunately, the crowd she'd imagined did not exist, and Steven's confession was witnessed only by her and the quiet of the afternoon.

He pitched forward and planted both hands in the cold mud that oozed up between his fingers. On all fours, he looked up, fire snapping in his eyes. He struggled to his feet and slung the mud off his hands, his face flaming and his mouth set in a grim line. Instant regret at the harshness of her words filled Willow, and she raised an arm to reach out to him, to explain; but the fury on his face made her hesitate and finally drop her arm to her side.

"I'm sorry. I . . . you startled me."

He didn't answer for several seconds that seemed to stretch longer, looking down at his muddy hands. "No, I apologize to you. I'm afraid I let an impetuous moment and the holiday get the better of my sense." He met her eyes, his expression colder than the day and just as bleak. "It won't happen again."

For some inexplicable reason, Willow's heart seemed to plunge to the bottom of her stomach. A small niggling of doubt gnawed at her confidence in her quick answer.

"Until you're ready, that is." He moved a step closer and Willow recoiled inwardly at the hardness in his bearing and in his eyes. "I know that somewhere inside that hard shell of nonchalance you wear, there is a warm, kind, and passionate woman. And she wants to get out. You're just too stubborn to hear her. And until you do, she's going to torment you and eat away at you with what-ifs that will bring you sleepless nights. Listen to her, Willow. She's the real Willow Dawson, held captive by fear and plain bullheadedness."

He moved closer again until he towered over her. She met his gaze squarely, letting him know he didn't frighten her. But now his eyes had softened into a gentle, gray sadness as he looked down into her face.

"I went about this in all the wrong ways. I never asked your opinion or what you felt. I thought I knew. I realized now that I don't know you as well as I had believed."

His words elicited a surge of compassion that almost made her agree to marry him—anything to erase that sadness from his eyes.

"So understand these things. I want you for my wife, no matter how long I have to wait for you to come to me. I want you to bear my children and share my home. All you have to do, Willow, is say you want me, and we'll find a way to handle the rest. Your fears, your need for independence. None of those things should stand in our way—if we want each other enough.''

He moved back a step and Willow waited, sensing he had more to say and needed distance to say it. "But the final outcome will be your decision. You already know mine.''

He pivoted and walked back toward the fort, his back stiff and his gait hard. Willow looked up at the threatening sky and wished she could disappear into the roiling clouds. A single, lazy snowflake floated to its death on the damp ground. So much death and misery. Everywhere one looked was evidence of the cycle of life. Birth, existence, and finally rejoining the earth.

She looked after Steven. He walked looking down, staring at the ground. Occasionally, he brushed at his pants and chafed his hands together. He reached the fort gates, nodded to the sentry, then disappeared behind the thick cottonwood stockade walls.

Hidden from view.

So like herself.

"A wedding? When?''

Emily stood in the center of the hotel parlor, her hand firmly clasped in Ben's big, rough one, and Willow's world reeled.

"We think maybe in May or June, after the thaw." She glanced up adoringly at the huge man at her side. "We're going to live here, in Fort McLeod, until Ben's enlistment is up in a year, then we'll move home and Ben's going to help Pa with the ranch.''

"But when ...?" Sensible sentences simply would not materialize in Willow's brain. Emily married? And gone from them? She'd suspected there was more between Emily and Ben than either let on, but marriage? And so soon?

"Ben and I have been discussing marriage for a few weeks now, when he'd come by on patrol. He asked Pa last night and me today. Of course I said yes."

The usually calm and sedate Emily looked about to jump up and down like a six-year-old, and Willow smiled. This was what Emily had always wanted: someone to love her and a home of her own. So little and so essential—at least to Emily.

"I'm so happy for you." Willow put her arms around Emily and squeezed her.

When she backed away, Emily narrowed her eyes. "Are you all right?"

The telltale flush crawled up her cheeks. She'd stopped in the stable for a good cry into Pat's mane. No one knew except her and the little mustang and she wanted it to stay that way. "No, I'm just very happy for you."

Emily's expression said she wasn't through with her, and Willow began inventing an explanation in her mind even as she shifted her attention to Libby and Cletis, both staring with wide, sad eyes. Except Cletis's were filled with tears.

"Pa?" Emily said, frowning.

"My little girl's getting married," he said wistfully. Then a wide, poignant grin split his face. "Congratulations, honey." He held out a beefy hand to Ben. "Welcome to the Dawson clan."

Ben beamed, grasped Cletis's hand and pumped

it enthusiastically. "Thank you," he rumbled. "Who's gonna feed us?" Libby said with a pout. "I thought she was gonna marry Steven and live with us."

"Steven? What on earth gave you that idea?" Emily asked.

"Well, caused he kissed you last night in front of the hotel."

"That was a quick peck between friends, Libby." Emily turned to Willow, started to say something, then demurely pressed her lips together. "Willow will look after you all for a year."

"We won't never get nothing to eat!" Libby rolled out her lip. "Nothing's gonna be the same."

"We won't ever get anything to eat," Emily corrected.

"We sure won't," Libby said with a sad shake of her head.

"We'll have to celebrate tonight at dinner before we start for home in the morning." Cletis rubbed his hands together, apparently very pleased with the sudden turn of events. "Invite young Constable Gravel, too."

"No." Everyone turned to look at Willow's outburst. "I think he said he had sentry duty," she finished weakly.

"That's right." Ben grinned. "I'll have to supply the charm for the both of us."

"Then it's settled. A celebration tonight at seven."

The bunk groaned as Steven lowered his body into the grass-stuffed mattress, stretched out, and sighed. Bagley's bunk overhead was empty, for the young constable was walking guard duty in his

place. Ben, determined not to celebrate his engage-
ment alone, had persuaded the young man to
switch duties.

Steven propped his feet against the supporting
frame and crossed his arms behind his head. But
as tired as he was, he knew sleep would not come.

Up in the exposed beams of the barracks, a soft
scurrying gave away a mouse's nocturnal route.
Willow's words echoed in his mind, drowning out
all the sensible arguments he would have made up
for himself.

She didn't love him.

She'd never love anyone.

To expect more from her was a fool's endeavor.

She was one of those women who'd endure her
husband's touch only long enough to conceive a
child and then not again until another conception
was necessary.

All these things he'd have liked to believe, for
belief would have freed his mind and his heart.
But he knew better. Willow would be a warm and
willing lover, a friend and a good mother. If only
she believed that.

Steven turned over and shifted his weight, looking for a comfortable place in the mattress. Perhaps
he was sore from sitting tense all during dinner.
Seated beside Willow, he struggled to keep his
hands from touching her, from allowing his fingers
one brief foray across the delicate skin on the back
of her hand. She needed kissing—hard, passionate
kisses. Yes, kissing her breathless might be a start
to winning her.

Across the room, another cot groaned and heavy
steps made their way to the potbellied stove. The
door creaked open and shadows danced on the
end wall. Then, the door closed and the steps

returned and stopped at Steven's side. Ben sat down on the empty bunk opposite him, a fragrant cloud of pipe smoke swirling around him.

"Want a smoke?" Ben asked and held out Steven's own pipe.

He hadn't lit it in weeks. The blend he smoked, had brought with him west, reminded him still of quiet evenings with Catherine curled in his arms.

"I put some of my tobacco in," Ben said.

Steven sat up, ducking to miss the upper bunk's slats, and took the pipe from Ben's hand.

"I didn't tell you congratulations," Steven said as Ben held out a glowing piece of wood he'd plucked from the stove. Steven cupped his hand around the pipe's carved bowl and sucked on the pipe stem. The tobacco flared, then glowed a warm orange, sending up ghostly tendrils of smoke.

"Thank you, lad. I'd anticipated this being a double celebration." By the light of their pipes, Steven could just make out Ben's face.

"Willow's not the marrying kind, apparently." Steven propped his elbows on his knees and stared at the floor.

"According to Emily, that's not true."

"Well, she certainly made it plain to me."

"Turned you down, did she?"

"Turned me down flat. Literally."

"Well, that was just the first askin'. You always have to ask a lass twice, once for her to make up her mind and once so she can say she made you beg."

"Did Emily turn you down the first time?"

"I have to say she didn't."

"Well, then you're one ahead of the game, aren't you?" Steven took another pull on the pipe and found that its comforting presence did nothing to ease his mind.

"Willow's a difficult lass, to be sure. Emily's told me some about her. Em believes she'll come around, though."

Steven shook his head. "No amount of asking is going to change Willow's mind unless she wants to change it. She's buried so far in her own fears, she can't see over them."

"Her Ma's dyin'?"

"Willow saw it all."

"Hard thing for a woman to forget, I'm guessin'. Still, she's not the first to put something like that behind her."

Steven studied Ben in the dim light. Despite their friendship, he wondered if he should ask the question he wanted to ask. "Is Emily afraid? Of having children, I mean?"

Ben shrugged, seeming to take no offense. "She wants children. She told me about her Ma, of course, but she didn't seem worried. I guess all women worry about that some, wouldn't you say?"

Steven shrugged. "I guess. I can't remember Catherine mentioning it when she found out she was with child."

"Depends on the woman."

Steven nodded. "Suppose so."

An uncomfortable silence settled between the two men. They lived in close quarters, and yet few men ever talked of personal things. Steven glanced around the barracks, now about half occupied since headquarters had been transferred to Fort Walsh. Of all the men sleeping there, he knew only cursory details about all but two or three, Ben counted in that number. Strange that women would put such stock in confiding in each other.

Or that they would feel the need. Catherine had been his confidante and he hers, for the most part. And yet she'd never mentioned her fears of childbirth, and rarely spoke of the impending birth except to emphasize to him she hoped she could give him a son. What terrors had she carried in her heart that she never shared?

He only knew one man and one woman who would tell him the details he needed to offset Willow's fears.

"I beg your pardon?" Colin turned from the small bench that held his mortar and pestle and stared straight at Steven.

Steven felt the color threaten to burst out of the top of his ears.

"I'm sorry." Colin wiped his hands on a cloth and pulled his suspenders back up onto his shoulders. "You just took me by surprise with that one. Come inside. I've got coffee warming."

Steven followed Colin through the room he used as a combination examination room and office and into the small room he and Maggie used as their kitchen and parlor. He poured dark liquid into two cups and sat down at the table.

"Where's Maggie?" Steven asked, glancing around the room and wondering why he hadn't thought to check before he blurted out the purpose of his visit.

"She took the baby over to Abigail Baker's house. They're working on a quilt for Mary."

Steven sat down opposite him and stared into his cup. "I'm not sure I can get the question out again, so I hope you heard me the first time."

Colin chuckled. "Actually, it's not an unusual

question at all. Limiting family size has been practiced for centuries. In fact, when I was in school in Edinburgh, a visiting professor from France presented a very interesting seminar on the subject of birth control. It's just never been a very public subject either in England or here in Canada. The real experts are the women. They pass this information between themselves and never let us poor rutting fellows in on the details."

"Maybe some women do."

"I take it you and Catherine never . . ."

"No. At least if she did, I knew nothing about any measures she took to prevent conception. We wanted a baby right away."

Last night, in the dark, this discussion had seemed like a logical, sensible idea. If you want information, ask someone who knows. If anyone should know about this subject, it should be Colin, a doctor trained in Scotland, exposed to a worldliness no one in Fort McLeod could match. But now, in the light of day, Steven felt like an even bigger fool than yesterday.

"Look, I'm sorry I asked." Steven shoved back his chair and stood.

"Sit down, Steven. This is obviously important to you."

Steven paused, then sat, feeling like the child chastised in front of the class.

"Speaking as a doctor, I wish more people would ask." Colin leaned forward and wrapped his hands around his cup. "Can you imagine the life of a woman who conceives every year? Or every two years. They're old women at thirty. Unless they have an understanding husband."

"How understanding?"

"May I ask if this has something to do with Willow?"

He'd trusted Colin with his very life more than once. Why was it so hard to trust him with intimate details?

"I've asked her to marry me."

Colin grinned. "Congratulations."

"Not yet. She turned me down."

"And her refusal has something to do with this?" Colin frowned. "Is there something wrong?"

Steven related Willow's history and Colin listened, his eyebrows knitted together in concern.

"Terrible thing to happen to a family."

"What do you suppose was wrong with the second twin?"

Colin shook his head and swirled his coffee. "No one but God knows. There's all sorts of old wives' tales and superstitions about deformed babies. Some Indian tribes, and some other cultures, believe it's the incarnation of an evil spirit. Others believe the mother saw some evil being that cursed the child. Some think the mother did wrong some time in her life and this is her punishment. I believe it's some unfortunate act of nature we've yet to understand. And yet its occurrence can destroy people's lives because of its rarity. They want to assign blame in an attempt to understand. Willow's afraid this will happen to her?"

"Yes, I believe she is."

Colin leaned back, crossed his legs, and hung one arm off the back of his chair. "Abstinence is the only certainty."

Steven shook his head. "Besides that?"

"There are things available, but none too common out here. Withdrawal's still the most common method."

Steven nodded.

"Hard on a man. And a woman, too, I'm told," Colin said with a small grin. "Not foolproof, either. A man has to have all his wits about him and resist temptation. Difficult thing to do in that particular situation."

Steven swallowed, images of Willow cavorting through his head. Could he make love to his wife, then leave her wanting and unsatisfied when she needed him most?

"There's a method used in the Arabian countries where a man holds—"

"No." Steven shook his head. "Don't tell me that one."

Colin shrugged. "I'm not sure I'd advise that one from a general medical standpoint. You know how varied the traders' wares are. Want me to ask around? From a medical perspective, of course. I'd be interested, now that you've brought up the subject, to see just what's made it this far west. I know for sure many devices are common in Toronto."

Steven nodded, not sharing Colin's obvious fascination with the scientific facts of the discussion.

"Have you told her she's this special to you?"

"What do you mean?"

Colin hunched his shoulders. "I wouldn't imagine doctors get this question from many grooms-to-be. Mostly from men burdened with too many mouths to feed. After the fact, so to speak. It's a rare man so interested in his wife's wellbeing from the start."

"I had hoped I could offer her . . . a guarantee. I guess I was hoping you had . . . modern information."

Colin leaned forward, pushed his coffee cup

away, and threaded his fingers together. "My personal opinion is there will never be any guarantees. Every time I'm close to Maggie, my first impulse is to take her in that bedroom and make love to her." He pointed toward the closed door at the end of the kitchen. "But I resist. Some of the time, at least. I can't say to you that I'm always the sensible doctor who holds back. Sometimes I'm a rutting bastard who just can't get enough of his wife's body." He leaned back in the chair. "Talk to her, Steven. Tell her you love her, with the same conviction it took to come to me today."

Willow threw her stirrup over Pat's saddle and gave the cinch a final yank. She patted his thick neck, received a soft grunt in response, then lowered the stirrup. The wagon was hitched and waiting for their luggage at the front of the hotel. They were going home and she should be happy. She *was* happy, she reminded herself. She'd have plenty of time to think and plan on the long ride home. She'd approach Pa about that land to the south as soon as they were unpacked and settled. By spring, she could have a cabin up, just in time for the spring roundup. By next winter, she'd be moved into her own place, answerable to no one. Gratefully alone.

But somehow, that prospect didn't bring the joy it once had.

"Let's go, boy," she said as she gathered the reins from where they were looped over a stall railing.

"I think Pat will wait a few more minutes."

Willow whirled at the sound of Steven's voice. He stood in the doorway, devastating even in silhouette. The buffalo coat gave him a bulkiness that cast a long, wide shadow.

"Could I talk to you a moment before you go?"

"Sure," she said, nodding and wishing for a way to disappear.

He stepped nearer until he was no longer a dark silhouette, but a man with slate gray eyes standing far too close for comfort. If she'd thought she could never want him more than that night he'd kissed her in the window, she'd been wrong. In the few seconds since his voice had reached her ear, desire had sent her fears scurrying away. And without those fears—those horrifying images that she nursed back into existence each time they deserted her—she'd be vulnerable to him, to his love, his offer of marriage, and the pleasures his body could offer hers. And she knew, without a doubt or experience upon which to base her opinion, that he would give her pleasure—a price she couldn't afford.

"I want to apologize for yesterday. I acted like a fool and you had every right to be angry. No man should ask a woman to marry him with no more forethought or warning than I gave you."

Shocked by the civility in his tone, Willow studied him a moment before answering. "I accept." Two words seemed very inadequate to smooth the misunderstanding between them.

"But my offer still stands. If and when you're ready."

He moved closer and Willow waited. For what, she didn't know. He took her fingers into his warm hand.

"I owe you a courtship—difficult when you're fifty miles away, but we'll find a way. If you're agreeable to let me call upon you."

She couldn't think this close to him, seemed unable to call up her defenses, to rally her suspicions and bravado. He rolled her fingers gently between his, mesmerizing part of her; then he leaned down and touched her lips with his. He smelled wonderful: smoky and male, powerful and soothing. He didn't pull her closer or deepen the kiss. And when their lips parted, he remained over her, his face inches away.

"I know what you fear most. You're afraid to become my wife for fear you'll conceive a child and suffer the same fate as your mother. There are things a man can do to prevent that, and I'll do those things if they will bring you to me. I don't want a marriage by name only, Willow, but I'll accept that as your terms if that's the only way I can have you. At least until I can convince you otherwise."

He pressed her fingertips to his lips, his breath hot and moist on her naked skin. "I'll take whatever part of you you can give. And hope I can earn the rest."

Then, with a stir of cold air, he walked away, leaving her reeling from his kiss and the intimacy of the words he'd whispered.

Marshaling her wits, she led Pat outside. Steven waited by their wagon, looking up at Pa and Emily.

"I would like to come and call on Willow, if that's agreeable to you, Mr. Dawson," he was saying.

Pa glanced at her with a strange expression. "What does Willow say to this?"

All eyes turned toward her. What could she say with everyone looking at her?

"I suppose it's all right," she said with as much nonchalance as she could still scrape together. She plopped her hat onto her head and turned to put one foot in her stirrup. A hand on her shoulder kept her from pulling herself into the saddle.

Without a word, Steven yanked her into his arms and planted his lips on hers. Her hat fell backward into the snow and her hair tumbled down around her shoulders. For a brief moment she parted her lips beneath his and tasted the warm roughness of his tongue. Then, he released her and stepped back. She reeled like a drunk and stumbled back against Pat who *oof*ed and shifted his weight.

"When I come to call on you, we'll finish this," he whispered, his voice heavy and rough. His hand slid into the pocket of her coat and left a small package behind to press against her side.

He nodded toward the shocked faces in the wagon and stalked away down the snowy street.

Chapter Twelve

Willow leaned against the door frame, watching her father at his desk. Head bent, he pored over an old newspaper for the third time, one of several he'd scrounged on their trip to Fort McLeod. Weak sunlight made a faint pattern on his balding head as he leaned forward with hunched shoulders, completely absorbed in the spiderlike print, giving her a rare chance to observe him.

The years and the sorrows had taken their toll, sculpting wrinkles around his eyes and aging his skin to a fine, ridged leather. Fingers, blunt and rough, tapped absently against the newsprint, defining hands that could be hard or gentle when required.

She would miss him the most.

Quick tears stung her eyes and she blinked them away. She wouldn't cry. Pa couldn't know her decision was fueled by anything but her desire for her own land. He couldn't know his oldest daughter was a coward.

"Pa? Could I talk to you a minute?"

Cletis raised his eyes. "Of course." He lowered the paper to the desktop.

Willow walked to her desk, pulled her chair out from underneath, and sat down facing him. "I want to talk to you about that land to the south."

Slowly Cletis folded the paper and laid it to the side.

"We've talked about my having it, building my own place. I'd like to do that in the spring."

Thoughts flickered across his face, all registering in his eyes as he studied her. "Are you sure that's what you want?"

No, she wasn't sure. In fact, she wasn't sure about anything anymore. Her carefully regimented and thought-out plans had all been disrupted by one kiss and a tiny piece of gold that now hung between her breasts, hidden underneath her shirt. Elegant and empty, the locket had been Steven's gift to her, the package he'd slipped into her pocket. Filigree etched the smooth oval cover that opened to reveal an emptiness begging to be filled. Tucked into the nest of shredded paper that held the locket was a simple note: "Hearts and lockets should always be full."

"Yes, I'm sure. We've talked about this before. It's time for me to go, Pa."

Cletis leaned back in his chair. "Your Ma was an independent woman. Irritatingly so, sometimes. Reckon I can't fault you for being like her. What about Constable Gravel?"

The warmth of embarrassment crept up her cheeks at the sudden memory of his public kiss. "What about him?"

Cletis frowned. "I thought . . ."

"Steven and I have no agreement."

Cletis nodded slowly. "I kind of thought, with the way he left you . . ."

Willow sighed and looked down at her hands. "He'd like more; that's a fact. But . . . marriage is not in my plans. You've always known that."

She looked up and saw deep concern in her father's face.

"Your Ma's death was a hard thing for me, Willow. She was the only woman I ever loved—or ever will. But I don't regret loving her. Or having you girls. Or the sons I lost, God protect 'em. I've said a lot of things to you maybe I shouldn't have." He paused and swallowed. "You're so like her." His voice was rough with emotion.

"This has nothing to do with Ma. This is just the way I want things."

Cletis suddenly leaned forward and clasped her hands between his two big, warm ones. He stared down at their joined hands for several seconds. "Your Ma died with a peaceful heart, Willow. She never gave up her Blackfoot beliefs, and they believe there's life beyond, just like we do. She knew when she conceived the boys what a chance she was taking. Libby's birth wasn't easy, but you don't remember that." He massaged her fingers. "Men get the credit for bravery, but it's the women, God help 'em, who are the brave ones."

He looked up and she met his eyes. "She wanted to give me a son. That meant more to her than the risk she was taking.

"You shouldn't 'a seen the things you saw that day. It's kept me awake many a night that that's made you the way you are."

"Pa—"

"If she were here," he interrupted, "she'd tell you this is a foolish idea, goin' off on your own like this."

Willow opened her mouth to protest.

"But she ain't here and I reckon it's my job to handle this. I ain't gonna tell you you can't do this, but I will tell you that that young man's in love with you and you'd be foolish to throw away what all of us seen in his eyes."

Willow looked away from his intense expression. She'd chosen a path and she had to stick with her decision or lose herself. Steven's offer was filled with dark unknowns, uncertainties she wasn't ready to explore. Ranching and cows and the wind in her face were things she knew.

And she'd take the known every time.

"I'm taking Emily to Fort McLeod tomorrow." Cletis said as he dropped her hands and leaned back. "She wants to shop for material for her wedding dress." The statement was more a question.

"I've got chores to do."

"Andy and Wilbur can do 'em. Wilbur's knee is good as new."

"No, Pa," Willow said with a shake of her head.

He sighed and shrugged. "It's your decision."

The Dawson wagon rattled out of the yard at first light the next morning, an unexpected chinook blowing temperate wind at their back. Emily turned on the wagon seat, a worried expression on her face, and Libby huddled in the back, a quilt over her head and drawn tight under her chin. Willow watched them go, a mixture of relief and regret surging through her. Emily's constant bubbling over her wedding ran Willow's emotions through a gauntlet ranging from joy to sorrow. A few days away from the preparations would be a welcome respite.

"You want to work on them fences now?" Andy asked at her elbow.

"Yeah. I'll be right there."

"How come you didn't go with 'em?"

Willow turned and started toward the barn. "I've got things to do here."

"You sure you ain't trying to avoid Constable Gravel?"

Willow stopped so suddenly that Andy ran into her back. "Who told you about Constable Gravel?"

Andy flushed and scuffed at the muddy ground with the toe of his boot. "Libby told me he kissed you right out in front of the whole dang town."

"Libby's mouth runs at both ends."

"Well? Did he?" Andy looked up, focused intently on her face.

"Yes, he did."

"Gosh."

"Now, can we get to work?" She started off again for the barn with long strides.

"What was it like?"

"What was what like?" she answered as she swung open the barn door.

"Kissing him. Did you like it?"

She paused with a hand on Pat's stall and swiveled to face Andy. Huge eyes stared back at her from a gaunt, boyish face. "It was all right. Why?"

Again Andy dropped his gaze to seem fascinated with the hay strewn about the dirt floor. "I just wondered 'cause I sometimes think about doing the same thing."

"Kissing Constable Gravel?" she said, suppressing a smile.

"No!" Andy jerked his head up. "Come on, Willow. You know what I mean. Kissing you."

Willow smiled at the flush of color that inched all the way up to Andy's hairline. But something twisted inside her at the raw admiration on his face. "You think about kissing me?"

Andy grinned crookedly. "Sometimes."

"I'm old enough to be your mother."

"You ain't. You're twenty and I'm sixteen. That's only four years."

"Okay, I'm old enough to be your older sister, then."

"Is that how you think about me, Willow? A little brother?"

She knew well the pain evident in Andy's eyes.

"You're part of the family, Andy, you and Wilbur. I think of you as . . . part of the family. What about Libby? I've seen the way you look at her."

Again Andy blushed. "Libby thinks I'm a pest."

"Well, she should know. She's the biggest pest around."

"Are you in love with Constable Gravel?"

Was she? Andy watched her earnestly, expecting an answer.

"No," she lied.

"That ain't what your eyes said when I mentioned his name just now."

Willow turned back to Pat, alarmed that her feelings were so plainly displayed on her face, readable even by a love-smitten sixteen-year-old. "Constable Gravel and I are just friends."

"Don't seem like it to me if he kissed you like Libby said."

"Libby's in love with love, at the moment. A result, I'm afraid, of reading Mr. Shakespeare's *Romeo and Juliet* three times. She read more into that kiss than there was. It was just a peck between friends.'' She grabbed Pat's halter and led him out of the stall, hoping Andy would give up on his questions and realize there was work to be done.

Andy took the hint and shuffled toward the back of the barn where his horse, Charlie, stared curiously over the stall, munching hay. ''Don't seem like no peck to me if your hat falls clean off,'' he muttered.

The chinook disappeared as quickly as it had come, changing to a sudden storm of snow and wind. Willow stabled Pat and walked to the house, her head bowed against the driving snow. She and Andy had repaired fence for two days in preparation for the spring roundup, still two months away.

The house was dark and cold when she hung her coat on a nail and stepped into the kitchen, careful to wipe her feet on the hooked rug. Fumbling in the dark, she lit a lantern and made her way to the parlor to light the fireplace. Tentative flames made dancing shadows against Pa's dark paneling.

Willow sat back on her heels and let the flames mesmerize her. This was how it would be alone. Every night a cold, empty house. A fireplace waiting to be lit. A meal waiting to be prepared. With a jolt, she realized that Emily and her quiet, efficient ways had spoiled them all. Living alone, no matter that it was her dream, would take some adjustment.

The jingle of tack rose above the soft swish of snow-filled wind, and the thump of boots on the porch brought her to her feet. She opened the door and faced a snow-covered Steven.

''What are you doing here?'' she asked, alarm

and joy spreading through her. "Is something wrong?"

"No," he said with a shake of his head that sent snow flying off the brim of his Stetson. "Your father asked that I check on you when I rode patrol this way today. May I come in?"

"Of course." Chagrined, Willow opened the door wider. He took off his buffalo coat and shook off the snow, then stepped inside onto another of Emily's rugs.

For all her efforts to put him out of her mind, to forget the feel of his lips on hers and the way his touch made her heart jump, one look at him undid all her valiant efforts. The broad-brimmed Stetson made him look taller, slimmer than the tiny field hat or helmet he'd worn before. Had his eyes always been this gentle shade of gray? Was his hair so wavy before, inviting one to run her hand across the gentle ridges? Did his cheeks always dimple this way when he smiled?

"How have you been?" he asked in a soft timbre that her insides remembered well.

"Fine. Where'd you see Pa?" Willow stepped into the parlor and threw another log onto the firedogs.

"He came to the fort yesterday."

"To see you?" she asked, avoiding his eyes while trepidation began to crawl through her.

"Yes."

She squatted and poked at the fire. "What about?"

Steven pulled off his white gloves and tucked them into his belt. "You." He moved to the fire and held out his hands.

Willow stood, replaced the poker, and moved a little farther away. They were alone in the house with no one else for miles save Andy and Wilbur.

If he reached for her, she wasn't sure she could—
or would—resist.

"He thinks he's to blame for your refusing my
proposal."

Willow folded her arms across her chest. She
didn't want to talk about this or even remember
how his heartfelt words had made her heart twist.
"He's not. I can think for myself."

Steven cocked an eyebrow at her. "He knows
you better than you think. In fact, he thinks he
put the notion of spinsterhood into your head."

"You say that as if a woman who never marries
is an oddity, someone to be pitied."

He chafed his hands together and stepped back
from the fire. "Only if she purposely chooses that
path to make herself miserable."

"That's not what I'm doing."

He took a step toward her. "What are you doing,
Willow? Why did you refuse me? I want to hear it
from you in plain talk."

Pa's desk was to her back and there was no graceful way to put distance between them. And she'd
not dash away like some frightened doe. So she
stood her ground and met his eyes.

"I don't love you."

"Liar."

"Why do you think I'm lying?"

He stood a few feet away and made no move to
come closer, but his gaze pinned her where she
stood all the same. She wanted to close her eyes,
to shut out the love she saw in his. "You say it in
so many ways, Willow," he said softly, with no trace
of the anger she expected. "The way you look at
me. The way you kissed me at Christmas. The way
you refuse to believe I love and want you. The way
you try to harden your heart against me. Only a

woman deeply in love would go to so much trouble. You'll have to come up with a better reason than that.''

"I told you I don't want to get married. I just don't want to, that's all.''

"You're afraid, Willow. Admit it and let me help you.''

"I don't need your help. I don't need anybody's help. I can do just fine on my own.'' Her traitorous voice broke then, belying the emotion churning within her. A frown wrinkled his brows and he stepped to within arm's reach of her.

"Tell me you want me to take you in my arms.''

"No.''

"Tell me, Willow.''

"No.''

He studied her face briefly, and his sigh was evidenced only by the slight rise and fall of his chest. "I'd appreciate it if I could bunk in with Wilbur and Andy tonight. I'll be on my way in the morning.''

She nodded. "You know where the bunkhouse is.''

He turned and walked toward the front door; then he stopped and turned. "I'm not giving up on you. No matter how many times you send me away.''

She watched in silence as he shrugged into his coat. "May I put Buck in the barn?''

"Of course. I have to check on Pat, anyway.'' Willow snared her coat off its nail and followed him out into the storm. The snowfall had slowed. A muddy scrape marred the surface of the snow in front of the barn, evidence the door had recently been opened.

"Andy?'' she called as she opened the door.

No answer.

Steven led Buck into the darkened interior and Willow lit the nearest lamp. A pile of firewood lay neatly stacked next to the barrel stove Pa'd installed in the barn for nights he sat up with ailing stock. *Odd*, she thought.

"Wilbur?"

The scrape of wood on wood sounded from the double barn doors. Willow ran to the door and shoved. It was braced from the outside. They were locked in together.

"Andy? Wilbur?"

"You didn't leave us no choice, Willow," Andy said through the door. "Me and Wilbur we talked about it and decided that you're too hardheaded for your own good. We don't want to see you living off someplace all by yourself. Constable Gravel there's a fine man. Now you two just work things out while you're in there."

"Andy, you let us out of here this minute! You don't know what you're talking about."

"Yes, we do. Libby told us all about what happened in Fort McLeod, that Constable Gravel proposed and you said no and want to go live on that land to the south. You know that ain't no fittin' place for you, Willow."

"When did you and Wilbur start taking advice from thirteen-year-old girls?" She smacked the wood with the palm of her hand. "Let us out of here!"

"Libby might be young, but she had the story straight's how I see it. She don't want you to leave, neither, seein's how Emily's moving to town and all. I knowed it plain, when I talked to you yesterday, that you loved him and not me."

"Andy, now you know I can't spend the night in a barn with an unmarried man. It's not right."

"I trust the constable there to be a gentleman, else me and Wilbur wouldn'a done this. Now you go on and talk to him and get all your trouble ironed right out."

Willow kicked the door and winced when her toe filled with eye-watering pain.

"I know this seems sort of odd," chimed in Wilbur's steady voice, "but sometimes other folks just gotta step in, and me and Andy figure this is one of them times. I've knowed you since you was a tadpole, and if you'll forgive me, Miss Willow, you has always sort of had the bit in your teeth. Now, you and the constable just settle what ain't right between you and then we'll just get on with this marriage thing."

"I'll kill you both when I get out of here. Do you hear me?" Willow yelled, full panic now in charge.

"Well, now that might be, but I figure I've lived a good and long life, and I'd just consider it an honor to die by your hand." The humor in Wilbur's drawled words just made her angrier. Had everybody taken leave of their senses?

Willow stalked away from the door, giving Steven a wide berth. He seemed unperturbed and began to unsaddle Buck. Willow paced and thought for a moment. *The back door.* She bolted down the dark interior, felt along the wall, and gave the door a shove. It, too, was blocked.

"Now, Willow, I thought of this one, too," Andy said through the door with maddening calm. "And don't go and try to jump out of the hayloft neither. Wilbur and me moved the wagon that was under

it and you'd just end up with a broke leg or something."

Steven watched Willow aim another vicious kick
at the door. He wanted to laugh out loud and have
her join him in sweet peals of laughter. He wanted
her to see how ridiculous the situation had become
and how much her family loved and cared for her.
But she was too angry and terrified to see the
humor of the situation.

"Come and sit down," he said as he dragged the
saddle off Buck's back. "They left us firewood. We
won't freeze. We'll just wait it out till morning."
He hoisted the saddle onto a saddle tree in the
tack room, then returned to light the fire in the
stove. "Surely then they'll see fit to let us out."

Willow stood by the door, arms crossed, listening,
as if she imagined they'd come to their senses and
release them. Arguing with her further was futile,
he decided, so he pulled up a stack of burlap bags
and sat down with his back against a post. In their
ridiculously desperate way, Andy and Wilbur just
might have provided him with the very tool he
needed to get through to Willow: her complete
and undivided attention.

"It's going to be a long night if you stand over
there the whole time."

She ignored him.

"Come over here where it's warm."

She threw him a glance, then scuffed at the floor
with the toe of her boot.

"Talk to me, Willow. We've nothing else to do
till morning. We might as well get to know each
other better. Ask me a question, anything, and I'll
answer you truthfully. Then I can ask you something and you'll have to tell me the truth. It'll be
a game. Deal?"

"That's ridiculous."

"Afraid?"

She narrowed her eyes and studied him speculatively. "No talk about marriage."

"All right. No marriage proposals. Tell me about when you were a little girl."

Willow stared at the floor, abject frustration in her stance. Then she sighed, walked over to the stove, and flopped down on a pile of bags he'd pushed in her direction.

"Why don't you tell me about your wife?" she countered with a taunting look.

"Fair enough. What do you want to know?"

Willow shrugged. "What was she like?"

Steven took off his Stetson and leaned his head back against the post. "We met at her nephew's birthday party. She was the hostess and I was the entertainment. It was love at first sight. We married six months later. Catherine loved to laugh, and I guess that's why she tolerated my being a clown, even though her parents said I'd never amount to anything and we'd all starve."

"You wanted children?" she ventured.

"Very much. Catherine especially. She loved children."

"What happened to her?"

Steven shrugged. "No one knows, I suppose. Complications, the doctor said. The baby was stillborn and Catherine died a few hours after the birth. I don't remember much about the next few months. Then I joined the police and here I am."

Willow watched him and he could almost see the thoughts churning in her mind. "Do you miss her?"

"Yes."

"Are you still in love with her?"

Steven drew in a breath. Maybe this wasn't such a good idea after all. "She'll always be with me, if that's what you mean. Just as your mother's always with you."

"Why would you want to risk that kind of pain again? Of losing her ... someone ... again, I mean."

He shifted on the bags. "Truth?"

Willow nodded. "Truth."

"I liked being married. I liked having my wife in my bed at night. I liked laughing under the covers and having her pinch me when she thought no one was looking and the thrill when she rubbed against me in passing, then pretended she didn't notice she'd done it."

Willow looked shocked, then glanced away from him. "You shouldn't be telling me these things."

"You asked me to tell you the truth."

"Those are very personal things about your life with your wife."

"They're true of every married couple in the world." He leaned closer and encircled her wrist with his fingers. "I like being intimate, Willow. I like someone knowing my body better than I do, knowing where I'm ticklish and how I got every scar. I like to be touched and to touch in return. That's how love is supposed to be. Sometimes babies come from such intimacy, and that's a fact of life. Not every woman dies in childbirth just like every woman who gallops headlong across snowy prairies doesn't pitch headfirst off her horse and break her fool neck."

Chapter Thirteen

Willow drew her hand away slowly. "It's not the same thing and you know it."

Steven leaned back. His heart sank at the fear and distrust in her eyes. Perhaps there was no way to reason through the doubts possessing her. Perhaps her father was right; she was destined to live out her life alone. He could almost see her slipping away from him.

"Do you think your wife was afraid of having her . . . your baby?" she ventured after a long pause.

"I don't know," he answered honestly. "If she was, she never said so to me."

"Did she like to be . . . touched?"

Steven squirmed.

"You said I could ask you anything." Large, dark eyes stared at him, waiting for wisdom. At least it was a step forward, albeit an embarrassing one.

"So I did. Yes, she liked it very much."

Willow licked her lips and threaded her fingers

together. "I can't imagine trusting someone that much."

"You can trust me, Willow."

She ignored the pointed look he gave her and glanced off into the dark. "Were you married long?"

"About a year."

"You and she wanted a baby right off?"

Steven nodded. "Yes."

She shifted her position and unclasped her hands to shove back her hair. "Truth?"

An alarm went off in Steven's head and he wondered briefly at the wisdom of agreeing to say the absolute truth. But he'd promised, and he'd not compromise the fine thread of trust that had developed between them.

"You said . . . in the livery in Fort McLeod . . . that there were . . . things a man could do. . . ." Her eyes darted away briefly while a deep blush crept up her cheeks. Then she swung her gaze back to his face and held, awaiting his answer.

Steven searched for an obscure explanation, some combination of words that would convey information and yet not violate the tattered shred of propriety still existing between them. How could he explain such a complicated thing to a virginal woman? He was about to say things to her he'd never discussed with anyone else, including his wife—things men did not even discuss among themselves, except in necessary circumstances, such as between father and son.

There was a quivering hope in her eyes, a tentative reach across her void of fear. How could he not offer an answer when he'd suggested the question?

"The most certain method is abstinence. A man doesn't touch his wife until they decide to have a child." The words came out in a rush, and he wondered if she recognized his nervousness.

Her brows flinched, but her eyes never left his. "Are there other ways?"

The trust she'd professed not to have was suddenly there, quivering on the air between them. Steven took a deep breath and ran a finger around the collar of his jacket. "There's withdrawal. When a couple are . . . making love . . . he withdraws from her body before . . . he's finished."

He dared not look away from her now, dared not show any signs of reluctance to answer whatever she might ask next—even though he knew his face was as red as hers.

Her eyes never wavered from his as she digested the information. "Does that hurt?"

"I don't know," he answered pointedly.

"Oh." Her mouth rounded the word. Then she shrugged one shoulder and tipped one corner of her mouth in a small smile. "Seems like it would. Pa told me things straight when I asked him a long time ago." Her face sobered. "You'd do that for me?"

"I'll do whatever it takes to make you feel safe with me."

"Are there other . . . things?"

"Sometimes couples count days . . . when a woman is most likely to conceive . . . and only make love then." He felt like a gangly boy again, struggling through a stumbling conversation with his father.

She nodded and said nothing.

"And there are things women can buy . . . to keep them from conceiving. Back east they're easy to find, but here . . ." He let his words drift off, recognizing the wisp of desire darkening her eyes.

"Having this conversation with you violates every remaining rule of propriety."

"I know." She looked down at her hands. "I appreciate your telling me the truth." She turned her hands over, seemingly fascinated with the ridges of her knuckles. "I don't know who else I could ask these things."

"Please tell me why you're so afraid, Willow."

She glanced away, and for a moment he thought she might scramble to her feet and bolt to the other end of the barn. "You already know."

"I want to hear it from you."

She swallowed and studied the frayed edge of a burlap bag for a few seconds; then she raised her eyes to his. "When I was nine, my Ma had twin boys, both born dead."

Steven waited for her to continue.

"It was just Pa and me with her. Pa knew right off something was wrong. He'd delivered the rest of us and said it was taking too long." She wrapped a raveled string around her finger, unwrapped it, then repeated the process again. "She was in such pain."

She looked up, unshed tears glimmering on her lashes. "Pa wouldn't leave her until we couldn't think of anything else to do. Then, he left me with her and he went after Uncle Lame Deer. Pa didn't believe in the Blackfoot ways, but he was desperate and Uncle Lame Deer was a medicine man."

Steven longed to reach across the space between them and pull her into his arms, to lay her down in the soft hay and convince her that the rewards of loving were worth the risks. But he didn't reach for her, even though he ached just to touch her hand.

"I look like Ma, Pa says. I've got her coloring

and her hair. He says I remind him of her every day." She smiled and looked down at the worried string. "After Pa built this house, Ma gave up some of her Blackfoot ways, but she never stopped wearing her buckskin dresses. I can still remember playing with the fringe and the sound of her moccasins on the wooden floor."

She'd veered away from the heart of the discussion, but Steven let her ramble, hoping she'd return to the source of her fears on her own.

"How about before your Pa built the house?"

Willow stared off into the dark recesses of the barn—reliving those days, he knew. "We wandered around a lot. I remember Emily and me riding the same pinto mare." She laughed. "Pa named her Bell. She was so fat and our legs were so short we rode with them sticking out at this funny angle. Pa said from a distance Bell looked like she had skinny wings."

"Her name was Bell? Like Libby's goat?"

"Yes. She died a few years ago of old age. Libby named her goat in her honor." Her bottom lip quivered slightly, barely discernable in the lamplight. "She was the last thing we had of the old life."

"You miss those days roaming the prairie?"

Willow pulled off her hat and fluffed her hair around her shoulders. The effect was devastating, and Steven swallowed hard.

"Sometimes, even though I don't remember much about it. Pa and Ma laughed a lot, I remember. Pa always made things funny, no matter how cold or wet it was. Now he just seems sad." The joy on her face faded.

"What happened to the babies?"

Willow stared at him unwaveringly for a span of

seconds, her dark eyes unfocused ... remembering.

"Tell me, Willow," he pursued.

"When Uncle Lame Deer got there, it was almost morning. A soft pink light spread over everything. He made Ma drink something. He and Pa argued about it. Not too long after that, Aaron was born dead." She smiled softly. "He was perfect and tiny. But he lay so still. I remember I wanted to pick him up and hold him close. Pa said not to touch him but I did. He was cold and hard and it frightened me." Her voice broke on the last word and she pressed her fingertips to her lips.

Steven again fought down the impulse to go to her, but her cleansing would be complete only if she offered up all her demons—alone.

"When the second baby came, I remember Uncle Lame Deer turned his chair over. I don't know why I remember that except it made a loud noise. He started speaking in Blackfoot and backed away from the bed. Pa yelled at me to bring him more water and towels." She sobbed and focused her gaze on Steven's eyes. "The baby was ... missing things."

Her hesitant tears spilled over and ran down her cheeks.

"Pa cried. His tears made little circles in the blood on his hands. He tried not to let me see the baby, but I did. Ma never knew. She died before Pa could tell her.

"That was in the winter. When spring came and the calving started, I put two and two together and started asking questions. Pa told me straight how cows got calves and how people got babies. I couldn't imagine Pa and Ma ... And when I got older, I couldn't imagine me ... doing that. Every time I'd think about having babies of my own, or a husband, I'd see Ma laying there in a pool of her own blood . . . in the bed where she and Pa slept and . . ." She spread her hands in a helpless gesture.

Steven's heart twisted. How could his love alone erase images time had not touched? A horrible loss witnessed by a child had been woven into a tapestry of fear. Adolescent curiosity and awakening had added to that tapestry until she'd wrapped herself tightly inside a contorted picture of love.

"How does Emily feel about all this?"

"Emily didn't see. Pa and I made sure of that. We cleaned Ma up before we let Emily come in."

"I meant about babies."

Willow smiled and shook her head. "Emily thinks a woman's place in life is to make a home and bear children. The outcome is the will of God, according to her, and we aren't meant to understand."

"Perhaps it is." He leaned to touch her arm and felt her muscles tense beneath the fabric of her shirt. "There will always be things we won't understand, things we will know with our hearts instead of our minds."

"No God I know made that . . . thing . . . we delivered from my mother's body."

"It was an accident, Willow, an accident of nature. As simple as a broken cinch strap or a spilled cup of water. A tragic accident, of course, but unavoidable and unforeseen." He tightened his grip and Willow met his eyes. "Don't throw love away over something that happened so many years ago. Don't break both our hearts. Do you remember what you said to me that night at Fort McLeod when we delivered the cattle? The night you spent at Maggie's?"

She glanced away then and he tugged at her arm. "You wanted me then. Thanks to Maggie's bootleg liquor, I saw a different Willow. Where were your fears then?"

A blush darkened her cheeks. "I don't know and I'd rather not remember that. Besides, I apologized."

"It's not an apology I'm after. You weren't afraid of me then. You begged me to make love to you. I wanted to, Willow, very badly. Do you remember that?"

"Yes. I was drunk." She pulled her arm out of his grip and walked to the door. "It was the liquor talking."

Steven rose and followed her into the shadows just beyond the lantern's light.

"No. That was the Willow who'd dare let herself be loved." He put both hands on her shoulders and peered into her face. "Has nothing I've said here tonight made any difference?"

She raised her head to look into his face. "Truth?"

"Truth."

"I can't erase a lifetime of fear in one night. I don't know why I remember things like I do. And I can't seem to reason it away. The thought of marrying you and finding out I can't be a proper wife . . . I couldn't live with that. I couldn't do that to you."

"I'm willing to take that chance. You're a caring, compassionate woman. I see it in the way you treat your family, your cattle, even Pat in there. Maybe you'll be afraid at first. Maybe you'll be terrified." He gripped her arms tighter. "But I have faith in the strength of my love. And I have faith in the strength of your love for me, even if you won't admit it. You love me, Willow, and nothing's going to stand in the way of that. Not you or your fears.''

Her eyes searched his face. "You've had enough sorrow, Steven. You deserve better.''

"I'm not sure I do.''

"Why?''

"Because Andy and Wilbur think me more of a gentleman than I am.''

He pulled her to him and covered her mouth with his. But this time his kiss was different. More urgent. More demanding. Her lips parted with the first gentle nudge of his tongue and she tasted him, rough and smooth, sweet and salty. Her thoughts swam as desire quickly took over, chasing away her objections and careful logic.

"If I can't convince you, I'll seduce you,'' he murmured into her hair as he nipped a ridge along her shoulder. "I'm a desperate man. I want to share my life and my confidences with you. I want you to have my children. I have only one thing left to offer you, Willow. You already have everything else.''

He put his hands underneath her hair and combed it through his fingers, allowing it to fall across her shoulders. She closed her eyes and shivered from the warmth of his fingers and the depth of his words. Perhaps if she could not see him, some semblance of sense would return to her rapidly mutinying body. When that failed, she attempted to conjure up all the reasons she'd carefully cataloged for not loving this man.

His fingers traced a path across her collarbone, stopping at the first button on her shirt. His knuckles rested against her bare skin. She opened her eyes and stared into his, now smoky with desire. "Tell me now, Willow. Do you want me to stop?''

He'd laid paradise at her feet and given her the key to lock or unlock the door to it. A thousand reasons not to follow her heart arose and sailed through her thoughts like weary spirits. But none was good enough to make her say no. She shook her head.

The first button popped loose, then a second, and on until her shirt lay open, revealing the top half of the knit union suit she wore in the winter. Deftly, his fingers worked loose those buttons as well and ripples of gooseflesh ran over her skin, now exposed to the cool air.

One large, warm hand slid inside. Callused hands rasped gently against sensitive skin, and his eyes closed. He stood still, holding her for so long, Willow reached up and pushed a strand of hair off his forehead, an excuse to touch him. "Are you all right?" she asked when his eyes opened.

"Do you know how long I've dreamed of touching you this way? Of having you trust me enough to allow this?"

With trembling fingers, Willow touched the brass buttons on his scarlet jacket. She worked the first one loose, then a second and a third and on until his coat hung loose from his shoulders. Emily's cautioning voice suddenly interjected into her scrambled thoughts with explicit instructions on how ladies did and did not conduct themselves. She pushed aside the words and slipped her arms around his waist, feeling the satin lining slide past her knuckles. His back tensed and muscles played across his ribs as he pushed her shirt off her shoulders and pulled her hard against him.

His kiss was a nibble against her lips, a tasting. Then he covered her mouth and swept her teeth with his tongue. Pressed against her, his body was tense and ready, and by the tremble in his shoulders, she knew he was fighting carrying things further. Were men the same hopeless slaves to their desires as women? Did his knees grow weak at her touch as hers did at his? Caught up in his passion, she cupped his face in her hands, beard stubble rasping against her palms. Suddenly, she wanted to go beyond where he resisted. She wanted to be held in his arms, loved and filled by him. She wanted to know what lay on the other side of her nightmares and slay them once and for all.

"Steven," she whispered against his lips. He lifted her into his arms and carried her to a pile of hay waiting to be used in the stalls. The straw crackled beneath her as he lay her in its fragrant midst and a summery scent rose, reminiscent of warm days and lazy insect sounds. He joined her on the fragrant pile and kissed the bare skin revealed between her breasts.

"If I don't stop now, I may not be able to," he whispered in a strained voice. "Tell me to stop."

"No. I want to know."

He pulled back a little to study her face. "This isn't a lesson, Willow. This is real. I don't take this lightly."

Willow pushed herself to her elbows. "Neither do I. I know exactly what we're doing." She touched his cheek. "I think I have to do this, have to know."

"How can I condemn you for what I'm about to do myself? You're giving me your most precious gift."

"And you're offering me your love with no guarantees. So who has the most at stake here?"

"There's still a chance you could conceive."

"I know." She wrapped her arms around his

neck and pulled him down to her. "Please, Steven, before I lose my nerve."

He stared down at her a moment, last-second doubts flickering in his eyes. She knew without asking that he'd lain with no woman since his wife. He was not a man who would take a woman outside marriage, and to ask him to do so now went against all he was. The fact that he would do so because she needed him was testament to the character of the man she'd now committed her heart to. He'd put her first, his ideals second.

He kissed her then, so tenderly that tears started in her eyes. All he'd professed was evident in the gentle way his lips took hers. She slid the jacket off his shoulders and he shrugged both arms out. Then, he stood and pulled her to her feet.

He unbuckled her belt and allowed her pants to drift to the floor, skimming his hands across her hips and down her legs. Her winter underwear hung baggy and loose on her frame. Gently he peeled away the top and followed it, too, to the dirt floor with his hands, the warmth of his palms leaving a trail of gooseflesh in their wake. With the last layer of clothes, she stood before him as naked as her emotions.

He encircled her waist with his hands and pulled her closer. His spread hands roamed down her back to cup her and bring her hips hard against him.

"This is what you do to me," he whispered, his teeth nibbling a line across her shoulder, stopping at her arm.

Willow slipped the tip of her fingers inside the waistband of his pants and unbuttoned his suspenders, noticing with a smile that he winced when she touched him. She followed the pants to the floor with her hands, as he had done to her, gliding her palms across narrow hips and down long, muscled legs. He bent and pulled off his boots and pants, then straightened and waited.

They stood in the shadows, away from the thin circle of light thrown by the softly crackling stove. Outside, the wind sang a soft lullaby as it whisked snow across the roof. She wished she could see his eyes, judge his reaction as she relieved him of each layer of clothing, but the only light fell directly across his chest.

She worked loose the tiny pearl buttons on his suit of winter underwear and pushed the fabric off his muscled shoulders and over his narrow hips. He stepped out of the garment then stood before her, as naked as she was. Abruptly, he took her hand and stepped toward the light, pulling her behind him. Bathed in the yellow glow, they no longer had any secrets from each other. He was magnificent: lean and sinewy, a body shaped by hard work and hours outdoors. Softly rounded muscles defined his upper arms. A soft sprinkling of curly hair scattered across a broad chest and a narrow waist led into lean hips. She looked up into his eyes and saw that the gentle gray had darkened to a dangerous shade of slate. That he wanted her was evident.

The first edge of panic budded within her and grew. She squeezed her eyes shut and forced the familiar images out of her mind. This was gentle Steven Gravel, the man who wanted to be her husband. He would take care of her. He'd promised.

He touched her breast, cupping her. His warmth was calming, soothing; his touch was gentle, light. His hand slid around her, settling at the small of her back, and his arm drew her against him. Coarse hair scratched against her in sensitive places.

"I love you," he whispered into the top of her hair.

"I love you, too," she replied, surprised at how easily the words came, without thought, without second guesses.

His chest contracted and his breathing paused for an instant. "As far as I'm concerned, you're already my wife, even though you haven't given me your answer," he said, his breath hot against her scalp. "I wouldn't be standing here, like this, if I didn't feel that way."

He was far taller than she and her cheek rested against the gentle swell of his breast, her ear pressed against the soft thud of his heart. What could she say in response? Yes? Could she pledge that at this moment with the surety he deserved?

No.

Hesitation gripped her and she heard the thundering voice of morality. She lifted her head, prepared to tell him this was wrong, that no good could come of what they were about to do, when he dropped to his knees, clasped her around her waist, and laid his cheek against her abdomen. He seemed so vulnerable, so fragile at that moment. She threaded her fingers through his silky hair and wondered if the sensation was the same as when he'd combed his fingers through hers.

He rose, trailing kisses across the swell of her stomach. She gasped at the intimacy of his actions and admired the play of muscle beneath skin as he stood and reached for his jacket. He spread it out across the hay, lining side up, and finished their bed with a piece of dusty canvas. Once again he lifted her into their sun-dried nest and settled

his weight lightly upon her. She sank into the softness, the hay crackling beneath her.

He kissed her again, open-mouthed and passionate. Drawn into his desire, she responded, kneading the muscles of his back. His breathing came
hard and shallow as he reached up and took her
hands off his shoulders. Lacing their fingers
together, he pulled her hands over her head until
she was stretched out before him.

"It'll hurt a little at first," he said, his voice hoarse
and tense. "But only for a second and then no
more."

She nodded, her fate in his hands. How could
she have feared this? she thought, anxious for him
to continue.

He was gentle, arousing her with hands and
mouth before he joined his body to hers. She ached
for more as he tasted her breasts, her lips, the
intimate parts of her body. Finally, he joined his
body with hers, hesitantly at first, slowly, carefully.
He stared into her eyes, measuring, weighing her
response. Then he paused and looked down into
her eyes. "Are you ready?"

She could only nod. Coherent thought had left
minutes ago. He dropped his forehead to her shoulder, squeezed her fingers, and pushed through the
barrier that separated them. A searing pain tore
through her, ripping her apart.

"It'll be all right," he whispered, and he settled
into a smooth rhythm. The pain faded quickly,
replaced by a sensation of reaching, soaring. He
was a gentle and eager lover, playing the thread
of passion that ran through her the way an accomplished musician might play a valued instrument.

Her body suddenly tensed, every muscle taut and
stretched, and fulfillment flowed through her in

a blaze of lights, seen only behind her closed eyes. He left her abruptly, then rolled to his side, his back to her. Willow turned her head. His shoulder flinched one, twice, and she thought he moaned softly.

"Steven?" she asked, touching his shoulder. He shuddered under her fingers.

"I'm all right," he said in a strange voice. One hand reached back, burrowing underneath her into his jacket, and withdrew a handkerchief from his pocket. He sat up, keeping his back turned for several more minutes. Finally he pivoted, facing her. "What about you?" He leaned over and kissed her, hovering over her afterward.

"I'm fine," she said with a smile, knowing now how a cat felt, sitting in the morning sun and licking milk from its whiskers.

"I'd say you passed the test, Willow Dawson. With flying colors, I might add," he said with a grin.

She fell back to earth with a thud. "Did you . . . ?"

"No," he said with a shake of his head.

She wanted to ask him more, to know the how and why of what he'd done. But an odd expression passed through his eyes before he glanced away. "I told you I'd take care of you."

She touched his arm and he flinched, his muscles tense.

"What's wrong?"

"Nothing," he replied and kissed her between the eyes, then swept her body with a glance that stirred awareness in the pit of her stomach.

"Would it always be this way?"

He laughed. "Well . . . I can't guarantee always."

"It was nice."

"Just nice?"

She smiled lazily, liking the way his eyes studied her mouth. She stretched a little, and his eyes darted to her breasts. Feeling an edge of power over him, she smiled up at him. "Very nice. Could we do it again?"

"No." Steven stood, alarm flickering through his eyes. "I mean . . . not until I . . . You could conceive if I . . . Not twice in a row. Oh, Lord, I've created a monster."

They laughed together; then Steven grew serious. "I can't offer you guarantees there will be no hardship or heartache, Willow. I can only guarantee I will stand by you through them."

She opened her mouth to reply, but Steven cut in. "I don't want an answer from you tonight or tomorrow or for a while. I want you to think, Willow—think about what we've done and why we did it. You and I crossed the first hurdle together; the rest you have to cross alone."

He kissed her fingers. "We better get some sleep. Andy and Wilbur might decide to open the door at first light."

They dressed quickly, the vulnerability of their situation suddenly dawning. Willow adjusted his belt, threading the spare end through the loops, returning to the place she'd begun. She stepped back, and he was again Constable Steven Gravel. But she knew she'd always see him as he'd been the moment he took her virginity—his head upon her shoulder, his fingers squeezing hers.

And in that moment of reasoning, Willow Dawson ceased to exist as an individual. The realization was jarring and terrifying. He'd be there always, in her heart and her thoughts, his voice joining the others in her head. She'd discuss things with him in her own thoughts, weigh his opinion by anticipating what she knew he'd say. Her independence was as irretrievable now as her innocence. In that moment of blinding pleasure that set her heart on an irreversible path, reasonable Willow Dawson lost her way.

They made their beds away from each other in case Andy and Wilbur thought better of their detention. Steven leaned against a post, a roll of burlap sacks against his back, his hat pulled over his eyes. Willow spent a sleepless night in her hay nest, haunted by the scent of him that clung to the dusty canvas beneath her.

The door opened with a squeak and Andy's shadow blocked out the early morning light. "Willow?"

"I'm here and you better be running when my feet hit this floor," she said, sitting bolt upright.

Sheepishly, Andy approached. "Me and Wilbur meant well, Willow. I know you're madder'n hell at me, but . . . Did you two work anything out?"

Steven tipped back his hat and looked up at Andy. "As a matter of fact, we did," he said with complete nonchalance.

Andy opened his mouth, then snapped it shut, apparently thinking better of delving too deeply into the subject. "Well . . . I got work to do." He edged toward the door as Willow slid to the floor and started toward him. "You gonna tell your Pa what we did?"

"No. At this point you'd be in as much trouble as I would." Willow pointed an accusing finger. "You remember that."

Andy hurried away with a backward look, apparently relieved that the confrontation was over.

Steven stood and stretched. "I have to be on my way, too."

They faced each other and Willow wondered at the void that now seemed to yawn between them. How did people go from being two separate individuals to joined souls and then back to individuals so easily?

He pulled her to him, holding her against his chest. "I love you. Remember that when your doubts get the upper hand." He leaned back to look into her face. "I don't regret a second of last night, and neither should you."

"I don't."

"You won't mull this over for a few days and decide you've made a horrible mistake?"

She shook her head.

"That'll do for starts." He kissed the end of her nose, then walked down to Buck's stall.

"I'll see you in a few weeks," he said as he shrugged into his buffalo coat and swung up into the saddle. Suddenly she was blind-sided by the ridiculous urge to cling to his leg. By dark, he'd be a day's ride away.

"Steven? I . . . love you."

He leaned down with a smile and kissed her lightly on the lips. "I haven't wanted another woman since Catherine . . . until last night. I want you to be my wife, Willow, but I want you to come to me satisfied in your mind it's the right thing to do. I've done all I can to convince you. The rest is up to you."

He swung Buck around and ducked to pass through the barn door. She followed him outside as he guided Buck up the incline behind the house and watched until he reached the top. He stopped and looked back. She raised a hand and he waved in return before disappearing over the crest. Tears flowed then, and she stumbled back to the barn, passing a bewildered Andy on the way.

Chapter Fourteen

"What do you think?"

Willow reluctantly turned from the window, where she could see the clouds lowering for another onslaught of snow. Somewhere out there, just beyond that last roll of gray, lay Fort McLeod . . . and Steven. Tears of loneliness sprang to the corners of her eyes.

Emily had draped a length of soft white batiste across her chest, pulling it snug to her waist.

"It's for my wedding dress."

"That's nice," Willow replied with as much emotion as she could muster.

"I was hoping for a little more enthusiasm from you. Libby barely gave it a glance before she went out to torture Wilbur." Emily rolled the batiste back onto the bolt and smoothed it with her hand. "I'm going to make it just like your dress with the pink rosebuds, only I think I'll make the rosebuds white. That way you can be my bridesmaid and our dresses will match." Emily grinned as if she'd just happened on the cure for smallpox.

"Uh huh." Willow turned back to stare out the window. A snowflake flattened itself against the glass pane, melted, and ran down the window in a miserable dribble. She wasn't sure which was the most painful: her aching insides or Emily's unbounded joy. All she could think about was Steven and the miles and miles between them. How could he have become so completely embedded in her thoughts in their few stolen moments? The dependency she'd feared grew with every passing minute.

Emily touched her on the shoulder and Willow jumped. "Where were you? Did you hear anything I said?"

Willow turned, hoping her eyes didn't give away her secret pain. "I'm sorry, Em. I guess I wasn't paying attention."

"Is something the matter?"

"No, nothing."

"Are you ill?" Emily placed a palm against her forehead. "Are you coming down with a fever?"

"No. I guess I'm just tired of winter."

Emily frowned. "You love the snow and the cold. What's really the matter?"

Willow pasted a smile on her face. "Nothing. Tell me about Ben and Fort McLeod."

Emily blushed furiously, walked back to the bed, and stacked the bolts of cloth she'd bought. "Ben is fine. He bought our . . . bed last week." She turned a deeper shade of rose and fiddled aimlessly with the cloth. "I never thought I'd be this happy." She bit her lip, her voice slipping on the last word. "I will miss you all so."

Willow crossed the floor, hesitated, then put her

arms around her sister. "We're all happy for you. You deserve this. You've looked after us for a long time. It's time we did some looking after ourselves."

"It's very frightening to put one's life in someone else's hands."

"Yes, it is," Willow said. Terrifying, she thought, was more the case.

Emily pulled back and looked into Willow's eyes. "You're always so sure of yourself and your decisions. I wish I had some of your confidence."

What a laugh that is, Willow thought. "And I wish I had some of your peace of mind."

Emily stepped out of Willow's embrace and returned to the pile of packages and boxes on the bed. She ran a hand over the batiste. "My mind isn't so peaceful right now."

A sense of foreboding swept over Willow, but she waited for Emily to continue.

"I've had relations with Ben."

Nothing on earth could have floored Willow the way those five words did. Sensible, proper Emily swept away by passion? She and Big Ben wrapped in each other's arms like . . .

"I don't regret it," Emily said with a firmness in her voice. "I love him and it's a long time until May."

Laughter bubbled up, but Willow stifled the urge to laugh with relief. So, Emily was just as vulnerable to sin as she.

"I already know all the moralities of what we did and the risks. If I've conceived a child, I won't be showing in May."

Willow couldn't believe the confession coming from her proper, mild-mannered sister. Had Pa brought back the right Emily? But one look in her eyes told Willow that this was, indeed, her beloved Emily, deeply in love. Emily, who seemed able to herd together all the details of life the way a hen herds her chicks. And then move the whole collection in one unerring direction, confidently following her heart. No bouts of self-doubt for Emily Dawson.

Emily finally looked up, embarrassment on her cheeks, but no regret in her eyes. "I never thought it would be . . . the way it was. It was like we were truly part of each other, not just for that one incredible moment, but from then on, leaving a little bit of ourselves behind with each other."

"I'm very happy for you, Em." The urge to leave before the discussion got any deeper sent Willow sidling toward the door. The last thing she wanted at the moment was to take out her raw, tattered emotions and hold them up for close examination.

"What are you going to do about Steven?"

"I don't know."

Emily gave her a motherly stare. "You must have some opinion on his proposal."

"I was flattered."

"Flattered? Nothing else?"

Standing in the center of the bedroom floor, there was nothing to grip or twist or fumble with to busy her nervous hands. She shoved them in her pockets and looked away from Emily, fighting to keep her pain private. "Steven's a good man. He'd make some woman a good husband."

"Some woman? You say that of a man that's all but cut out his heart and laid it at your feet?" Emily advanced on her, stopping only when they stood nearly toe to toe. Willow expected Emily to jam her hands on her hips and let loose with a scolding. But instead, Emily calmly studied Willow's face.

"I think perhaps we have done you a great wrong."

"What do you mean?"

"You're the one who's kept this family together and a roof over our heads. You've been running this ranch since you were old enough to do sums and sit a horse. And Pa was perfectly content to let you."

"I did what I did because I wanted to. You know I was never comfortable with cooking and sewing. Pa didn't have anything to do with it."

Emily narrowed her eyes. "Pa had everything to do with it. Pa tried to mold you over to become the son he lost."

"You sound like you hate him." Suddenly, everything was changing too fast.

"No, no," she replied with a frown and a shake of her head. "In fact, I doubt he's even aware he's done this. He couldn't bear the burden of both his grief and the ranch, so he was happy to shift some of the load to you. You seemed delighted and happy and he never doubted it was true. But I know you better."

"What do you mean? I'm perfectly happy with things the way they are."

Emily smiled. "You're a compassionate, loving woman, Willow. I see it in the way you treat Libby and Wilbur and Andy. In the way you treat Pat and the cows. And I know you're in love with Constable Gravel."

"Just because you're in love with Ben, don't try and—"

"All your bluster and denials won't change my mind," Emily said, unflustered. "I see it now, in your eyes when you look out the window toward the west. You're thinking about him."

"Nonsense. I was wondering if it was going to snow tonight."

Emily encased Willow's rough, callused hands inside her smooth ones. "It's all right to love him, Willow. It's all right to want to marry him and have his babies. It's all right to laugh with him over something silly and rub his back at night. The world doesn't revolve around cattle prices and grazing practices. The world revolves around human hearts and what's in them. Say yes to him, Willow."

"You won't guess who's downstairs!" Libby burst into the room, her hair in disarray and flecked with straw. "Come quick!"

Willow started for the door, but Emily stopped her, still holding her hands. "Think about what I've said," she implored.

Willow nodded briefly and followed Libby downstairs. Baron Von Roth stood in the foyer brushing snow from his coat.

"My goodness," Emily said from the second landing. "We weren't expecting you."

He grinned and waved a dismissing hand at her. "Do not concern yourself with niceties. Your sister impressed me so much with her ideas, I came to see for myself the empire of Cletis Dawson and his lovely daughters."

"Where's Pa?" Willow asked Libby.

Eyes wide, face white, Libby gaped openly at George.

"Libby?"

"He's in the barn reshoeing Nelly," she mumbled. "Are them real fox skins?" she asked, staring at George's fur collar, which stared back at her with glass eyes.

"Yes, my dear lady, they are." He unwound one

of the furs from his neck and squatted down. "Would you like to have it to wear?"

Libby threw a terrified glance up at Emily. George looked up, too. "I'd like her to have it, if it is all right with you."

"You may say yes," Emily replied.

"Yes," Libby echoed and took the soft fur from him as if it were a piece of delicate china. "Thank you."

George stood, grinning. "My wife and I hope for many children. We would like a daughter just like her."

"God help you," Willow muttered under her breath.

"I have brought you a present, also, Willow Dawson," he declared with sparkling eyes. "Come outside and see."

Willow walked down the stairs and out onto the porch. Standing peacefully in the yard were a black Angus bull and cow. Huge brass rings pierced their noses and they were secured by ropes held by a cowboy mounted on a dun horse.

"This is John, one of my hands," George said, and the silent John nodded.

"They're beautiful," Willow breathed, moving to the bull. She ran a hand down his sleek side. He was strong and fit, with a stout chest and clear eyes. The cow was plump, obviously due to calve in a couple of months, Willow judged. "But this is too much. I can't possibly accept such an expensive gift."

George smiled. "I have many bulls, many cows. I would like to see the breed grow here in Alberta. I make them a gift to you for that purpose."

A simple thank-you seemed very inadequate for

a gift that fulfilled one of her dreams. "Thank you," she said anyway.

"And for you, Emily Dawson. My wife sends a gift." He ran a big hand inside his elegant, black fur coat and produced a small silver box.

"Won't you come inside out of the cold?" Emily said, obviously flustered at her lack of manners.

"No, no." He waved a hand. "I have small amount of time. I will go to Fort McLeod tonight." He handed Emily the box. She opened it and lifted out a silver locket that winked even in the fading light. "My wife is expecting child in fall and is not feeling well now." He grinned broadly. "I understand you are to be married to one of our fine Mounted Police in spring. Anna wishes you to have this as wedding present."

"It's so beautiful. Please, tell her thank you. If you have time, I'll pen a quick note to her."

He shook his head. "I will tell her you are very happy. I was hoping Willow would show me her ranch before I have to go."

Pa appeared, summoned by Libby, wiping his hands on a cloth. While he greeted George, Willow glanced at Emily and found her staring back at her. The cattle were what she needed to get started. She'd run a few head of Herefords and shorthorns and breed the Angus. She could have a shack built and a barn up before summer. Next winter she could look out across her own snow-covered hills dotted with grazing cattle. This was what she'd wanted and prayed for. Ben and Emily would have moved home by then, and Pa'd have someone to replace her. Plans were falling into place like a line of dominoes. Why, then, didn't the prospect bring her the joy she'd expected?

* * *

"This is beautiful land. Beautiful," George remarked, gazing around the rolling hills. She'd led him to the place she'd always imagined as hers. Pa called it the Buffalo Wallows, because of the numerous patches of churned dirt. In the summer, buffalo came to roll and tumble in the soft dirt, filling their thick and tangled coats with dust to choke out pests. A small herd almost always spent a great portion of the winter here. Protected in the lee of a ridge, the area received less wind and snow than other places.

"You will build a house there?" He pointed to an area that backed up against the ridge. Sloping hillsides of land came down beside it in gentle rolls.

"Yes." He'd picked the exact spot she'd imagined.

"Hmm. Good protection from the wind and snow. Facing south for the sun. Good choice." He turned and smiled at her, the wind ruffling the black fur of his coat. "And you plan to live here alone?"

"Yes."

He shook his head and stared off across the prairie. "A woman is not safe here alone."

"I'll be fine."

He turned back to her. "You do not want a husband?"

Was everyone going to ask her that question? Why was that such a strange idea? "I want something that is mine, that I built first."

"If a woman and a man build something together, it is good for both. I left my Anna in Germany and come here to build ranch. I thought

I had to have fine house and large ranch before she would marry me." He smiled softly. "She say she would have rather had little house and me sooner. I spend many lonely nights in large, fine house before I go back to marry her."

"I'm used to being alone."

"Riding horse alone and sleeping alone are two different things."

Willow colored at his words, inappropriate but heartfelt, she knew. George Von Roth was a man obviously in love with his wife.

"Here in Territories, a woman needs a man."

Willow bristled at his condescending words. "Do you think a woman cannot run a ranch or her life without a man's help?"

George turned, no animosity on his face. Rather, he looked puzzled. "No, never did I mean that. After my papa died, Mother ran our estate alone. She directed servants, bred and sold horses, and raised my brothers and me. She was strong woman and smart. No, I mean a woman needs a man for companionship, friend, helper. I am sorry if I have angered you."

"No . . . I'm not angry. I'm sorry. I misunderstood you." Her nerves were on edge, put there by the growing feeling that perhaps she couldn't live alone the rest of her life. Perhaps she couldn't go another day without a glimpse of Steven's face or the touch of his hand. She rubbed fingers across her forehead, caressing a budding headache.

"This is fine place." George straightened in his saddle and gathered up his reins. "I must be on my way. Emily has invited us to wedding in the spring. If my Anna feels well enough, we will come and make big party." He grinned, flashing a brilliant smile.

* * *

The feeble fire provided little warmth and sorry company. Steven pulled his coat closer around him and stared into the dancing flames, little defense against the bone chilling cold. What had he expected? he asked himself. That one night of passion would erase all Willow's doubts? That one night in his arms would prompt her to accept his proposal immediately?

Of course not, his common sense said, but that did nothing to ease the gnawing emptiness he couldn't define. He shifted his position on the log he'd pulled up to the fire and cursed his reawakened desires. Grief, hard work, and constant danger had dulled desire for years, but now that he'd again known intimacy, Willow was all he could think about. She'd been soft and warm, ready. And the moment their bodies had joined, he'd known she'd forever be part of him, no matter the miles or doubts between them.

And yet the emptiness nibbled away at him.

Steven rose and walked away from the fire, seeking the cooling effects of the frigid night. There'd been no promises between them, no understanding of purpose or future. He'd promised her he'd protect her, promised he'd take every precaution known to him, and yet the result had left him empty and unfulfilled. And feeling a little dirty. Somehow, unfinished lovemaking just didn't seem natural.

"Too cold for ye, lad?" Ben asked as he stepped around his horse's ample rump. They'd spent the last two days trailing a lone, bedraggled whiskey trader as he went from village to village trying to ply his illegal wares. So far, he'd disappeared as soon as they had his trail. For once, Steven was glad for the slippery nature of bootleggers. It helped keep his mind on something other than Willow.

"No. Just a muscle cramp."

Ben threw him a quizzical glance. "Ye've been mighty quiet lately."

Steven forced a smile. The last thing he wanted to do was discuss the cause of his aching body and the dissatisfaction eating through him. Least of all with Ben McGavin, whose grin was now perpetual with his wedding only weeks away. "I guess I'm just tired of the cold. How are the wedding plans coming?" That would get Ben going in another direction. These days, Emily seemed to occupy his every waking thought. Why was it a woman could so completely disrupt a man's life?

Ben colored, suspiciously nervous at the indirect mention of Emily. "Churning along. I bought a bed from I. G. Baker last week." His color deepened.

"Sounds like everything's in order."

Ben didn't comment, unduly occupied with the tangled bridle in his hand.

"You were once a married bloke," Ben began, and Steven groaned inwardly. Ben had been dropping hints for days, edging closer and closer to asking a question Steven was sure would be embarrassing. Apparently, despite his colorful past and unorthodox path to service in the Northwest Mounted Police, Ben McGavin had navigated that twisted path as a virgin. Or so he'd hinted.

"I was intimate with Emily."

The announcement came like a thunderbolt. "I beg your pardon?"

Poor Ben turned another shade of red and fiddled with the bridle until it was hopelessly entangled. "We couldn't help ourselves," he said with outspread hands, as if asking for divine judgment. "I'm a rake. I've despoiled my bride."

Steven covered a laugh with a cough. No one walking this earth was any less a rake than poor, conscience-stricken Ben McGavin. "I don't think it's quite that bad, Ben. What does Emily say?"

"Poor, innocent lass. She's doesn't realize the graveness of our sin. When she left Fort McLeod, she was smilin' and puttin' up a brave front."

Steven chuckled outright then and shook his head. "Emily Dawson is one of the most sensible women I've ever known. I doubt seriously she was putting on any kind of front, except maybe to keep Cletis from asking why she was grinning from ear to ear."

"Do ye think she'll still marry me?"

Steven sat back down on a log and stretched his booted feet out toward the fire, unable to resist teasing Ben just a little. "Well, I don't know. Did she seem happy . . . afterwards?"

Ben's wide face split into a grin. "That she did, for sure." Quickly, he wrestled his smile back into a contrite expression.

"Then I seriously doubt she'll leave you at the altar."

Ben sat down beside him and dropped the bridle to the ground. " 'Tis a wonderful thing this feeling between a man and a woman."

"Yes, it is," Steven said with a nod, wondering if, at the moment, *wonderful* was quite the word that applied.

"I'm ashamed to say that's all I can think about now, and the wedding two months away."

"Cold nights," Steven said with a nod. "Cold nights, hard riding, and difficult work will take care of those thoughts. Keep things off your mind."

"You make it sound like work, lad. I admit it's hard to keep my mind on what I oughta, but 'tis not totally unwelcome thoughts."

"No, no. Of course not," Steven hurried to add.

An ember popped and bits of charred wood shot out from the campfire to smolder on the ground.

"Has Willow given you an answer?" Ben ventured, his voice hesitant.

"No. Sometimes I wonder if she ever will." He'd said too much; he knew it the moment the words were out of his mouth.

"Ye aren't giving up on the lass, are ye?"

When did a man give up on the woman who disturbed his sleep and haunted his days? A week? A month? A lifetime? Did he go to her again, or wait for some message from her?

"No, I'm not giving up. At least not yet."

Chapter Fifteen

An insistent tap, tap, tapping worked its way into Steven's scattered dreams. He cracked open an eye and stared at the iron monster squatted in the center of the barracks floor. Glimmers of orange flames outlined the door of the heater and hinted at a hole here and there in its bottom. An ember popped with a tiny explosion and a log fell against the inside of the heater with a thump.

He rolled over onto his back and stared up at the beamed ceiling, sorting through foggy thoughts. Had he actually heard something or was he still dreaming? From across the room, Ben's snores came soft and regular. Outside, the soft plop of snowflakes against the windows beckoned him back into sleep.

Tap, tap, tap.

This time the noise was louder, more regular, intentional and not some night sound. Steven swung his feet to the floor and sat up. Soft rustlings whispered against the heavy wooden door. Reaching for his revolver, Steven stood and padded across the floor barefooted. Placing an ear against the door, he listened. Perhaps an animal was foraging for a midnight meal.

Someone tapped the wood directly beneath his ear and he flinched.

"I'm right behind ye, lad," Ben's voice whispered softly in his ear.

Without looking around, Steven nodded and eased the door open. A fur-shrouded face peered through the crack, human eyes glimmering just beneath the snarling grin of a wolverine pelt. The shock jolted through him and he heard Ben mutter "Holy Saints" behind him.

"Steven Gravel come," the Blackfoot man whispered.

"I'm Steven Gravel," Steven answered. "What is it?"

"You come."

"Come where?"

"You come to Dawson house."

"Cletis Dawson's ranch? Why?"

"Oldest daughter missing. You come."

Dread filled his veins like icy water. What damnfool thing had Willow gone and done now?

"Willow is missing?"

"Yes, Willow. Sister Emily send me to get you. You come."

"Wait here." Steven crept back to his cot and picked up his rifle and scabbard, then shrugged into his jacket and buffalo coat.

"I'm coming with you," Ben said softly, already dressed and at his side.

Steven scooped up his boots and socks and hurried out to the porch. Leaning against the wall, he pulled on first one boot and then the other while the Blackfoot looked on.

"Who are you?" Steven asked, his thoughts clearing enough to realize this could be some sort of trick.

"I am Crooked Stick. Cousin of Dawson women."

"Cousin?" Steven stepped out into the snow and waded toward McLeod's office. "Where is Cletis?"

"Gone to Benton to get bull. I watch house."

"Does Cletis know you watch the house?"

"No."

Steven threw him a glance, but the man stared straight ahead. "What happened to Willow?"

"She go to place she is building, to see about black cows. Not come back. Sister send me for you."

"Building? Where?"

Crooked Stick struggled through the snow at Steven's side. "Place called Buffalo Wallows. South of Dawson house."

Steven ground his teeth.

So, she'd chosen independence.

"How long has she been gone?" Steven stepped up on McLeod's porch and brushed the snow off his pants legs.

"Two suns."

Fear joined the dread already in command of his knees. Two days, and it would take another one to get there. Steven rapped on McLeod's door and received a sleepy "Come in" from the other side. He pushed open the door and found McLeod sitting on the edge of his bed in an undershirt and his uniform pants.

"What's the matter, Constable?" he asked, raking a hand through his sleep-tousled hair.

"Willow Dawson is missing and her sister Emily has sent for me to help in the search."

McLeod looked between the men standing before him. "Who is he?" He nodded at Crooked Stick.

"Her cousin, sir."

McLeod pulled a hand across his beard stubble. "Take Constable McGavin with you and go."

The sunrise had been gray and dull, the sun a weak disk behind heavy clouds. As light chased away the dark, snow still stung their faces, flung by a vengeful wind. Steven had been in the saddle all night and his body was stiff and cold.

The yellow lights from the Dawson house were a welcome sight in the early dawn as they rode down off the ridge and into the yard. Hope flared momentarily as Emily flung open the door and flew out into Ben's arms, nearly knocking him over the moment his feet touched the ground.

"I'm so glad you're here," she sobbed into his shoulder.

"She hasn't come home?" Steven asked.

"No," Emily mumbled into Ben's jacket, then lifted a tear-stained face, droplets quivering on her dark lashes. "Where's Crooked Stick?"

Steven jerked his head back over his shoulder. "Out there waiting. He wouldn't come into the yard."

Emily stared into the dark. "No, he wouldn't." She left Ben and gripped Steven's forearms. "You have to find her."

"I'll find her."

Andy stepped out of the house, eyes on the porch boards, his hands shoved deep in his pockets. Wilbur followed, a slight limp the only evidence of his injured knee. "I shoulda kept her from going," Andy mumbled.

Emily stepped back and wiped her cheeks with the hem of her apron. "Nonsense. You know how she is once she sets her mind to something. Neither one of you could have stopped her."

"Where is this place Crooked Stick is talking about? He said she was building a house?" Steven asked.

Emily glanced at Ben. "Baron Von Roth brought her a pair of black Angus. She bullied Andy into helping her put up a cabin on the land Pa promised her."

Steven swallowed, rage and disappointment warring for his attention. "Did she say why?"

Slowly, Emily shook her head. "No," she answered softly. "I'm so sorry, Steven."

"Why did she go in the face of this storm?"

"Them black cows of hers got out of the barn"— Andy threw an accusing glance at Libby's face pressed against the parlor window—"somehow and wandered off. Nothing would do 'ceptin' she went after 'em. Said they wouldn't go far and she'd be back long before dark. She thought they mighta gone south, down to that pasture her Pa's Herefords stay in. She was worried 'bout them, too, afraid they'd want to bunch up in a little coulee down there and what the snow didn't get the wolves'd pick off."

"We'll start looking there, then."

Andy shook his head. "Me and Wilbur's done been there. We rode in this morning. Didn't see no sight of her."

"Come inside and get warm. I've got coffee ready

and hot food.'' Emily said, twisting a dishtowel in her hands.

"No," Steven said, shaking his head. "We should make use of the remaining light."

"It'll do her no good if you freeze to death."

Steven stared down at the leather reins laced through his fingers and knew, reluctantly, that she was right.

"Andy'll get you fresh horses by the time you've eaten and warmed up. You can leave then."

He looked up at Emily; her lips were quivering slightly. Even in a crisis, Emily thought good food would solve everything. Or at least make it all more endurable. And maybe she was right.

Warmed and full, Steven and Ben stepped from the house a half hour later, just in time for Andy to arrive with three fresh horses.

"I want to come along," he said firmly, his jaw set. "I can show you where she mighta gone and where she'd hole up to last out the storm, even though me and Wilbur's done checked all them places."

Steven glanced at Ben and then at Emily, who nodded her agreement. The wind howled around the corner of the house, driving a brutal sheet of snow before it and whipping Emily's skirt tight around her legs.

Ben put an arm around Emily's waist, pulled her tight against him, and kissed her soundly with no pretense of propriety. Then, he stepped off into the snow and climbed into his saddle.

Steven hooked one foot in the stirrup, then looked back once more to Wilbur and Emily on the porch.

"She ain't Cletis Dawson's daughter fer nothin'," Wilbur said with a confidence Steven didn't feel. "She'll know what to do to live. She's got her Ma's blood, too. Pure Blackfoot. Thrive in snow, they do. Willow's all right, just holed up someplace till the wind dies down." He punctuated his comments with a curt nod, then limped back into the house.

"Kate! Boris!" Willow yelled into the wind, pulling her knitted muffler down just long enough to shout the words. "What self-respecting bull is going to answer to a name like 'Boris' anyway," she muttered to herself, pulling the material securely back across her face.

Given the privilege of naming the pair, Libby had quickly dubbed the bull Boris, after the tortured character in a book Pa'd brought her from Benton, and the cow Kate, just because she liked the sound of it. "Libby thinks they're big, black dogs," she complained to Pat. "If she hadn't let them out, we wouldn't be in this fix, would we?" She leaned forward to stroke Pat's neck and he stopped and pricked his ears forward.

Squinting into the swirling storm, Willow could barely make out the tree line in the distance, much less anything in between. She heeled Pat's sides and he ignored her, his lungs heaving in a snort, his muscles tense.

Gripping a little tighter with her knees, Willow reached back and slid her rifle from its leather scabbard. She cradled the weapon in her arms and again scanned the dark line in the distance.

Nothing moved in the storm, save the ice and the wind that drove it. The temperature was dropping, and she'd already ridden farther from home and been gone one day longer than she intended.

"Well, let's go find out what you see," she said and punched Pat again. Stepping cautiously, he moved forward, ears up, muscles trembling.

They rode under the first dangling tree branches, and the forest muted the wind's fury. Sticks cracked under Pat's hooves and he shied, nearly unseating Willow. Her heart hammered against her ribs. Pat's instincts were seldom wrong. Had he seen Boris and Kate? Or a pack of hungry wolves?

A faint cry rose above the wind, sending goose-flesh running over Willow's skin. She pulled back on the reins and listened. Snow filtered down through bare branches. A puff of wind shook the treetops, sending blobs of snow plunging off the branches.

There it was again. A soft plea, a human voice. "Hello?" she cried. "Is anybody there?"

"We are here. Please help us," a voice answered from deeper in the woods.

Willow studied the dense thicket before her. Who was *we?* She glanced around. And where were *their* horses? She cocked the rifle and urged Pat forward, heeling him hard to force him to overcome his reluctance.

Blankets lay across a bramble thicket as a make-shift shelter. As she drew Pat to a halt, the blanket lifted and a man climbed out of the tangle. Willow raised the rifle, aiming at the center of his chest.

He was Blackfoot, by her reckoning. Young, barely older than Emily, he wore a fox skin on his head, the teeth bared. "Please, my wife," he said in broken English with hands spread helplessly. "Baby come."

She glanced on either side of her and saw no one. "What are you doing here?"

"We travel to her family's village. Baby should not come until spring, but he wants to come out now."

Willow's heart lurched into a wild flutter, and if not for the pounding in her chest, she might have laughed at the irony of the situation. She shoved her rifle into her scabbard and dismounted, wrapping Pat's reins around a convenient branch.

The young Blackfoot held up the edge of the blanket and Willow ducked underneath. In the heart of the thicket a pregnant woman sat spraddle-legged on a blanket, her hands holding her bulging belly. Despite the cold, her hair was plastered to her forehead. She was even younger than her husband—about Libby's age, Willow guessed.

Squatting down, Willow spoke softly in Blackfoot, and the woman smiled slightly.

"How long have you been in pain?" Willow asked.

"Long time. Since last night," she said, her voice breathless and weak.

Willow swallowed and took a deep breath.

"You know what is wrong?" the woman asked, her dark eyes intent on Willow's face.

"The baby might be breech, sideways." Willow swiped her hand across her own stomach. The woman's eyes grew larger.

"What's your name?" Willow asked, moving closer.

"Little Rabbit," she replied.

Willow laid a hand on the woman and slid her palm across the bulge, imagining the baby where it should be. Tiny feet kicked against her palm on the side. Willow sat back on her heels, willing her heart to behave. The baby wasn't breech, but he wasn't head-down either.

She closed her eyes and imagined all the births she'd ever witnessed. Cattle, horses, dogs. Her brothers'. The familiar image returned, complete with sweaty palms and chilling fear. But then a strange calm descended on her, pouring over her, soothing. Perhaps today, this second, was the reason that image of blood and pain had always haunted her.

Little Rabbit closed her eyes and her face paled as another pain gripped her.

Willow turned to the husband. "What's your name?" she asked.

"Running Bird," he answered, his eyes on his wife, and concern knitting his eyebrows together.

"Do you have some furs with you? Cloths?"

"Yes," he said, nodding.

"Get them."

As he unrolled a bundle she hadn't seen before, soft, silky furs poured out, apparently the take from his trap line.

"They'll do just fine," Willow said, glancing around inside the little shelter the couple had found.

"Put the furs here." She patted the ground in the center of the small cavity.

While Running Bird spread the furs, Willow grasped the woman's hand and pulled her forward. "Stand up, then squat down like me," she said, bouncing on her bent knees.

Little Rabbit struggled to her feet, then squatted, her stomach hanging between her legs. Willow laced her fingers with Little Rabbit's and held on tightly, using her body to balance them both.

"When the next pain comes, push down," Willow said.

Eyes full of fear stared into Willow's. "You have children?" she asked.

Willow opened her mouth to say "no," then thought better. "Yes, a boy and a girl," she lied.

"They were born this way?"

Willow swallowed and made a quick plea for forgiveness. "Yes, both of them."

Little Rabbit's face paled again. She set her jaw and grunted deeply.

"Come here," Willow said to Running Bird and nodded to a space beside her. "When the baby comes out, catch it in those furs."

Running Bird gawked at her as if she'd lost her mind. "A warrior does not—"

"Right this second, I don't give a damn *what* a warrior does. This is your baby here. She didn't get this way by herself. Now, you get down here and catch him."

Running Bird looked shocked for a second, then obediently got to his knees and looked up into his wife's face.

"Baby is coming," she groaned and arched her back.

A tiny head appeared. "Push harder. Harder, Little Rabbit. Don't stop," Willow coaxed and gripped Little Rabbit's fingers tighter.

The tiny baby boy slid into the world and his father instantly wrapped him snugly in the furs. While Running Bird admired his son, Willow cut the cord and swept the afterbirth out of the way. She helped Little Rabbit lean back against the rough alder trunks and covered her with the remaining furs.

Turning her attention to the baby, she pushed aside the furs with one finger and looked down into the face of a large, full-term baby. She glanced at Running Bird's adoring face as he gazed down at the son he held in his arms. Obviously, the baby hadn't been early. The marriage had been late.

She took the baby from him and jerked her head toward his wife. He moved to Little Rabbit's side, picked up her hand, and spoke soft, sweet words in Blackfoot.

Bloody but perfect, the baby wiggled one tiny fist free and Willow ran a finger across the soft hand. So tiny. Joy born of pain and fear. She glanced over her shoulder at the couple and envied them this bond now between them. Looking back down at the baby, she saw her own child: dark hair, slate gray eyes. Steven's child. Perhaps such a gift would be worth the risk.

Stark fingers of wood sprawled across the smooth blanket of snow, half buried in high drifts. The skeleton-like frame of a small house stood trembling against the brunt of the wind.

Willow's house, Steven thought with a sharp twist of his heart. So, he hadn't put to rest her doubts after all. He'd lost the battle and the war to a piece of rolling, treeless Canadian prairie.

He circled the homesite, but no tracks marred the snowfall. No sign of life stirred save a piece of ragged burlap that twisted in the wind, straining against the nail that held it securely to a board.

She wasn't here.

He looked over the leaning structure with its awkward construction and amateur nailing. "When did she plan to move in, Andy?"

When Andy didn't answer, Steven turned in his saddle to stare at the embarrassed young man.

"She said as soon as Miss Emily's weddin' was over," he mumbled.

He wanted to curse the house, Willow, the cattle, and everything associated with all of them, but none of that mattered at the moment.

"Where's that coulee Wilbur mentioned?"

"On down yonder, south of here."

"Let's go, then," Steven said, and pulled Buck around to head back out onto the storm.

Crooked Stick rode at their side, silent and observant, his eyes darting from side to side as they rode. Steven remembered what Wilbur had said about Willow, about her having Blackfoot blood in her. And he wondered at the mysterious, silent connection between Willow and her mother's people.

The horses waded through drifts up to their bellies; in other places the wind had swept the ground clean, exposing dark-brown soil. Somehow, this land Willow so loved was tragically beautiful. It was hard and unforgiving but generous with sensual pleasures. Perhaps that was why she loved it enough to turn away his love.

"Yonder's the coulee." Andy pointed to the west, where a group of bare, skinny trees clawed at the sky. A steep bank curved gracefully around the depression, providing adequate cover from a storm. Steven's spirits lifted and he roused himself from the half-sleep that had claimed him hours ago.

They rode into the coulee, where dark-blue shadows clung to softly sculpted piles of snow. At the end of the depression was a huge, dark shadow just beneath the surface of the snow. Bits of brown fur stirred in the wind. A group of Herefords lay frozen and stiff. Part of Cletis's herd, no doubt.

"Dear God," Ben said.

"Willow!" Steven called, then strained to listen. No voice called out, and Steven cursed the howling wind. If she was hurt or weak, he'd never hear her.

"Willow!" he tried again.

As silent as the graveyard it was; the coulee gave up no secrets.

Ben and Andy dismounted and brushed snow away from the bodies of the cattle, hoping that perhaps Willow had crawled underneath for protection from the storm. But there was no sign of her and no sign of Pat.

"Did Pat come home?" Steven asked, and Andy shook his head.

"There's another coulee just south of here. Maybe she went into that one," Andy offered as they rode back out onto the open prairie.

By the time the sun clung to the western horizon, they'd exhausted every possibility Andy could conceive. Spent in mind and body, Steven knew they couldn't search through another night. They'd have to return home and look in another direction come morning.

Chapter Sixteen

Steven padded across the wooden floor in his sock feet, the cup of coffee in his hand long since grown cold. Starlight flirted with him from outside the open curtains, but his worry was too deep to notice the clear, beautiful night.

Where else could they have looked? he asked himself for the thousandth time. Or what had they overlooked? He stopped in front of the fireplace, staring at, but not seeing, the leaping flames. While he was in here, warm and full, she was out there, cold, maybe hungry.

He'd wanted to go back out, planning on pausing only for a fresh horse and another blanket. But Emily and Ben had interceded, arguing that before morning they'd be out searching for him, too. Emily declared she didn't have any worry left to spare. And so they'd chased him inside. Then, he'd been bone tired, exhausted. Now he couldn't sleep.

A scraping at the door caught his attention. He

glanced out the window and saw only the moon reflecting off the snow. Must be Bell, he concluded and returned to contemplating the fire.

Another scrape ended in a solid thud against the door. Setting his cup down on a table, Steven hurried to the door and flung it open. Willow stood on the porch, the arm of a young Blackfoot man draped across her shoulder. Head dangling limply, he barely stood and she sagged under his weight.

Steven pulled the man's other arm across his shoulders and half-dragged him inside.

"His wife's outside on Pat," Willow said with a grunt as they eased him onto the couch. "She's just had a baby."

Steven hurried back outside. She was barely older than Libby, he thought with a jolt as he reached up for her. She leaned down to him with no resistance.

Scooping her into his arms, he strode back into the house and gingerly deposited her in Cletis's large leather chair.

Willow knelt at the fireplace, laying more wood on the flames, rubbing her hands together briefly before she straightened and crossed to Little Rabbit's side. She parted the bundle of furs, then motioned to Steven with a crooked finger. He moved to her side, oblivious to all but the fact she was safe and here with him.

He glanced down at the tiny face that peered up between soft rabbit furs, then turned his gaze back on Willow. How could she infuriate him nearly beyond endurance and seduce both his thoughts and his anger at the same time?

"Isn't he beautiful?" she asked, her eyes shining. "And I delivered him."

The string of curses Steven had ready withered

on his tongue. Footsteps pounded down the stairs behind him.

"Dear God," Emily said, her hair loose around her shoulders, her wrapper flung around her. "Quick, Libby. Bring me all the quilts off my bed. Then put your shoes on and go get Ben from the barn."

Kneeling, Emily cupped Running Bird's cheek and lifted his head. "He's just cold and tired." She pivoted on Willow. "What happened?"

"I was out looking for the Angus—"

"Which you shouldn't have been doing," Emily interrupted.

" . . . when I came across them in a thicket," she finished, frowning at Emily. "She was in labor and in a bad way. She's so young, she didn't know what to do. The baby wouldn't come down."

Willow turned to Steven and searched his face so intimately, he could almost feel her hand on his skin. "So I made her squat down like I saw Ma do." She paused abruptly as her eyes filled with tears. "And the baby came."

Emily put a hand to her mouth and blinked back tears, too. "Oh my," she breathed.

"What's going on?" Libby asked, peeping over the bundle of quilts in her arms.

Emily snatched the covers away and draped two over Running Bear's shoulders. "How did all of you get here on poor Pat?" she asked as she tucked the material around him.

"We put Little Rabbit in the saddle and Running Deer and I walked." Willow chafed her hands together and turned back to the fire.

"How long have you been walking?" Steven asked as he lifted another quilt and draped it across

Little Rabbit's shoulders, then slid her chair closer to the fire.

Willow shrugged and moved to the side. "A couple of hours. Maybe three."

Steven grabbed her hands and yanked off her gloves. He felt each finger, examining it closely. Then he squatted down, picked up one foot, and snatched off her heavy leather boot.

"What are you doing?" she asked, hopping to keep her balance.

"Checking for frostbite." He peeled off three layers of socks. Underneath, her feet were chilly, but far from cold. He held her foot for a moment, content just to touch this much of her skin, allowing the fear to drain from him. Shaking his head with relief, he stood and faced her. "Your feet are fine."

She flashed him a brief, wicked smile. "I always wear three pairs of socks when I know I'm going to be gone for a time."

"I'll just put some water on to boil," Emily said, straightening.

"No, Willow and I will do it," Steven said with a firm hand on Emily's shoulder.

Emily glanced from one to the other. "If you want . . ."

"I do," Steven answered without taking his eyes off Willow.

She followed him to the kitchen, bracing herself when the door swung closed behind them.

"Who sent for you?" she asked, hoping to get in the first comment.

He stood with his back to her, hands jammed on his hips. "Crooked Stick came for me. Emily sent him."

"Oh."

"Where were you all these days?" He turned, his eyes filled with anger and anguish. He'd been frightened for her. Terrified, if she read him correctly. No one had ever worried about her like that before. They'd always assumed she could take care of herself. Suddenly, her decision to venture out alone seemed very foolish and very selfish.

"Did you ride out looking for me?" she asked, dreading the answer.

"Of course I did. Wilbur and Andy rode all night, searching for you at the Wallows."

So, he knew. "You saw the house?"

He nodded slowly. "I saw."

She moved away from him, hoping to escape the disappointment that oozed from him. "I wanted to tell you about that myself, to explain."

He turned, yanked open the door to the firebox of the cookstove, and tossed in a log that struck the back of the chamber with a clunk. He jammed in a bit of kindling, then slammed the door closed. Bracing both hands on the stovetop, he stared down into the feeble flames that licked up through the stove eye.

"Damn it, Willow. Do you ever stop and think about what you're doing?"

"Of course I do."

"Did you ever once think that if you rode out into that storm and stayed gone for days, the rest of us would worry?"

"I had no way of knowing she'd send for you. Besides, Emily knows I can take care of myself."

"That doesn't mean she doesn't worry."

He turned around to face her. "What was so all-fired important about finding the Angus right then? They're big pets. They wouldn't have wandered far from home anyway."

"I couldn't let anything happen to them. They're going to be the start of my—"

"The start of your herd. Is that what you were going to say?" He pounced on her words like a cat on a lizard.

"Yes."

He stared at her a moment, then turned and dropped the kettle onto the stove with a loud clank. "You're determined to do this alone, aren't you? You're going to shut me out of your life, just snuff out all that we could have had together." He hunched his shoulders and watched the kettle begin to steam. "I made love to you, Willow. I took your virginity. That's not something I take lightly. I treated you as if you were my wife, legally mine to take. Do you have any idea how difficult it has been for me to convince myself I did the right thing? That you'd see love was nothing to fear and something deeply intimate between a man and a woman?"

He turned around, leaned against the stove, and crossed his arms over his chest. "You take out your fears and hold them up between us when it suits you, when what you feel for me frightens you. You were no cowering innocent that night in the barn. You wanted me as badly as I wanted you."

He shoved away from the stove and took a step toward her. "You're not afraid of childbirth, Willow."

"What do you mean?" she asked, backing up a step as his voice rose. "I told you—"

"I have no doubt you were afraid, for a time. But then, as the years passed, you found it made a good excuse to avoid the subject of marriage. Anytime Emily brought up the subject, you'd whip out your collection of excuses. And your Pa let you get by with it, encouraged you in your little game.''

"Leave Pa out of this," she warned. "You don't know me. You don't know any of this is the truth." The accuracy of his accusals was jarring. Somehow, he'd crept into her head and unearthed all her secrets. Even some unknown to her.

"You're afraid somebody other than you might have a little say over what you do and when you do it. You've run things for so long, you can't imagine anybody else doing anything as well as you."

The damp warmth of the kitchen suddenly began to take its toll on Willow's tired body. She leaned a shoulder against the door frame, tempted to slide down and sit on the floor. "I'm not building the ranch just for me. It's for—"

"Us? You're doing this for us?" He laughed bitterly. "No, you're doing this for the iron-willed Willow Dawson."

Her eyes drooped heavily as she fought off sleep. "Of course I am. It's just . . ."

The anger suddenly drained from his face and he made one step toward her before she did indeed slide down the stout wooden frame and sit cross-legged on the floor.

"I'm all right," she said, holding up a hand when he reached down. "I'm just tired is all."

He bent to lift her, but she shoved his hands away and scrambled to her feet alone. "I'm going up to bed. Without any help."

"What on earth is going on in here? You two are waking up the ba—" Emily shoved open the kitchen door. "Willow!" She reached for her, but Willow shrugged off her grip, too.

Traveling on pride alone, Willow stumbled to the foot of the stairs and cast a glance over her shoulder. Little Rabbit sat in the chair smiling down at her son. Running Bird had recovered enough to kneel at her side with an arm around her waist.

Tears stinging her eyes, Willow gripped the banister and hauled herself to the second floor, Steven's harsh words ringing in her mind. He was right. Utterly right. She was a selfish brat. Emily's sweet efficiency at simple tasks had always rankled her and she'd countered by tackling a seemingly monumental problem and bringing it to heel. She broke horses, roped cattle, drove herds of beef all the way to Fort McLeod. But she couldn't simply be a woman, soft and pliant in the arms of the man she loved. No, she had to best him before she'd feel secure in giving herself to him completely.

And she hated him for proving it to her.

She was strangely warm, and something soft curled around and beneath her. Her confused thoughts spun backward. Where was she, and how had she gotten here?

A soft *flap, flap, flap* called her from sleep. What was that sound?

She opened one eye to peer through her lashes. Steven sat at her side, his head bowed. His hands moved quickly over the quilt, producing that intriguing noise.

She forced open the other eye and squinted to focus. A line of cards lay spread out across the patchwork pattern, their colorful pictures in contrast to the soft hues of the fabric. His nimble fingers flipped them all with one turn, then flipped them back, producing the soft fluttering sound she'd heard. Fascinated, she continued to watch.

His hair was mussed and shaggy, and more than a day's growth of beard darkened his cheeks. He wore a soft undershirt and his uniform pants with suspenders dangling at his sides. Fatigue haunted his face. Regret for yesterday's sharp words bit her.

Steven gathered up the cards, shuffled them, then put them down and pulled one card from the top of the deck. Magically, the card flitted through his fingers, then disappeared completely. Steven opened his hand and smiled, finally lifting his head. Tired circles rimmed his eyes.

"How—" Her throat was dry and sore. She cleared it and began again. "How long have I been asleep?"

He smiled at her. Was that relief she saw in his eyes? "About a day, give or take an hour."

"Where are Running Bird and Little Rabbit?"

"They've gone on to her village. We lent them two horses." He leaned forward and took her hand in his leathery, warm one. "How are you feeling?"

"Thirsty."

Steven stood and lifted a glass off a table by the bed. He slipped a hand underneath her head and brought the glass to her lips. She took a sip and closed her eyes as the cool liquid slid down her tortured throat.

"Running Bird told me about how you delivered the baby." He lowered her back onto the soft pillow, briefly fussing with the quilt at her throat before he sat back down with a soft groan. "That was quick thinking."

"She was in trouble. I couldn't just leave her there."

"No fears?"

She looked up into his beautiful gray eyes and shook her head. "No, no fears. I didn't even think about Ma, except to remember what she did. I guess that's good use of old memories. Right?"

He squeezed her hand. Tiny flecks of black darkened the gray of his irises. Funny, she'd never noticed that before. But then her best opportunity had been in a darkened barn when passion had robbed her of all powers of observation. Except for the way he'd moved within her or the sweet pain of giving up her innocence to him.

"Steven, I need time to think." She needed silence in which to turn out her thoughts like the cards he'd fanned out across the quilt. *Pick one. Pick a future.*

"Willow." His palm cupped her cheek and urged her face back to look into his. "I—"

"No. I don't want to know what you're going to say."

"I'm sorry for the things I said yesterday in the kitchen."

"Don't be. You were right." She found a loose string on the quilt and began to roll it between her fingers. "You were right about all of it. You made me see things I didn't want to see before. I'm better off for it." She raised her eyes to his. "Thank you."

A quick frown flitted across his face. "Willow, I didn't mean—"

"Yes, you did. I've treated you badly when all you gave me was love and consideration. I want to bring something to our marriage, something good."

"You'll be bringing you."

"That's not enough and you know it." She smoothed her hand across his hair, little thrills running up her arm at the silkiness of it. "I need time."

"Will you ever have had enough time, Willow?" he asked softly as he rose from the bed.

He stalked to the window and braced a hand on either side. "My enlistment is up in May. I want a home, Willow, and a family. I want to leave something behind when I'm gone. Children. Some mark that I was here. I want to come home at night and have someone waiting for me. I want *you* waiting for me. But I won't beg, Willow. Hell, what am I saying? I've already done that." He turned to face her. "If you don't know by now, after what we did, after all I've said, whether or not you love me enough to be my wife, you'll never know."

Willow felt the bottom drop out of her heart and panic edge into her veins. She was losing him.

He paused and she felt every second that ticked by.

"I'm coming to Emily and Ben's wedding in May," he said in a tight voice. "If you can't give me an answer by then, I've made arrangements to buy some land near Fort Walsh. I've waited a long time to live a normal life again. I have to start someplace, with or without you."

"Willow!" Her room door banged back against the wall and Cletis rushed in, snow still clinging to his beard. He scooped her up into an embrace, sprinkling her with droplets of icy water. "Emily told me what happened," he said, his voice oddly tight. "What would I have done if I'd lost you?"

He held her so tightly, she thought for a moment he'd squeeze the breath right out of her. "I'm all right, Pa."

"What possessed you to do such a fool thing?" he asked, releasing her and stepping back from the bed. Anger had replaced concern.

"Libby let the Angus out of the barn and they wandered off. I went to bring them back."

"That was a damn-fool thing to do." Cletis said, unwinding a knit scarf from around his neck. "Damn the cattle and your hardheadedness."

He threw Steven a glance, then rounded on him. "Can't you do anything with her? She's going to be your wife."

How had Pa found out? "Pa—"

"Actually, Mr. Dawson, Willow has not yet agreed to marry me."

"And why the hell not?" Cletis turned back to Willow and she wished she could shrink up under the covers.

She glanced at Steven, but he offered no assistance, only watched her with his calm gray eyes. "I just don't feel like I'm ready, Pa. How'd you find out about this, anyway?"

"Ben told me," Cletis huffed, and ran a hand through his thin hair, setting it on end. "You're twenty years old, lass. I'd say it's about time you got yourself ready."

Appalled that her father had deserted her side of the argument, she looked between the two men glowering down at her. She could always depend on her father seeing things her way. When had the tide of the discussion shifted against her? "I . . . wanted to get my ranch on its feet first," she said, looking from one to the other, Steven's unanswered ultimatum hanging in the air.

"I'd say young Constable Gravel here needs to concentrate on getting you off yours." Cletis shook a finger in her face, then slung his coat to the floor with a string of curses.

"Pa!"

"Don't 'Pa' me, Willow Carrie."

Willow shrank from the name he only used when he was at his wits' end. She'd long ago learned that it signaled the beginning of the end of Pa's good humor.

"Constable, could you give us a few minutes alone?" Cletis asked.

"Of course. I'll just go down for some coffee." With the ease of a cat, Steven glided from the room without a sound.

Cletis glared at her a second longer and she instinctively slid the quilt up to her neck. Finally, he sat down on the side of the bed with a heartfelt sigh. "What kind of game are you playing with the constable here?"

"I'm not playing a game, Pa. I . . . just want something of my own first. I'm not ready to get married."

"Why?"

"What do you mean?"

"I mean why aren't you ready? Give me a reason."

Willow glanced away from her father. "What if he were to die, like Ma?"

"Lord, Willow. What if he were to suddenly rise up with butterfly wings."

Willow threw him a disgusted glance.

"You can't cover every possibility, child."

"I can try, Pa. I wouldn't be a good rancher if I didn't try to plan for every misfortune, now would I?"

Cletis raked a hand through his hair. "God bless the man raising daughters." He rose and walked to the same window Steven had just vacated. Shoulders sagging beneath the faded, baggy shirt, he braced one hand on the wall and the other on his hip.

"I should have talked to you girls about this a

long time ago,'' he said, his breath fogging the glass. He paused and Willow glanced up at him. He stared out across the sun-sparkled snow, and for an instant she could imagine him as a young man. Slim with wavy auburn hair. Dancing blue eyes.

"Your Ma wanted another baby in the worst sort of way about the time Libby was two. She'd given me three beautiful daughters, but she thought she'd let me down by not giving me a son. I told her it didn't matter none, especially since Libby's birth was so hard; that I couldn't love a son more than I loved the three of you. But her people value boys. In their eyes, a man just ain't a man without a son to carry on his name. And a wife who couldn't give her husband a son weren't no kind of woman, in her way of thinking.''

Cletis paused again and cleared his throat. "So I did what she asked and she conceived the boys.''

He left the window and came to sit on the bed at her side. "I knew right off something weren't right. Some days she couldn't get out of the bed.''

He smoothed the quilt with his rugged hand. "But she died thinking she'd done the right thing, Willow. She never once regretted her decision to have another baby. It was me had the regrets. What if I hadn't given in to her?'' He lifted his face and met Willow's eyes. "I've carried that guilt all these years. I reckon that's why I didn't sit you girls down and explain all this to you. You especially. But I'm explaining now.'' He picked up her hand. "You've got her strength, Willow. It was your Ma got this place started, her that wanted a home for you and Emily. Me, I'd have spent the rest of my life roaming the prairie, I reckon. And I missed her awful when she died. But now that I've had time to think about it, I don't regret none of it. I reckon things happened just the way God intended, and it weren't my place to second-guess Him.''

"You've got a good man wanting to marry you, Willow. He loves you, from what I've seen. Don't let your pigheadedness get in the way of that.''

Pa abruptly rose and left the room. Willow looked out the window, sensing the conversation was far from over and wondering what he was up to. He returned quickly and pressed a shell ornament into her hand. A long, worn rawhide string was attached.

"That was yore Ma's. She wore it in her hair the day I married her. I kept it all these years cause I ain't got enough of her things to give something to each of you. But I reckon you need it the most.'' Cletis sat on the bed and looked down at the board floor. "You got an uncle in the Blackfoot village to the west. I reckon you oughta go have a talk with him.''

"I know,'' Willow answered.

Cletis looked up at her. "I suspected you did. I've seen the things you brought back to your sisters, even though they tried to hide 'em. He shook his head. "I reckon I had to blame somebody for her dying, and Lame Deer was handy. 'Cause of my pigheadedness, you girls ain't never known your Ma's people, and they're good people.''

Cletis rose. "I better let you rest. You ain't never been afraid of nothing in your life. I got no doubt you could take a horse, a gun, and a pack of matches and build yourself an empire. But just 'cause *I* know ain't no good. You gotta know it yourself.''

He turned and walked to the door, then paused in the doorway. "Lovin' a man and havin' his babies takes a whole lot more gumption than building a ranch, Willow. Takes a different kind of courage. You got it and so did your Ma.'' Then he closed the door behind him and his steps faded down the hall.

Chapter Seventeen

Willow eased the door closed behind her and stepped carefully across the patches of snow, holding the quilt high enough not to drag in the mud. Dangling an unlit lantern in one hand, she fumbled with the barn door until it opened with a gentle swish and she slipped inside.

Passing the first stall, she peeked over the top rail to see Boris standing trancelike, staring at a corner. Sprigs of hay hung out of both sides of his mouth as he raised his head to look at her with calm eyes. She moved to the next stall and scratched the curly black hair on Kate's head, touched the belly full of calf. Gratefully hefting her weight against the boards, Kate closed her eyes momentarily, enjoying Willow's ministrations.

The ladder to the loft was directly beside Pat's stall. Willow pulled the quilt up around her neck and climbed the wooden rungs.

Above, Steven slept in the hay, intending to

return to Fort McLeod in the morning. Ben had conceded to take the guest room, but Steven had insisted on the barn. *Now who's the stubborn one?* Willow thought with a smirk as she poked her head above the floor of the hayloft.

She lit the lantern with a match she'd tucked behind her ear, turned the wick down low, and walked softly across the hay, the soles of her bare feet still stinging from the cold wet ground.

Steven slept on his side, one arm beneath his cheek. A blanket lay beneath him and another covered his shoulders. In sleep, his face was peaceful and unlined. Willow sat down cross-legged at his side.

His lashes formed dark circles on cheeks stained with a day's growth of beard. The wind and snow had chapped his face until it was red and rough, and the aroma of one of Emily's cremes floated about him.

The circle his body formed between bent knees and outstretched arms looked inviting, and she longed to crawl into that curve and rest her head on his arm, to feel his body pressed against her back.

There'd be long days of work, she imagined, days when building their home would tax them both to the end of their strength. She'd learn to be different. She'd learn to let him shoulder some of the load. Night would bring welcome rest in each other's arms. No more mornings would she awake alone. No more nights would she lie down wanting him with an ache that filled her body and tormented her mind. And one day there'd be babies to feed and change and tickle.

She smiled, imagining him with pins in his mouth and not enough hands, struggling with tiny flailing arms and legs. What woman would not want such a picture tucked away amid other precious memories? Had her mother had such notions of her father? Was that what had prompted her to risk another pregnancy?

Willow leaned forward to wake Steven with a chaste kiss, but as she tasted his skin, she knew her intentions had never been innocent. She'd come out here to make love to him. No sense in lying to herself. She wanted him inside her again, to hear and feel his groans as he dropped every shred of his cool self-confidence, then melted and reformed in her arms.

"Willow?" Steven said softly. "What are you doing out here in your underwear?" He pushed himself to his elbows, his eyes soft with sleep. "You'll catch your death. Didn't you do a good enough job last night trying to kill yourself?"

Willow glanced down at her baggy winter underwear. "I . . . wanted to see you. You didn't come back after Pa left."

He watched her with dark eyes that made her shiver. He wasn't buying her excuse.

"Come here."

She stood, hung the lantern on a nail, and moved to his side. He patted the blanket beside him and she curled up facing him inside the envied curve of only moments ago. He covered her with her quilt and draped his coat over her shoulders.

"Warm enough?"

She nodded, feeling his body stir to life beside her.

"Now, why'd you really come out here?"

She kissed him softly on the lips, but his eyes didn't slide closed and he didn't return the kiss. "Make love to me again, Steven," she whispered.

His gaze flitted across her face. Up to her eyes, down to her mouth, and pausing there. "No," he said softly.

"Why?"

"Because you're not a whore, Willow, and I'm not some randy buck. If you can't make up your mind, making love won't help."

She slid a hand between them, hesitated when he flinched and drew in his breath, then continued down until she touched him. "You want me."

"Yes, I do," he answered in a tight voice. "God help me, I do. But I want more than this." He kissed her and she felt his pulse jump beneath her hand.

"I meant what I said." He encircled her wrist with his fingers and pulled her hand away. "I won't use you, Willow, and that's what it would be."

"No, it wouldn't. Not if I was going to be your wife."

He watched her, suspicious. "Empty promises again?" he asked bitterly.

She swallowed and wondered briefly if she'd done more damage than could be repaired. "No, but I am going to ask you a favor."

He sighed and rolled onto his back. "Do I have a sign pinned to me that invites you to break my heart at every chance?"

Willow waited.

"What is it?"

"When you come for Emily's wedding in May, decide then if you still want to marry me. If you do, I'll marry you that very day."

He rolled back to his side and propped his chin on his hand. "Okay, I'm intrigued. But what are you up to between now and then?"

"I'm going to get to know my Blackfoot family

better—learn about my mother and maybe a little something about me. You were right about me. Everything you said. I've been selfish and bossy and stubborn.''

He stroked her hair. ''I told you I was sorry about what I said.''

''No, you were right. I don't know if I can change those things about me, but I can put them to better use.''

''Willow—'' She cut off his words with a kiss that he returned eagerly. She plucked open the buttons of his undershirt and slid a hand inside, across the rough hair of his chest to the soft skin that stretched over his rib cage.

''Steven,'' she whispered against his lips as she slithered over to lie atop him.

With trembling fingers, he opened her buttons and cupped her breasts briefly before tasting each. A tiny impulse sped to her center, unleashing desire that flowed through her like warmed syrup.

His arms folded her flat against his chest. ''You're my greatest weakness, Willow. Don't tempt me if you don't mean it,'' he whispered into her hair.

She ignored his warnings and attacked the rest of his tiny white buttons. As they fell victim to her fingers, he shoved the top of her underwear off her shoulders and down her arms to bunch at her waist. She shivered in the cold air as he nipped at the smooth skin on the inside of her arm and left a trail of little bites up to her shoulder. ''You've made me an evil man, Willow Dawson,'' he muttered as he directed his attention to her breasts.

The first touch of his warm mouth sent shards of desire through her, sharp and painful in their urgency. His hands encircled her waist, his fingers digging into her skin.

"What are we doing?" he asked, his voice thick with emotion, moving his hips to slide her across his stomach.

"You're taking off your clothes." She stood and stepped out of her remaining clothes while he wriggled the garment down his body and kicked it off.

She stood over him a moment, gazing down at his muscular body. He was hers for a word, a promise. He placed tender trust in her, a delicate bond, betraying all he held honorable to please her.

She straddled his waist. At the touch of her bare skin against his, he jerked his head back and his eyes flew open.

"No, Willow."

She ignored his complaint and angled her body to take him within her, marveling at how perfectly they fit together and the way his eyes helplessly drifted shut. She sensed she held a strange power over him and the knowledge made her bold. Her palms planted on his chest, she copied the rhythm he'd shown her, her own response immediately intense.

She leaned down to kiss him, teasing his sensitive skin with the ends of her hair, but he found her lips first. Cupping the back of her head with one hand, he devoured her mouth, passion flowing through him. He attempted to roll her over, to tuck her underneath him and gain control, but she pushed his shoulders back flat against the hay.

"I won't be able to stop. . . ." he whispered hoarsely, his fingers digging into her hips, guiding her, moving his body to meet hers halfway.

"I know," she whispered. "I don't want you to."

Willow quickly passed the point of caution, plunging headlong into the unknown. She danced on the edge of daring, taking the man she loved, bending him to her will as easily as he bent her to his. The fact she might conceive faded into the background of her concern.

He moaned softly and his grip on her skin tightened. "Now, Willow. Move off me now."

"No," she said as her own pleasure began.

He arched his back, his whole body rigid, and the warmth of his seed flowed into her. She clung to him until he relaxed and rolled her underneath him, their bodies still joined. "How can you not want to do that every day for the rest of our lives?" he said breathlessly.

"I do," she answered, and combed a hand through his hair. "I'm just giving you an out in case you don't."

He shook his head slowly. "Never." He kissed her once more, then withdrew from her and snugged her against him. The emptiness of his body leaving hers was almost overwhelming.

"I've been recalled to Fort Walsh."

His words fell like a thunderbolt, splitting apart their warm cocoon. Willow plucked hay from her hair. "What do you mean?"

Steven tucked the quilt around them both. "Sitting Bull and his people are causing some trouble. A rider brought a message for me this afternoon. Walsh thinks since Braden and I have dealt with them before, we'd have the most success now."

"When were you going to tell me this?"

"I certainly had no intention of telling you like this," he replied with a cocked eyebrow, lifting a stray piece of straw from her hair.

Tears gathered behind her eyes and she fought for control of her raw nerves. "How long will you be gone?"

"I don't know. I hope to be back in time for the wedding . . . and to hold you to your promise."

Willow began to tremble, partly from cold, partly from the realization she had squandered precious time. "Will it be dangerous?"

Steven looked down, refusing to meet her eyes. "I won't lie to you. It could be. I don't know what we're getting into."

"Take me with you." She gripped his forearm. "We'll find somebody to marry us there."

He kissed her lightly, sweetly. "What happened to your gracious plan to give me an out?"

"I take it all back. You're stuck with me the way I am."

He laughed, then slowly sobered. "You know I can't take you with me."

"I know," she said, her voice betraying her with a hitch. "Oh, God, Steven, I've wasted so much of our time." A tear trailed down her cheek.

He stood and pulled her to her feet. She put her arms around his waist and lay her head against his chest.

"There'll be plenty of time for us when I come back." He held her for several silent moments and the air grew heavy with unspoken words. "You know you could conceive from what just happened."

She raised her head. "I know. I hope so."

He looked into her eyes. "You'll send for me?"

She shrugged in his embrace. "I won't know for sure until you're already back."

"Are you going to tell Emily?"

She shook her head. "No."

"You're going to wait it out alone?"

"It's something private between us." Tears smeared across the soft hair on his chest. "Just us and no one else. I'd like to keep it that way. I don't regret what I did, Steven. I want you to take that with you.''

He rubbed his cheek against the side of her face, his beard chafing gently, leaving behind a suspicious dampness. "God, you're hard on a man's heart."

"Tell me about my mother."

Lame Deer raised an eyebrow and drew deeply on the clay pipe clamped firmly in his teeth. The tobacco in the bowl glowed red for a moment and then a stream of white smoke escaped from his lips. He breathed out slowly, closing his eyes to savor the taste, then snapped open his eyes and studied her. "What do you want to know?"

"Did she love my father?"

Lame Deer sucked again on the pipe stem, billowing another cloud of white that drifted up to the smoke hole in the top of the teepee. His long dark hair was streaked with gray and silver, but his face was that of a younger man, with eyes alert and filled with humor. Sitting here cross-legged on his floor, Willow felt closer than she ever had to the mother she barely remembered.

"Ah," he said finally. "You want to know about trouble she caused."

"What trouble?"

"Your mother and father cause much talk, much worry."

"They did?"

Lame Deer laughed. "You are pleased they cause trouble. Maybe because you have caused trouble for your father?"

"Pa says I'm stubborn just like her."

Lame Deer smiled softly. "Pretty Water was stubborn child that grew into stubborn woman. When she is little, she cross arms"—he folded his arms across his chest—"like this, and say 'no' and shake head. People think she is funny, but our mother and father do not think she is funny."

Willow laughed, imagining the faceless woman in her mind as a little child, jaw set, dark hair swinging side to side as she defied the adults bending over her.

"What did she and Pa do?"

"The first thing they do is be alone together. This is bad in Blackfoot village. Cletis Dawson find her on prairie gathering food. He follow her to stream and old women find them there."

"What were they doing?" Willow leaned closer.

Lame Deer laughed. "They were sitting together on rock talking," he said with a smirk.

"Oh."

"But that is bad to old women. They hurry back to village. Spread word. Our mother was very angry and father threatened to kill white man who dishonor daughter. But your father follow Pretty Water home and ask Mother and Father to marry her."

"What did they say?"

Lame Deer guffawed and laid his pipe on his bent knee. "They were very angry. Father march around teepee and Mother cry. They send him away and then Pretty Water cry, but he was back next day and ask again."

Willow glanced up at the dark-haired young woman watching them from the other side of the teepee. Her aunt, Makes Fire, was large with child and sat with sewing spread across her expanding stomach. Her uncle had taken her as his wife a little over a year ago, after the death of his first two wives to smallpox. His face bore the marks of a close brush with the white man's curse. Willow watched her aunt shift on the reed mat that cushioned her, and wished she knew her better, understood the secret contentment on her face.

"Did they agree?" she asked, pulling her attention back to Lame Deer.

"No. He come back for one moon; every night he is here. He bring food, horses, pots, beads. Father say Cletis Dawson is as stubborn as Pretty Water and they deserve each other. So he give your mother to your father."

Lame Deer picked up a branch and threw it onto the fire. Despite the cold outside, the teepee was warm and comfortable, the floor spread with dried grass and furs. Lame Deer glanced at his wife and smiled softly as she adjusted the bulk of her stomach with one hand. His first wife had given him only one son, her cousin, Crooked Stick, and he'd always wanted more children. He glanced at Willow again and traced a figure in the dirt at his feet. "You want to know about Pretty Water's death? That is why you came?"

"Yes."

Lame Deer jabbed at the figure he'd drawn. "Your father come to get me on cold night. I never see a man so afraid. He say baby is stuck, can't come out. I come and bring medicine."

He swallowed and blinked. "When I get there, Pretty Water is in great pain. Baby stuck. I try to pull out, but baby does not come. Then, I give her medicine to make babies come faster. First baby, son, is born dead. Then, there is another baby. Two babies." He held up two fingers, the remembered terror in his eyes.

"Second baby is . . . not baby. Something else."

"What do you think happened?" Willow waited, hoping her uncle's wisdom could put to rest her fears.

He hesitated, seemingly fascinated with scratching marks in the dirt. "One time when I am boy, I see buffalo cow giving birth. She is laying on side, breathing hard." He imitated the heaving breaths of labor. "Calf come out, then another. Cow tear bag off first calf and it stand. Second lay still and mother not tear off bag. She and first calf leave. I go and look at second." He paused and stared into the fire. "Second calf had no legs, no eyes. I think about this for long time."

Willow closed her eyes against the half-remembered bits and pieces of horror that flashed through her mind.

"I go away to find wisdom on this. I was gone many days and do not eat. In my vision, I see man make love to his woman and put two spirits into her. Then while woman's belly grows big, spirits fight to see who is strongest. Strongest one wins and they agree to become one body. When child is born, strong spirit is man's courage; weaker spirit is his fear, all in same body." He nodded, as if satisfied. "I believe this is the way of the spirits."

Willow thought about what he'd said, weighing his words against what she knew to be true. He was confident in the explanation he'd found, placing all his sorrow on the shoulders of ones he considered wiser. Perhaps he was right. Perhaps man would never know the true nature of what went on in the womb. How, then, did that explain her brothers' deaths?

"The spirits saw that both your brothers were strong, brave spirits and could never live in same body peacefully," Lame Deer continued as if reading her thoughts. "So, he say your mother should decide which would die." He shrugged. "Your mother had already grown to love both and could not decide, so the spirits took her to look after them until they would go into a woman again."

The fears that had haunted her, Lame Deer had explained to himself by simple faith. Faith that there is a reason for every sorrow. Faith that from every sorrow grows hope.

"You come now and ask these questions. Do you carry a child?"

Instant denial sprang to her tongue. "I don't know," she replied instead.

"You have lain with the red coat?"

"Yes. He has asked me to be his wife." She met his gaze without faltering.

"And you said no to him."

"You know?"

Lame Deer smiled and shrugged. "Your cousin, Crooked Stick, trades at Fort McLeod. The constable is good man; why do you not marry him?"

Willow shrugged. "I was afraid, at first. Afraid what happened to Ma would happen to me. Then it seemed to me that women become shadows of their husbands with nothing of their own, no thoughts or lives of their own. I guess somehow I thought one led to another. I don't know now what I thought."

"You think different now he has put his seed into you?"

She nodded. "I guess."

"Blackfoot woman owns her teepee, her property. She has mind and life of her own." He shook his head sadly. "Your mother was not there to teach you how things should be."

"I'm going to marry him when he comes back from Sitting Bull's camp."

Lame Deer raised his eyebrows. "He has gone to talk to Sitting Bull?"

"He was one of the men who helped the Sioux when they came to the Grandmother's land."

Lame Deer nodded, picked up his pipe, and examined the elaborately carved bowl. "I watch you and sisters grow into women. Your father did not know I watch. I promised your mother I would keep watch over all." He stuck the pipe stem back in his mouth and drew in a breath of smoke.

"You act like man. Brave woman." His tone was sarcastic, and Willow frowned at this sudden shift in his mood.

"You are fearless, ride into snowstorm. Ride long ways without man. Throw rope around cattle. But in heart, you are afraid of being woman."

Anger surged up within Willow even as she acknowledged he was right.

"When I am young man, I do things young men do to prove they are brave. I fight enemies, ride wild horses, do foolish things. As I become old man, I realize it takes more courage to raise family and be good father than steal horses or defeat enemies. Takes more courage for woman to bear babies, raise strong men than rope cattle and ride horses."

"That's what Pa said."

"Ah, then Cletis Dawson is wise man, too. We think of same good things." He chuckled, then leaned forward and touched her shoulder. "You want to know if you are like Pretty Water?"

"Am I, Uncle?"

The old man's face softened. "Yes, you are like her. She was stubborn, want own way, but only when about ones she love. Never for herself." He picked up the pipe and put it back in his mouth. "She have big heart like you." He nodded. "Name all horses in camp. Make young warriors mad, woman name their horse. They are afraid she steal their spirit," he said in an imitation of an indignant young man.

"No one come to court her because they are all afraid of her." He shrugged one shoulder. "Then spirits send Cletis Dawson to her."

He studied the opposite wall of the teepee for several silent seconds. "Maybe you are brave woman meant to carry spirits of dead brothers. Maybe Steven Gravel was sent to put them into you."

Chapter Eighteen

"Get that goat out of my flowers!" Emily howled
from the front porch.

Libby dashed to Bell's side and hauled her out
of the flower garden, stolen treats hanging out of
her mouth.

"There ain't no flowers on 'em, Em. They ain't
bloomed yet."

"I don't care if they haven't bloomed. I don't
want goat ... dung ... where I'm going to be
married."

Willow eased open the barn door to eye the confrontation. Cool, serene Emily Dawson was about
as rattled as Willow had ever seen her. Half her
hair streamed down her back and the other half
was piled on her head in a graceful upsweep. Clad
only in her wrapper, she gestured at Libby and
Bell with a clutched hairbrush.

"Reckon any of us are safe until after the weddin'?" Cletis asked at her elbow.

"Nope. That's why I'm here . . . in the barn."

"She's got poor Andy in the kitchen stuffing some sort of little doodads."

Willow nodded. "Yep, I saw him captured early this morning. I tried but I couldn't save him. Emily threatened to curl my hair if I interfered."

They laughed together and eased the barn door shut before their hiding place was discovered. Cletis pulled out his pocket watch and checked the time. "We gotta hide only about two more hours and the deed'll be done." He snapped the watch closed. "Why've you got Pat saddled?"

Willow checked the cinch and lowered her stirrup. "I thought I'd ride out to my place before the ceremony."

"Emily'll have your skin if she finds out. Besides, what kind of daughter would desert her Pa at a time like this?"

Gripping the saddle horn with one hand, Willow placed the other on the saddle apron and stared down at the ground between her feet. "The kind of woman who wants to make sure everything's perfect . . . in case he comes."

"Aw, honey. You know he's coming. He said he'd come back, didn't he? That is, if he can."

"I know, Pa. It's just . . . I haven't heard a word. Ben's heard nothing at all from him. Not even Commissioner McLeod knows exactly where he and Braden are. I'll be back before the wedding. I'm taking my dress with me in case I'm late. If he shows up, send him out, will you?"

Cletis touched her shoulder lightly, then slid an arm around her and hauled her tight against his chest. "I wish I'd a done a better job with you girls."

Willow dropped Pat's reins and wrapped her

arms around her father's waist. "You did fine, Pa. We all did just fine." With her face buried in his chest, she closed her eyes and said a quick prayer. If today didn't go the way she hoped, she'd need her father more than she ever had.

"Go out the back," Cletis said, releasing her and stepping quickly toward the back barn door. "That way you'll be out of earshot before Emily realizes you're gone."

Willow swung into Pat's saddle, then ducked as he stepped delicately through the small doorway. She paused just outside and looked back. "If I'm not here, don't hold the wedding up for me. Have the father go ahead with the ceremony. Emily'll be mad, I know, but she'll be married either way."

"Willow . . ." Cletis began, then fell silent, as if searching for the words. "Did you tell Steven what was in your heart?"

"Yes, Pa."

"Were you honest with him? No puttin' on a big front?"

"He knows I love him."

Willow started forward, then stopped again and looked back at her Pa, still standing in the open door. "Pa?"

"Yeah, baby?"

"I've spent a lot of years bossing all of you around, missing dinners, making you worry. I'm sorry."

Cletis smiled. "Go on now before Emily catches us and makes us stuff them doodads, too."

She turned Pat and rode around the outbuildings until she was out of sight of the house, then swung south.

Spring had scattered wildflowers across the prairie, dots of color to break up the unending carpet of newly green grass. Songbirds had returned and the sun was bright overhead. A beautiful day for a wedding. Why, then, did she carry this dread that threatened to snatch away the joy of the day?

She was pregnant.

She'd known the day after she and Steven made love that she carried his life within her. Lying in her bed that next morning, she'd closed her eyes and imagined the moment of conception. And now that tiny being lay within her, sleeping and waiting, its existence now confirmed.

Pat trotted to his usual place at the hitching post outside her house and stopped. She dismounted, climbed the steps, and pushed the door open. All was as she'd left it yesterday and the day before that. A new quilt stretched across the bed. A jar of flowers sat in the center of a rough-hewn table. The floors were swept clean of shavings and the whole house smelled of fresh wood. Now all she needed was a husband, she thought as she backed up and sat down on the edge of the bed.

Tears came hot and unwelcome. She yanked a handkerchief from her pocket and swiped at them. She'd done that a lot lately, cried for no reason. Poor Andy didn't know what to think of that or her refusal yesterday to rope a calf on foot and bounce along behind like she'd done a hundred times before. Frankly, neither did she. She was starting down a long, dark path. And possibly a lonely one.

Glancing sideways at Ben, Steven smiled inwardly. Poor Ben rode looking straight ahead, admiring neither the spring offerings nor the

sunny day. Pre-wedding jitters had completely consumed Big Ben McGavin.

Steven had arrived at Fort McLeod from Sitting
Bull's camp just in time to leave with Ben, McLeod,
and Constable Jackson last night, but he'd had to
ride straight through the night before to do it.
The thought of Willow's stricken face watching the
empty horizon had kept him awake in the saddle
despite periods of dozing.

"Ben? You all right?" he asked, and Ben turned,
his face a sickly shade of white.

"What?"

"Are you all right?"

He nodded mutely. "I'm fine. Just a little nervous, I guess. Reckon I shouldn't a eat all them
biscuits last night."

"I haven't lost a bridegroom yet," chimed in
Father Flannigan. Following along behind them
on his doddering but adored dun mare, the good
father had consented to perform the ceremony
uniting Ben and Emily.

"How long have you been in the Territories?"
questioned Commissioner McLeod, and the father
launched into a tirade on his adventures.

Ben heeled his horse into a faster shuffle and
Steven moved to keep pace, realizing they were
moving out of earshot of the other three men.

"There's something I've been wantin' to ask
you," Ben said, turning his now slightly green face
toward Steven.

"Ask me anything, Ben."

"On a lad's wedding night . . . how does he . . .
approach his bride?"

"I thought you'd already crossed that bridge."

Ben looked horrified and Steven regretted his
flippant answer.

"That was . . . a lustful encounter. Fact is, I don't remember just what was said." Ben added pink to the bouquet of color on his face. "By either one of us."

"She loves you and you love her. The details will work themselves out."

Ben belched and placed a hand over his mouth. "Excuse me," he mumbled. "What I mean is, do I reach for her first or wait for her to come to me?"

Reach for her. By all means, reach for her and hold onto her. Don't let her or anything else come between you. Despite his vow not to think of Willow, her head thrown back in passion as she took his life inside her, he did. And winced at the way his insides twisted. The question of whether or not she carried his child was eating away at him. He should have been there with her, he thought, when she either confirmed or denied she was pregnant. But she'd had to face the truth alone. Like so many things in her life.

"Go to her. Take her in your arms and let her know you'll always want her there."

Ben suddenly yanked his horse to a stop and dismounted. He strode behind a scraggly patch of brush and Steven heard him retching. Turning in the saddle, Steven looked back at McLeod, who slowly shook his head. Ben reemerged on wobbly legs and Steve reached over, unhooked his canteen, and held it out to him.

Ben took it, rinsed out his mouth, then poured water into his hand and wiped it across his face. "I think I'm all right now."

He remounted his horse and cleared his throat. "Just a few jitters. I can't believe she's marrying me. Big, dumb Ben McGavin."

"She adores you, Ben. I am convinced you can't

say or do anything to change that. No matter how hard you try."

"What if I don't do . . . it . . . right?"

Steven laughed out loud. "There's not a right or a wrong for 'it.' Stop worrying. Besides, Emily's a lady. You're the only basis for comparison she's got."

Ben's face brightened. "That's a fact, ain't it? I hadn't thought of it that way. No, I hadn't thought of it that way at all." He smiled and his color slowly returned.

The Dawson house was festooned with white ribbons fluttering on the afternoon breeze. Andy met them at the hitching rail.

"I sure am glad you're here," he muttered under his breath. "Ain't none of us been safe all morning."

Steven squinted at a white streak smeared across Andy's cheek, and the boy started off toward the barn, leading the horses. He suddenly stopped and turned. "I told her I didn't know how to stuff them little things." Without another word of explanation, he resumed his shuffling gait.

Steven and Ben exchanged glances and Ben's color faded. They stepped up onto the porch and Libby barreled through the front door, hair and ribbons flying, and plowed a path through their group. Father Flannigan teetered on the edge of the porch for a moment, then plunged backwards, landing spread-eagled in the newly turned flower bed. Commissioner McLeod lost his balance briefly, but grabbed a porch post at the last moment.

"Not to worry," the father said as he sprang up and dusted off his vestment. "Only a little dust."

Libby stopped and whirled around to face them. She wore the same white battle scars as Andy. "I hope Emily don't never get married again, and if she does, I hope everybody starves clean to death." Hands clenched at her sides, she stomped off toward the barn.

Cletis appeared in the doorway, his vest streaked with flour. "Welcome, gentlemen." He cleared his throat and looked after his retreating daughter. "It would appear this occasion ain't goin' too smoothly."

Constable Jackson stepped forward, hauling to full height his boyish frame. "I've had some experience in these occasions. Perhaps I can be of assistance."

Cletis put an arm around the lad's narrow shoulders. "Fresh recruits are welcome." Then he led the boy toward the kitchen.

Steven, Ben, and the father stepped into the house. A layer of white powder dusted the usually spotless floor now dappled with dainty hoofprints.

"Bell," Steven and Ben said at the same time.

Steven looked up the stairs. "Stay here," he said to Ben, and he took the steps two at a time.

When he reached Emily's door, he rapped softly. "Come in," came weakly from the other side.

He pushed open the door and peeked around it. Emily sat on the edge of her bed, her veil attached to a crown of golden curls, her flowers gripped tightly in her hand. She stared at the floorboards, her face nearly as stricken as Ben's.

"You look beautiful," Steven ventured.

"Thank you," she answered in a stricken voice. "Nothing's going right."

Steven sat gingerly on the bed beside her, careful

to move the voluminous skirt out of his way. "It's a sunny day and your groom's waiting downstairs."

"The food's a disaster. Andy ruined the stuffed canapés and Libby spilled all the flour. Bell got in while she was sweeping it out and—" Her voice broke and tears spilled over her lashes.

"We're not hungry, William's in the kitchen, and Bell's safely grazing by the barn."

"Not in my flower garden?"

"No, the father was in the flower garden."

"What?"

"Never mind." He slipped an arm around her shoulders. "Everything will work out just fine."

Emily raised the thin veil that covered her face. "Constable, may I ask you a question?" Her face flamed red and Steven's stomach sank.

"Of course."

She studied his face for a moment and swallowed. "Ordinarily, I'd never ask this of a man, I mean with the subject being what it is. There's just no one else to ask, and Willow, well she's not here, and Pa . . . I just can't ask Pa this. No, I definitely can't ask Pa. I'd never dream of discussing this with Wilbur, and Andy, well, he's just a boy. So that leaves you, Steven. I can call you Steven, can't I? I mean, with what I'm about to ask, I feel we should be on a first-name basis—"

Steven grabbed her shoulders. "Everything will be all right, Emily. Ben loves you."

"What does a man expect on his wedding night?" she blurted, blushing deeply.

Steven smiled and pushed aside a stray curl that had worked its way loose to bob over one tearful eye. "He expects his wife to love him, to take him in her arms, hold him close. He wants her to want him as much as he wants her. To know that when he lies down with her, she'll become part of him, a part he'll carry with him no matter how many miles separate them."

"That's beautiful," she sobbed, releasing a whole new crop of tears that she wiped away with the heel of her hand. "But Ben and I've already . . . I mean . . . what if—" She hiccuped. "I'm a soiled bride."

Steven leaned forward and sniffed. Emily Dawson was not only soiled, but soused as well.

"It won't matter. Tonight will be different."

"Really?"

"Really."

"Oh, Steven. You have to go to Willow." Emily flew up from the bed, nearly unseating Steven in her haste. Crossing to her dressing table, she returned with a note in her hand. "She left you this."

Steven took the piece of paper and unfolded it. Willow had penned two lines. "Come to the Wallows. Please?"

"Oh, Steven, you have to go to her. I think she's pregnant." Emily clamped both hands over her mouth.

"Are you ill?" Steven said, glancing frantically around for the chamber pot.

"I didn't mean to say that. Oh, damn. Now I'm vulgar, too." Tears streamed down her face as she flopped back down on the bed.

"Pregnant? You think she's pregnant? Why?"

Emily glanced up at him through her tears. "Well, she was sick yesterday. I saw her run outside. And Andy said she's been crying a lot." She leaned closer. "Willow never cries. But he said she cried when he branded a calf yesterday. Now, don't that seem sorta odd?" She attempted to put a finger to her lips and jabbed herself in the nose. "I won't tell a soul 'cause I think I am too," she finished in a whisper, her language slipping into her father's style. "Now ain't we a fine crowd?" Her mood suddenly shifted. "We're the pregnant Dawson sisters," she roared, waving her bedraggled bouquet for emphasis.

"Why don't you lie down for a while before the ceremony?" Steven took the battered flowers away from her and stood.

"I was awful to her this morning," she said as he pulled off her slippers and smoothed her dress as best he could. "She stood there in that doorway looking at me . . . so calm. I just can't stand the thought of her waiting out there. All alone. Watching for you." She sobbed, then hiccuped to punctuate her alcohol-enhanced plea. "I know she's annoying and infuriating and stubborn and . . . but I love her. She's my sister and I'm her sister." She stabbed at her chest. "And I want her to be as happy as I am." Emily sobbed and put the back of her hand over her mouth.

"Emily, I love Willow. I want to marry her. As strange as that might seem," he finished under his breath.

"You do? She'll be so happy." She lunged up and grabbed a handful of his coat. "We could all get married at the same time."

"We might not be back in time for your wedding."

"We'll wait." Emily gripped his arm so tightly he winced. "I'll just take a little nap till you get back." She fumbled with her veil.

"Here, let me." Steven reached up and removed the hairpins that held the veil in place. Before he had time to grab her, Emily flopped back on the bed, her eyes closed, her breathing even and shallow.

"The groom wore scarlet serge and the bride was drunk," he muttered as he spread a quilt over her.

The wind's song was a gentle hum instead of the primeval howl it had been the last time he rode this way. Steven spotted the rise of land that marked the beginning of Willow's ranch. He rode around the gentle hill and drew Buck to an abrupt stop. A tiny, neat cabin nestled against the protective rise of land. A porch stretched across its width, bordered by newly turned flower beds. Pat waited patiently by a hitching post, his head hung down in rest.

Steven's heart rose into his throat. "I'll be damned. She did it, Buck. Built her house, her ranch. She's independent at last. Question is, does she still want me? And is she carrying my child?" He patted Buck's thick neck. "Guess I won't find out asking you, will I?"

Heeling Buck into a trot, he soon covered the distance to the hitching rail. He tied Buck alongside Pat and stepped up on the porch. The door was ajar. He pushed it open and stepped inside. Willow sat on the wide bed, hands demurely folded in her lap, wearing the white-and-pink dress she despised. Her dark hair was upswept and unruly wisps dangled down in defiance.

"I got your note," he said, then thought how ridiculous that sounded.

She rose and crossed the room to stand in front of him. "You said to me once that you wanted a home and a family."

"I want you, however I can have you."

"Well, I've built you a home." She spread her hands to encompass the small room. It was neat and adequate, furnished with necessities and few luxuries. Firewood lay stacked on the hearth and a jar of early flowers sat on a crude table.

He swallowed the emotion that rose to choke him. The bed was large enough for two, its swelling tick covered with a colorful quilt. Willow branches, bent and twisted and lashed into a pattern, formed the headboard. He closed his eyes to shut out the erotic vision of her hands wound into the stripped yellow wood, knuckles white, gripping while he made love to her in their bed. She'd done all this for him. For them.

"Don't you have something to ask me?"

"Don't you have something you want to tell me?"

Her face blanched. "How did you know?"

"Emily told me."

Willow gasped. "How did she know?"

"Well," he began as he sank down on one knee, "probably, first, because you're alternating between throwing up and crying on a regular basis, and second, because she thinks she is, too."

"Emily?!"

He held her hand for a moment, not even the good-natured conversation enough to quell the emotion threatening to rise up and steal his voice at the most important moment of his life. "Willow, will you be my wife? And the mother of my children? Though not necessarily in that order."

She smiled down and ran a hand through his hair. "Yes to the first question. Yes to the second, and I'll ignore the comment."

He rose, pulled her into his arms, and rested his

chin on the top of her head. "A baby." The woman he loved carried within her his immortality.

And her father's name.

Her eyes widened as he grasped her wrist.

"Where are we going?" she asked, hurrying to keep up as he pulled her toward the door.

He lifted her into his arms at the porch's edge, carried her to Buck's side, and hoisted her into the saddle. Then he swung up behind her and leaned down to untie Pat's reins.

"Steven, what are you doing?"

"We can't let this baby be fatherless for one minute longer than necessary." He wheeled Buck around and headed for the Dawson ranch, Pat following them at a slow lope.

Libby sat on the steps, elbows on her knees, fists jammed into her cheeks when Steven and Willow rode into the yard.

"Where's Emily and Ben?" Steven asked as he drew Buck to a halt.

Libby raised her head and her face split into a smile. "Pa! They're here!" she yelled and scrambled for the front door.

Cletis appeared on the porch, slightly rumpled and yawning.

"Did we miss the wedding?" Steven asked.

Cletis shook his head solemnly. "Groom's out with his horse. Bride's asleep across her bed."

"No I'm not, Pa." Emily swept out the door, wilted bouquet in hand, veil askew. She wobbled for a second, then smiled. "You found her."

"Yes, I did," Steven said with a smile and a soft "oof" as Willow wiggled deliciously against him. "Libby, go find Father Flannigan."

"He's in here with Mr. McLeod." She dashed away just as Ben emerged from the barn.

Willow shifted her weight to dismount.

"Uh-huh," Steven said, looping an arm around her waist.

"What?" she asked, turning to look at him over her shoulder. Tendrils of soft hair spilled down her back, enticing him to misbehave in the middle of a yard full of milling people.

"You're not getting off this horse until you're legally my wife. You're not getting another chance to go off on some damn-fool adventure."

She shifted around farther, her brows furrowed together. "I can't get married on a horse," she said, her face inches from his.

"If you don't stop doing that, I won't be able to get off poor old Buck here even after the wedding," he muttered between clenched teeth.

Willow smiled slyly, shoved against him once more for good measure, then turned around and sighed innocently.

"Do you, Steven and Ben, take these women as your lawful wedded wives?"

Steven looked down at Willow, her head cradled against the scarlet of his jacket. "I do," he answered.

Ben turned to Emily, wobbling and clinging to his arm. "I do, saints help me."

"And do you, Willow and Emily take these men as your husbands, to have and to hold, for better or worse, for richer or poorer, in sickness and health until death do you part?"

Willow turned to look into Steven's face, and his

breath caught for an instant as she hesitated. "I do," she said with an impish smile.

Emily grinned up at Ben, her veil now well over one ear and her flowers long since nothing but stems. "I do."

"Then I pronounce you, finally, husbands and wives. Gentlemen, you may kiss your brides." The father slammed his Bible shut and wiped his forehead on the sleeve of his vestment. "Not quite sure I ever had to work so hard at a wedding."

Chapter Nineteen

Willow gripped the coiled pattern in the headboard and puffed against the onslaught on her body.

"Just a little more," Steven's calm voice said through the fog of pain.

"Are they on the way?" She felt his cool hand smooth across her forehead and follow it with a damp cloth.

"Yes, they should be here any second."

She fumbled and grasped his arm, his hair brittle and rough against her skin. "Is there any sign of the baby? Is anything wrong?"

"No, darling. Nothing. Everything's fine," he whispered.

A cold sweep of air chilled the room as the door banged open and then shut quickly. A dark face hovered over her: skin the color of tanned leather, and long dark hair. Gentle hands gripped her tortured abdomen; long fingers probed her skin, testing the lump that was her child. Then, the touch was gone.

"Ma?" Willow asked the fog around her.

"Put pole here," the voice demanded from a distance away.

Steven looked up at the beams of his ceiling, then back at Braden Flynn and his Sioux wife, Dancing Bird. "Is your wife crazy?"

Braden shrugged. "I dunno. The lass made the same demand of meself the day before she went into labor. I learned, 'tis best to just obey."

With the December wind ripping at his clothes, Steven dragged a planed fence rail in through the front door, stood it in the center of the room, then securely nailed it to an overhead beam, tottering on a chair while he completed the task.

"Now, all men out," Dancing Bird said with a wave of her hand.

"I'm not leaving Willow."

"How long, Dancing Bird?" Braden asked.

She shook her head. "I do not know. Hours, maybe."

"I'm not leaving my wife." Steven went to sit on the edge of Willow's bed, then bent to brush the damp hair off her forehead.

A gentle hand touched his shoulder and Dancing Bird's face leaned close. "She senses you worry," she whispered. "She is thinking of you and not herself and what she must do. You go with Braden, now. I will call you when it is time."

"Come and show me this new barn of yours," Braden said, lifting Steven's coat off a nail by the door.

They stepped out into the storm and, heads bent, struggled toward the partially finished structure. The heavy door swung shut, muting the fury of the storm. Steven sat down on a barrel and sank his head into his hands.

"And how is the queen of the ranch?" Braden asked, scratching Kate on the curly hair between her large, dark eyes. A young heifer peeked around its mother's hindquarters. "And the princess?"

"She's scared to death," Steven muttered.

"I don't know, lad. She looks perfectly calm to me."

"What?" Steven asked, looking to where Braden stood at the cow's stall. "I meant Willow."

"I know what ye meant," Braden said as he sauntered over and pulled up a barrel. "Sure she is. So was Dancing Bird. So was I. Frightened half out of my wits, I was."

"Were you there when your daughter was born?"

Braden grinned. "Aye, caught her meself. There was nobody but me and Dancing Bird. And she demanded a pole, just like she did in there. Couldn't figure it for the life o'me. When her time came, she squatted down, calm as you please, and out the little one came, right into me waitin' hands."

He propped his elbows on his knees, clasped his hands together, and stared at the ground between his feet. "Couldn't tell fer a minute or two if she was a lass or a laddy for the tears in me eyes."

A silence stretched between them and Steven put a hand on Braden's back. "What made you decide to come back to Fort McLeod after all?"

Braden clasped his hands together. "After April, I got to thinkin'. A lot of us that came out in seventy-three are gone." He jerked his chin in the direction of the house. "I wanted to get her away from the White Mud area. Things aren't goin' well for her people. Only a matter of time, I figure, before the Sioux are forced back across the border onto reservations. Especially after that ruckus last April."

"Well, you've got great timing."

Braden laughed and shook his head. "Timing had nothin' to do with it. Dancin' Bird had it figured down almost to the day."

Steven turned to look at Braden. "How did she know Willow was expecting a child? I didn't even know in April when I was there at Fort Walsh."

Braden grinned. "Well . . . ye told me what had gone on between ye, and well . . . a smart man tells his wife everything. Ye'll do well to learn that early."

Steven turned back to staring at the closed door. "I don't mind. I just appreciate that you're both here."

"She'll be fine."

Steepling his fingers over his mouth, Steven sighed. "She's so big and she's been so sick. Her mother died in childbirth. She's never been able to quite shake the fear, even though she hasn't mentioned it once this whole time."

The afternoon wore on. Steven gave Braden a detailed tour of the barn and then another one an hour later. Finally, as twilight stained the clouds and cast a yellow pallor, Dancing Bird called them, her voice faint over the receding storm.

Steven started out the door, then paused when Braden didn't follow.

"I got no place in there," he said.

Steven ran across the snow-covered expanse, leaped up onto the porch, and hurried through the door.

"Quickly, come." Dancing Bird shoved a handful of soft cloths into his hands, and tugged him to where the pole commanded the center of the small room.

Hair plastered to her head, Willow squatted, clinging to the rail.

"Steven," she gasped.

"What are you doing?" he asked, alarm ringing through him. "Why isn't she in the bed?"

"This is the Sioux way. Better for baby. Better for mother." She placed a hand on his shoulder and pushed him down into a squatting position.

"You hold hands under her like this." Dancing Bird took his hands in hers and positioned them underneath Willow. "Baby will come here. You catch."

He'd delivered more than one baby in his years in the Mounted Police, when necessity gave him no other choice. He'd been present when Colin delivered a baby or two, but this was worlds different. This was his wife.

"Won't this hurt her? Or the baby? I can't do this," he said, looking up at Dancing Bird, panic getting the better of him.

She put a hand on either side of Steven's face and forced him to look at her. "Do not let her hear fear in your voice," she whispered. "You will be her strength now." She smiled. "This is how my daughter was born. Braden did this for me. Now, you do for your wife."

She rose and moved to Willow's side. "This time

when the pain comes, push baby out into Steven's hands.''

"What if something's wrong?" Willow asked frantically, her fingers clutching the pole to balance her awkward body.

"Nothing is wrong. Keep your thoughts on your baby. He is ready to go to his father."

Dancing Bird faded into the background and Steven looked into Willow's pale face. "He's ready, Willow.''

Her knuckles whitened around the sapling pole. She arched her back and groaned deeply, keeping her eyes on his. A tiny, red baby slid into Steven's waiting hands.

Dancing Bird moved in, tied off the cord, and sliced through it with a sharp knife. Then she turned the baby onto his stomach and patted his tiny back. "You have a fine son."

The baby gasped a breath and mewed softly, then squalled loud and lusty.

"Dancing Bird. Something's wrong," Willow gasped, struggling against another pain.

"It is the afterbirth. Just let it come," she reassured.

"No, it's something else. Steven!" Her eyes were wild with fear as Dancing Bird tested her abdomen.

"There is another child," Dancing Bird said, alarm edging into her voice.

"I can't," Willow pleaded, dangling from the pole, sagging to her knees, her strength sapped.

"Go behind her," she commanded Steven with a hard shove to his shoulder. "Squat down, put your knees under hers. Hold her back against you while the baby is born."

He did as directed, pulling Willow's soaking, trembling body against his chest. The contraction rippled through them both, its intensity stiffening her.

"Steven, I'm so scared," she gasped. "What if—"

"Don't. Don't even think it, Willow. This is you and me. You and me and our children."

He pressed his lips to her neck, tasting the saltiness of her skin. His feet were numb and his knees screamed for relief but he clung to her as another pain clawed through her.

"I'm going to die, Steven," she gasped between pains, "just like Ma."

"No, you're not," he answered with as much determination as he could shove past the panic. "You're going to have this baby."

"What if it's not a baby?"

"It's a baby, a fine boy like his brother. They'll fill up this little house so quickly I'll have to build another one."

Willow strained again, her body so rigid he had trouble holding her against him. She groaned loud and long and then fell back against him so hard he nearly took them both to the floor.

"It's another boy," Dancing Bird said, rising from her knees with the baby wrapped in more clothes. "A fine, healthy boy." She bent and held the baby so Willow could see.

"Can you finish with her on the bed?" Steven asked. Dancing Bird nodded.

Steven picked up Willow's exhausted body and stumbled to the bed, praying his own aching knees wouldn't send them both plunging to the floor. Bending, he pressed a kiss to her forehead as he lay her down. "You were wonderful."

Willow frowned and gripped her stomach.

"You go see your sons," Dancing Bird said, pushing him out of the way.

He folded aside the swaddling cloths, baring the tiny bodies to his sight. Carefully he counted every finger and toe, tested every little arm and leg. Then he lifted both babies from their shared cradle, one on each arm. Tears blurred his vision. A sob stole his breath as he put the tiny, soft faces next to his. They were absolutely perfect.

He cried with relief and joy and exhaustion, his shoulders shaking with the effort.

Stars twinkled overhead, their silent music filling up the wintry sky. Steven puffed a breath of vapor and took a sip of his rapidly chilling coffee. Willow was asleep and so were the babies. Moments like this, peaceful and quiet, would come infrequently from now on. But he didn't care. He wouldn't trade the last few hours of confusion for all the peace in the universe.

He stepped back inside, closed the door, and set his coffee cup on the table. Willow slept peacefully on her side, and as Steven approached, he realized she'd fallen asleep with a baby at her breast. Firelight cast a soft glow, turning them both into angels.

The baby made gentle sucking noises at her bare breast, his tiny hands kneading her white flesh. Steven slipped into the bed beside her and propped up his head with his hand. Now was that Aaron or Adam?

"No, you're not next," Willow said softly and opened her eyes.

"I was just thinking that he's giving me some serious competition here."

"These are off limits to you . . . at least for a year or so."

Steven rolled out his bottom lip, then grinned. "But I can have the rest of you, can't I?"

"Not for the next two months."

He rolled over onto his back and put the back of his hand over his eyes. "Good thing I've got plenty of wood to chop. On very cold winter days."

"Well . . . I've been thinking. There are other ways."

Steven peeped out from under his hand. "The last time you were creative in this particular area, it got us these two guys."

"Do you regret any of it, Steven?" she asked, her voice soft and wistful.

He rolled back on his side to face her. "Not for a second."

Her cheek was soft against the palm of his hand. "You?"

"No. Never."

"We've got a lot of work ahead of us." He dangled a finger above the baby's face and he crossed his eyes.

"Do you miss the force?"

"I miss the people some, but most of them are within a day's ride. Colin and Maggie. Braden and Dancing Bird. This is where I was meant to be, Willow. Here with you and my babies."

"Do you know that tomorrow is Christmas Eve?"

"I'd completely forgotten. But I think Santa's already been to this house, hasn't he, Aaron? Or are you Adam?"

"Do you mind me naming them?"

"No, of course not. Did your father ever know you named the other baby?"

She shook her head, her hair moving softly against the pillowcase. "No. It just didn't seem right for him to have no name. So I wrote it on a piece of paper and slipped it under him when Pa put them in their casket. I wondered how God would know who he was when he got to heaven if we hadn't given him a name."

She pushed to a sitting position, winced, then tucked her breast back inside her gown.

Steven watched her immodest motions, supposing there was some benefit for him in this after all.

"Do you think Uncle Lame Deer was right? Are these babies the souls of my brothers?" She picked up the baby, placed it on her shoulder, and patted his back until he responded with a loud burp.

The sight of her in firelight, her hair soft and loose, the baby on her shoulder, brought unexpected tears to Steven's eyes.

He turned away quickly. He'd cried more today than he had in his entire life.

"Steven?"

He'd been caught.

"Put him back in the cradle. He's asleep."

Steven took the sleeping baby and placed him beside his brother in the cradle by the bed. He paused to touch both tiny heads.

Willow held up the covers. "Come to bed."

Steven slipped off the work clothes that now replaced his scarlet uniform and slipped into the warmth beside his wife. She lowered the quilt and snuggled up facing him. "I love you."

"I love you, too," he whispered around the lump in his throat.

She remained silent a few seconds, soothing his cheek with her soft hand, a hand that could give so much pleasure and that now began a slow slide down his body to touch him in sensitive places. "You realize I only married you because you looked terrific in your uniform."

"Well, maybe I should have kept it."

"Uh-uh. I always liked you better out of it," she said, grinning impishly as he sucked in his breath.

"This is going to be a long two months."

Author's Note

This is the last book of my Mountie series. I hope you have enjoyed reading these stories as much as I have enjoyed watching these characters evolve. However, the true heroes were the actual characters I borrowed from history.

James McLeod, whose name the settlement of Fort McLeod bears, was beloved by his men until his resignation on October 31, 1880, to become a stipendiary magistrate for the Northwest Territories. He died in Calgary on September 5, 1894.

James Morrow Walsh, probably the only white man Sitting Bull ever trusted, was removed from Fort Walsh by the prime minister with strict instructions to have no further dealings with Sitting Bull when his compassion for the plight of the refugees encouraged them to remain in Canada. He retired from the Force in 1893, but with the discovery of gold in the Klondike in 1897, the government made him administrator of the Yukon. He was rein-

---

stated as superintendent of the Northwest Mounted Police and given command of the force in the Yukon. He died at Brockville, Ontario, in 1905.

Resplendent in their scarlet dress uniforms, the Mounties preserve a taste of their history in the Musical Ride. Developed by early members of the force to amuse themselves, display their riding ability, and entertain the community, this colorful horseback drill was developed from basic British cavalry maneuvers. The first known display was given in 1876 by a troop trained by Sergeant Major Robert Belcher. Since then, it has become one of the last symbols of the force's past as recruit equitation was discontinued in 1966. The Ride is performed by thirty-two members and is based at the RCMP Rockcliffe facilities in Ontario.

In 1904, the Northwest Mounted Police were granted the prefix *Royal*. In 1919, they became officially known as the Royal Canadian Mounted Police, the title they proudly carry today.

Deepest thanks are in order to William McKay, curator of the RCMP Centennial Museum in Regina, for his help and patience with my endless questions.

You can write to me at **Ribbons@aol.com** with your comments.

Look for Kathryn Fox's next novel,
a Zebra Ballad book,
coming in January, 2002

Lauren has traveled halfway across Canada to rejoin the man who left her with a kiss and a promise two years ago. But the Northwest Mounted Policeman waiting for her at the train bears little resemblance to the Adam McPhail she remembers.

Reaching out for Lauren is a hardened, cautious man hewn from the Canadian frontier, no longer the gentle Constable McPhail of two years ago. Adam has seen what the frontier does to women and children and fears the same fate for Lauren if she stays and becomes his wife.

Lauren had promised her dying father to stay at his side until the end. She never knew he would linger unconscious for two years. Now, upon his death, she is determined to salvage the love she and Adam once shared and to make a life with this man who has fallen in love with the Northwest Territories.

Kathryn Fox likes to hear from her readers. You can e-mail her at *ribbons@aol.com*

COMING IN JANUARY 2002 FROM
ZEBRA BALLAD ROMANCES

__THE BRIDE WORE BLUE: The Brides of Bath
by Cheryl Bolen   0-8217-7247-3 $5.99US/$7.99CAN
Felicity came to the aid of Thomas Moreland after a band of highwaymen left
him for dead. Now he's determined to convince her that there's more to life
than assembly rooms, matrons, and matchmaking. But what Felicity doesn't
know yet is that her greatest desire of all is to spend the rest of her life in
Thomas's arms . . .

__PROMISE THE MOON: The Vaudrys
by Linda Lea Castle   0-8217-7266-X $5.99US/$7.99CAN
Held captive by Thomas Le Revenant, and betrothed against her will to his son,
Rowanne Vaudry is doomed to a life of misery. Then fate—in the form of
Brandt Le Revenant—steps in, rescuing her as she journeys to meet her fiancé.
How can Rowanne know that Brandt, a knight newly returned from the Crusades,
has his own reasons for helping her?

__NATE: The Rock Creek Six
by Lori Handeland   0-8217-7275-9 $5.99US/$7.99CAN
When Josephine Clancy met Nate Lang, she couldn't help but offer her friendship. Haunted by the War Between the States, Nate was the kind of man who
needed someone. But Jo hadn't counted on falling in love with the hurting,
secretive stranger—or the lengths she would travel to rescue him from the
melancholy that threatened to destroy him.

__REUNION: Men of Honor
by Kathryn Fox   0-8217-7242-2 $5.99US/$7.99CAN
Lauren often thought of the hardships she would face as the wife of a Canadian
Mountie. But she never imagined that her first challenge would be her own
betrothed, for Adam McPhail now seems distant and cautious. Lauren wonders
if the marriage she's dreamed of has ended before it has begun.

Call toll free **1-888-345-BOOK** to order by phone or use this coupon to order
by mail. *ALL BOOKS AVAILABLE JANUARY 01, 2002*
Name _____
Address _____
City _____ State _____ Zip _____
Please send me the books I have checked above.
I am enclosing $ _____
Plus postage and handling* $ _____
Sales tax (in NY and TN) $ _____
Total amount enclosed $ _____
*Add $2.50 for the first book and $.50 for each additional book. Send check
or money order (no cash or CODs) to: **Kensington Publishing Corp., Dept.
C.O., 850 Third Avenue, New York, NY 10022**
Prices and numbers subject to change without notice. Valid only in the U.S.
All orders subject to availabilty. **NO ADVANCE ORDERS.**
Visit our website at **www.kensingtonbooks.com**.

DO YOU HAVE THE
HOHL COLLECTION?

Contemporary Romance by
Kasey Michaels